SHADOWS OF PASSION

Carolyn sighed—time to go in. Yet before she could take the first step back toward the castle, a hint of motion over by the rose garden caught her eye. She grew still, staring.

He stopped two paces in front of her, this man out of every woman's secret dream, tall and powerful and oblivious to the buffeting wind, in a black suit recalling the grandeur of elegance and of ages past. Yet he did not smile. His eyes, when distant lightning exposed his features, were the haunted eyes of a caged bird of prey.

He held out his hand, and she placed her own in it without thought, without question. As though it were the most natural thing in the world, she let him draw her close and into the dance.

He led flawlessly, without misstep over the uneven ground of the cliff top. Soft layers of skirt whirled around her legs, tangling in the wind, and an odd constriction tightened around her chest, stifling her breathing. The hand holding hers grew tighter, warmer, drew her closer, drew her closer....

Other *Leisure* and *Love Spell* by Sabine Kells:
A DEEPER HUNGER

SHADOWS ON A SUNSET SEA

SABINE KELLS

LOVE SPELL NEW YORK CITY

*This one is for Hermi, as always...and
for the real Lily.*

LOVE SPELL®

October 1994

Published by

Dorchester Publishing Co., Inc.
276 Fifth Avenue
New York, NY 10001

Printed in the United States of America.

SHADOWS ON A SUNSET SEA

Prologue
The Past

Thornwyck Castle, Ireland, January 9, 1732

Tiernan flung open the door to the library, heedless of the resounding crash of solid oak into wall paneling. Like a baited, wounded panther he stormed into the dimly lit room and slammed to a halt in front of the gray-haired man in the black leather armchair. The flames of the candles on the mahogany side table flickered wildly with his approach, as if heralding the imminent battle.

"Ye'll no' force me into this, Da! No' in this life! I'll kill that *Sasanach* bitch afore I'll wed her, or bed her!"

The earl slowly lowered the leather-bound book to his lap and looked up. He'd been expecting this, Tiernan realized with sudden, cold dread; had been expecting him to rebel against marriage to an English bride.

Breath quickened in anger, Tiernan stared down at the pale green eyes meeting his from under bushy, furrowed brows—angry, silent, condemning eyes. He hated the thick brogue of his own words, as clear a sign of his fraying control as a fist driven into the wall; hated himself for revealing to his father how the old man's cursed ploy had betrayed him. Yet the O'Rourke said nothing at his outburst, only continued fixing him with those clear, commanding eyes.

Shaking with rage, lips tightening into a bloodless line of disgust, Tiernan clenched his fists and took a single step back. It was not a retreat; it was an instinctive distancing from something loathsome, vile, for fear that the taint might defile him too. "Ye might have pressed Bryce into this ungodly alliance, might be coward enough yerself t' have sought it, but I'll be havin' no part o' it!"

His voice was shaking now. Another moment and it would break. Whirling, Tiernan stalked back toward the door but caught himself after only two steps and spun back. He could feel the fury he could not master twisting his features into a devil's mask, surely no kinder than the grotesque gargoyles carved into the black Killarney marble of the mantelpiece. Yet he faced his father squarely, a mere pace distant, his own stormy green eyes narrowed to slits as words spilled like lifeblood from his throat.

"Ye started all this! Turnin' on yer own kin afore Grandda's body was even cold!" He exhaled fury, drew in a short breath. His voice did not break; it grew stronger. "And t' think that I've yer traitorous blood in me veins! God's wounds, the O'Rourkes dead six hundred years surely spun in their graves at yer deeds. They gave *kings* t' this land, long afore even the Normans ever set foot on it! And look at ye, Da! Pantin' in yer efforts t' please the English dogs, forsakin' yer own land and God—"

The earl of over threescore years surged up out of the chair, moving with the sudden power and agility of a youth. The blow came too quickly, too unexpectedly for Tiernan to dodge or block—not that he had ever dared raise a hand against his father. He reeled backwards with the force of it, into the mahogany shelving of the library wall, and tumbled to the polished wood floor. Books spilled out of their racks, rained down around him even as he pushed to his elbows and half turned, hand rising in disbelief to his face, the taste of blood in his mouth. The eighth Earl of Thornwyck stood towering over him, fist raised, face mottled with rage, while the wind drove hail and sleet against the mullioned windows veiled by wine-dark velvet drapes.

"I've had all I'll take out of you, lad. For that's all you are, and you'll bloody well mind your tongue when speaking to your sire!" The O'Rourke stepped back, gestured angrily around the room, his breathing harsh enough to set the candle flames to dancing. "Next time you think to throw temper tantrums, look around you! Look at Ross Castle, at the dozens of other estates that once belonged to the Irish! They're gone! Gone, all of them! And do you know why?"

Tiernan shoved to his feet, a rush of blood staining his neck and cheekbones, fury and shame intermingled. "I know *they* fought back! They—"

"They are *dead!*" The earl paused, regaining a measure of control, folding his arms across a chest still broad and powerful beneath the fine wool of his frock coat. "Most of them. Others, exiled. Only the ones that knuckled under, as you'd call it, yet remain. And they've become tenants on their own holdings! Thornwyck, even as it stands now, is among the last castles in all of Munster that's left in Irish hands."

"But at what cost!"

For an instant, Tiernan was certain the earl would lash out at him again for his rebellious words. He clenched his jaw but did not flinch. He'd not cowered before the old man since he'd been old enough to wear breeches, and he wouldn't start now.

But no blow came. His father had ever been a shrewd man; he understood a man's mind, knew well where to strike without ever raising a hand. Eyes bright with righteousness fixed upon Tiernan mercilessly.

"Go, then," the earl challenged him harshly. "Go live in poverty; go work your hands to the bone, with too little to eat and no ease in life! Go, live like one of them, little better than slaves, and then tell me of the price! I've kept this family alive, and better than alive—I've kept us living in relative ease to what's all around us! I've had the means to feed and clothe our tenants, when they could not do so for themselves, and to give aid to those even on English estates."

He paused to glare at Tiernan. "Think you my pride is so dear to me that I'd let so many suffer if I could help it?"

Tiernan stared at his father mutinously, unrepentant. After an instant of silence, the O'Rourke shook his head slowly, scowling. Yet when he spoke again his voice was quieter, calmer, a lull in the storm.

"Go, take your horse, that costly blooded stallion that your nearest Protestant neighbor could have bought for five pounds, were I still Catholic. Go and ride out, and look around you. And open your eyes, lad. Look at the wailing babes, the young women old afore their time. And then tell me you'd see your lady mother working for some English lord, taking out kitchen slops or tending the fields!" The earl's voice was rising again, harsh and cold like the sleet whipping against the windows. "Tell me you'd have your sister servant to one, and cleaning his laundry and obliging him in his bed!"

Tiernan's jaw remained clenched, ensuring silence. The O'Rourke stared at him for another second, breath coming hard and fast, anger palpable in the air around him. Then, suddenly, there was no more rage, no more strength at all. Tiernan watched his father turn away and sink wearily into one of the leather chairs facing the draped windows on the far wall. Without deigning to face his son again, he gestured tiredly toward the door to the hall.

"Go. And speak no more to me of rebellion. You'll be schooled and registered a Protestant, as Bryce was, and be legally wed by a minister of the Church of Ireland to an Anglican bride. And if you'll 'be having no part of it,' you'll no longer be a son of this house. I've grown tired of trying to beat the pride out of you. But I'll see Thornwyck and all upon it safe if 'tis the last thing I do."

Tiernan swallowed an oath and glared at the back of his father's head defiantly, only to be momentarily taken aback by the contrast of graying hair against the rich black leather of the chair.

Then the instant of softening was gone, frozen by the storm. Tiernan's mouth curved into a bitter smile. "Dinna forget, Da, I am yer only son now."

It was the lowest blow he could have struck. He full well knew it—despised himself, even, for the words, with Bryce's death so recent still. He could see the earl stiffen where he sat, yet his father did not so much as spare him a glance.

"I'll take a bastard, if needs be, so long as he be willing to turn Protestant."

The quiet promise drove the breath from Tiernan's lungs. Mute with disbelief, he stared at his father's back for long, painful moments. Then he spun and stalked wordlessly from the library, the sound of his boots on the marble tiles of the hall like the thunder echoing outside as he flung his cloak around him and all but ran into the howling storm that raged across the snow-clad cliffs of Thornwyck.

Chapter One
The Present

Thornwyck Castle, Ireland, September 7

The sharp raps of her high heels on the wooden stairs and then on the marble tiles of the hall echoed crazily around her, matching the frantic pounding of her heart. No one saw her flee down the hall, out into the darkness of the night, where the cold sea wind tore at the flowing fabric of her wedding dress—no one but the man from whom she fled, the man who would possess her, body and soul, with ruthless cruelty. He was following her now, steps quick but uneven from too much drink, following her across the cobblestone courtyard, laughing out loud because he knew there was no place she could run to, nowhere she could hide from him, no escape for her anymore. . . .

Carolyn woke with a gasp, lost for a wild

moment in an overwhelming sensation of panic, of utter hopelessness and terror. Yet the nightmare faded even as she blinked into the darkness of the room, its details vanishing irretrievably into the hazy void between wakefulness and oblivion. The emotions, however, were less quick to fade.

With a ragged sigh, Carolyn sat up, finger-combing tousled strands of hair out of her face while her heartbeat reluctantly returned to normal. The next instant she realized what was amiss. It was dark . . . too dark.

Rolling out of bed, Carolyn padded toward the window to pull the drawn drapes halfway open. No wonder she'd had a nightmare in this utter, inky blackness. She never slept with the drapes fully closed. . . .

But then, these weren't her drapes.

She paused halfway across the room, gazed blindly into its unfamiliar depths, and felt her lips curve upward in a dawning smile.

This was not, precisely, her room.

She wasn't in her downtown apartment in Vancouver. She was in a chamber older than any building still standing in all of British Columbia, was in a castellated mansion halfway across the world from the place she called home.

Ireland. Thornwyck Castle . . . and Aunt Beth.

Carolyn's smile widened, then slipped slightly as a sliver of vivid, unwanted memories intruded.

Her mother had hated Lady Elizabeth, after things had gone bad. But to Carolyn the child, Aunt Beth had been a fairy godmother living in a faraway land of castles and princes and knights in shining armor, a land to be dreamed about on quiet Sunday mornings when no one else was awake in the house.

Carolyn frowned disgustedly, crossing the remaining distance to the windows. She'd stopped believing in knights and princes and happily-ever-afters about the same time she'd recognized those sappy fairy tales for what they were: figments of some overenthusiastic optimist's imagination, with no more shred of truth than their sugar-coated endings. So she'd been a bit slow with that realization—hadn't caught on to it, in fact, until her early teens, when from one day to the next, life as Carolyn the child had known it had ceased to exist. First Dad had left—

No.

Carolyn yanked on the cord, opening the drapes with a good deal more force than necessary. A shaft of faint, milky light seeped through the foot-wide gap in the thick velvet, illuminating her wristwatch enough for her to make out the time: 3:15 a.m., GMT.

Carolyn summoned back her smile, and with a practiced shrug banished the intruding memories of a past she had long since put behind her. Leaning closer to the window, she stared out into a landscape of lantern-lit mist for a moment before turning back toward the beckoning warmth of the bed.

Not three steps away from the window a motion at the edge of her vision caught her eye. Reflexively, she glanced around, and jumped when she found herself staring at a face floating at eye level beside her.

An instant later, her mild, grumbled curse broke the silence of the room. Carolyn took a step closer to the wood-framed mirror resting atop a dresser, then made a face at her own reflection in the shadowed looking glass.

Yet there was something odd about the reflection, something that made her hesitate and take a second look. Her features looked softer, less angular, and the blue eyes held an air of innocent wonder that she had lost a decade ago. The straight blond hair that barely touched the tops of her shoulders was mussed up and sleep-tousled . . . but there was something like a shadow falling past her shoulders, as though the reflection of an identical twin with long, curling hair were merging with her own. . . .

Carolyn frowned and leaned closer still; the face in the mirror frowned back, a true reflection distorted only minutely by flaws in the ancient glass.

Shaking her head, smiling crookedly, Carolyn padded across the carpet and slipped back into the cozy warmth of the huge, ornately carved four-poster bed. Then, with a long sigh, she lay back and soaked up the sensation of the ancient chamber.

There was more to it than the faintly musty smell of oiled wooden furniture and wall paneling, more than the unaccustomed nearness of the heavy, tied-back curtains on the antique bed. This room held the memory of centuries, the weight of time and of lives forgotten in its passing.

Carolyn drew a slow, deep breath, listening to the unaccustomed silence. No bass echoes of her upstairs neighbor's stereo blasted into the early hours, no car horns or police sirens wailed in the distance. And yet the night was filled with sounds, fainter sounds, texturing the darkness, more vivid because of it. There was the steady, hollow tick of a wall clock, the occasional creak of wooden floorboards or beams, the gentle patter of rain against the window panes—

—another night in the solitude of her marriage bed, a night filled with the terrible voice of thunder—

Carolyn blinked, frowned puzzledly at the alien thought that had flickered through her mind. Thunder? The rain outside was heavy drizzle, at best. And marriage bed? Of all the absurd—!

She exhaled sharply, grim humor in the tightening of her mouth. Nothing could be more alien to her than the thought of marriage. She'd worked damned hard for her independence, financial *and* emotional, and had no intention of giving up the freedom of her own schedules and rules only to have some man run her life, telling her what to do when. She wasn't like her mother. She'd never be dependant on anyone but herself.

Carolyn rubbed her eyes, shaking her head at her uncharacteristically dismal frame of mind. She should be happy, for God's sake! She was really here, in Ireland, in Aunt Beth's fairy-tale castle complete with Rolls-Royce, maidservants, butler, and resident ghost.

The last traces of her frown disappeared and made way for a crooked smile at the memory of that tidbit of gossip once mentioned by her mother. A ghost, really.

Carolyn shook her head. She'd have to make a point of asking Aunt Beth about this outrageous advertising scheme . . . tomorrow, when she was awake enough to be considered one of the living again.

Being in good physical condition was supposed to help overcome jet lag, but Carolyn now knew that to be just another myth. Her arrival at Thornwyck was no more than an indistinct blur in her mind—proof of her exhaustion. After all, the only time her near-photographic memory flunked the grade was when she was overtired.

She faintly recalled being hustled up to this room by the tiny, fragile-looking lady who was Aunt Beth. No, thank you, she really didn't need any supper, and yes, she'd be just fine, if only she could curl up under the covers of that huge four-poster and sink into blissful sleep.

Carolyn sighed again. God, but she'd been so tired. . . .

The thought was father to the deed. Carolyn yawned, stretched, and was about to slide under the down duvet again when a faint motion on the far side of the room caught her eye.

She stiffened, scowling into the inky darkness near the door, straining to discern something beyond the vague, shadowy outlines that filled the room.

Then she did, and wished she hadn't.

There was someone there, in front of the door, someone veiled by the colors of night . . . someone slowly coming toward the bed.

Chapter Two

It was like a shadow shifting amid deeper night, a barely visible black outline of a human form gliding silently across the floorboards and carpets.

Carolyn's hands clenched on the covers as her breath caught somewhere in her chest. She wanted to laugh and call out, ask who was there, who was up playing a stupid practical joke at this ungodly hour of the night, but she had no voice. She wanted to reach for her purse, for the pepper spray in it, but her body refused to move, to draw attention to herself.

The hollow ticking of the antique wall clock ceased as the shadow passed by on its way toward her. Carolyn's heart lodged in her throat, pounding so hard she couldn't draw breath. Wide-eyed, she watched the shadow come to a stop at the foot of the bed, blocking the faint lantern light floating through the parted drapes. It was a man dressed in an oddly styled black suit, a man with long, dark hair and a face she couldn't see, a man reaching out a hand to her—

" . . . ssahh . . ."

Shivers tumbled down Carolyn's spine at the hollow whisper. It was not an intelligible sound, might have been no more than the hiss of breath surging into her own lungs—

She blinked, and he was gone.

With a choked cry, Carolyn lunged across the bed to turn on the lamp on the night table. Yet the light made no difference, revealed no hidden presence; it only hurt her eyes. She squinted against the brightness, blinking as her eyes watered, but still no shape loomed cold and dark at the foot of her bed or in the shadows by the door. She was alone in the ancient room.

Carolyn gave a shaky, whispered laugh as her heartbeat hesitantly returned to normal. Alarm ebbed into disbelief, and then embarrassment.

Good God, she was so exhausted from her trip, she was starting to hallucinate. This was worse than the time she'd driven home all night from that computer seminar in Oregon and had seen a Tyrannosaurus rex on the freeway just south of Seattle.

Grumbling an unintelligible curse, Carolyn switched off the light and curled up under the covers again. Oh, yes, she knew well how lack of sleep could mess with a person's mind— especially hers. No wonder sleep deprivation was one of the oldest forms of torture!

Yet despite that perfectly logical explanation, Carolyn found herself staring into the darkness by the door and listening to the stillness of the ancient chamber for a long time before once again drifting into sleep.

Warmth touched her face, warmth and light. Eyes still closed, Carolyn smiled, a slow, dreamy smile of contentment. There was no more glorious way of being woken up than by sunshine.

A pounding heartbeat later, Carolyn was scrambling out from beneath the covers. She was halfway out of bed before the realization that she wouldn't be fatally late for work or class dawned on her.

With a silly grin and a sigh of relief, she sank back and once more scooted beneath the toasty-warm down duvet. Why, she hadn't slept in like this for years!

That was precisely the reason she was here. To relax, take time off, maybe even let go of that iron control for a little while.

Carolyn sighed. Perhaps that was why memories of the dark years had crawled up out of her past so vividly last night. Perhaps it was a time of soul cleansing, of leaving behind her past in this ancient place, and facing a future free of shadows. . . .

The thought trailed off, suddenly unimportant. With eyes widening in awe, Carolyn gazed around the room that would be hers for the next two weeks, a room bright with sun slanting in between the half-drawn royal blue drapes.

This was what the grand chambers of princesses had once looked like. Carolyn was willing to bet that, with the possible exception of restorations and the addition of electricity, the room had seen no significant changes for two, perhaps three centuries.

The bright ray of sunshine that had woken her highlighted in blinding white the lace curtains behind the velvet drapes. On the wall beside the bed a black marble fireplace held a grate filled with coal, as if awaiting the touch of a flame; above her, elaborate plasterwork, brilliant white in the morning light, framed a ceiling painted in pale lavender. Furniture of carved dark wood matched the paneled walls and gleaming floor. Two Oriental rugs added shades of red and blue to the color scheme, while the whitewashed walls above the wainscoting were decorated with a delicate network of painted green vines and lavender blossoms that looked lifelike in the dusty light of the solitary sunbeam crossing the room.

Carolyn bit her lip as her gaze touched on the ornately carved tall-case clock by the door, remembering . . . something. Shadows?

Then she scowled, caught between guilt and elation as her eyes relayed the position of the clock's hands to her befuddled mind.

Talk about sleeping in—it was noon!

Good God, what a slugabed Aunt Beth must think her! Here she'd come halfway around the world to visit, and she was sleeping the day away.

Shaking off the last vestiges of a vaguely disconcerting, unremembered dream, Carolyn scrambled out of bed to greet her first day at Thornwyck.

The only occupants of the dining room were an elderly couple sitting at a table by the window in dusty-golden sunshine. Carolyn gazed across the huge, wood-paneled hall at the black marble fireplace, which housed a lively coal fire, then way up to the high, coffered wooden ceiling. She should probably pinch herself, to make sure she wasn't still dreaming—

"Oh, Miss Carolyn! Good morning to you!"

Carolyn snapped her mouth shut and turned to see a dark-haired woman in a bright flower-print dress coming toward her from the still-swinging kitchen doors, teapot in hand.

"Gracious, luv, but you can't have had much sleep. Lady Elizabeth told us not to expect you afore noon!"

The cheerful, open smile of the Irish hostess did not fit with sarcasm, Carolyn decided with a mild frown, tucking a strand of straight blond hair behind her ear. Perhaps the motherly woman was kindly trying to ease her embarrassment about having slept in so late. Or was there some conspiracy afoot to afford the most amount of R&R to one overworked, stressed-out, distant Canadian relative of Lady Elizabeth's?

"The sun woke me," Carolyn finally replied, smiling at her own thoughts before quickly tacking on a "Good morning." She'd met the

29

hostess last night, along with the rest of the staff, in the echoing, marble-tiled, two-story front hall. Lydia? No. Cathy? Rats. Carolyn frowned distractedly. She really must have been more asleep than awake.

"Ah, yes, 'tis a brilliant day we've out there." Seemingly oblivious to Carolyn's mental acrobatics, the hostess gestured at the two dozen or so empty tables, her smile as bright as the crisp white tablecloths.

"You go on, find yourself a place. Except for the Bartons, nobody's usually down here this early, unless 'tis a group o' hikers, or businessmen like our Mr. Chandler. He's from America, too, you know. Comes by a couple o' times a year on business. He's booked again next week, so you'll get the chance to meet him. Oh, he's ever such a charming man, you'll see, and so handsome, too. . . ."

Only half listening to the hostess's easy chatter, still covertly staring around the room, Carolyn preceded her across the gleaming wood floor toward a table by the large mullioned windows.

"I've a grand raspberry char here," the Irishwoman commented while filling a rose china cup with steaming, dark red liquid once Carolyn was seated. "From our own gardens, mind you. Best you can get."

"Mmh. Thank you." Basking in the dusty sunshine, Carolyn inhaled deeply of the delicious aroma, sending up a futile wish that the tea might actually taste as rich. In her experience, that was about as likely as real-life fairy tales.

The hostess, returning from a quick trip to a wall cabinet, set down crystal-cut milk and honey jars on her table. "Here's some *bainne* and honey, too, if you like, but watch out for the gray. Now, what can I get you for breakfast?"

Thornwyck was a dream come true, Carolyn decided over breakfast, a childhood dream she'd given up on over a decade ago. It had begun with Aunt Beth's letter—which wasn't in itself a surprise, since unlike her mother and father, Lady Patricia Elizabeth Warrington had never forgotten her birthday. But the contents of that envelope had been like a ray of golden sunshine bursting into the hectic hours of her busy working-day life, reminding her of a forgotten time of cloudless childhood days before the realities of life had intruded.

In addition to wishes for a happy 27th birthday, there had been a present: A beautifully old-fashioned formal invitation whose calligraphic script summoned one Carolyn Elizabeth Masters to visit Thornwyck Castle at her leisure, and an open, two-way air ticket to Ireland.

The smile faded slowly from Carolyn's lips. She stabbed her fork into another piece of French toast and chewed with determination.

She'd stood at Vancouver International's departure gate within days of receiving Aunt Beth's letter. Perry, her boss of four years, had been only too happy to give her the two weeks off, sending her on her way with best wishes and orders to relax and lighten up for a change. Had it come right down to it, she probably would have quit her job to get away.

And that scared her. The fact that she—rational, logical, *responsible* Carolyn Masters—had come so close to taking such an utterly irrational, illogical, and financially irresponsible action should be enough to make her run, not walk, straight to the nearest psychiatrist.

The idea of quitting work struck her as being as crazy now as it had then, reassuringly reaffirming her sanity. But the silent longing that had woken in her with Aunt Beth's invitation, the yearning that had drawn her here, knew nothing of logic, nothing of hesitation or modesty in accepting this generous gift. As though following the pagan belief that one's soul returned to one's homeland after death, she had returned to the ancestral home she'd never seen before.

And now she was at Thornwyck—and feeling as though she'd waited for this moment all her life. As though this place was her home, had always been her home . . .

Ridiculous, of course.

Carolyn tore her blind gaze away from the Warrington coat of arms hanging above the fireplace and shook her head. Forcing a smile, she dismissed the odd sensation of familiarity as stemming from a picture she must have seen of Thornwyck at some time. Her memory was good at playing tricks like this on her.

By the time Carolyn had finished her French toast and her second cup of heavenly raspberry tea, she was the only guest in the dining room.

Lucy—her memory had finally supplied the missing name of the hostess—and a teenage girl named Heather were clattering around in the kitchen to the accompaniment of lively Irish jigs and reels. Carolyn was just about to take her dishes in and see if she could lend a hand when the fattest Persian cat she had ever seen shouldered open one of the dining room's double doors and made a beeline for her table.

"Meow. Mrrroww. *Eeowww!*"

"Good God." Mouth dropping open, Carolyn stared down at the gray feline whose girth would have made a pasha proud. Its dignified, regal bearing extended even to its voice.

"Aren't you something." She smiled and reached down to make the furball's acquaintance, but found her hand utterly ignored. Brows high, she sat up again, theatrically miffed. "Well, fine. Be that way."

Seeing that no tidbits were forthcoming, the gray shot her an affronted look, tail twitching. The next instant it defied gravity by majestically launching itself into the air and streaking across the tabletop, toppling the honey jar to the floor with deadly accuracy.

Before Carolyn could more than leap up, an appalled cry from the vicinity of the kitchen door sent the cat bounding for the hallway, claws scrabbling for purchase on the polished floor.

"Serendipity!" Lucy rushed across the thankfully empty dining room, hands clapped to her face. "Oh, you terrible beast! Wait till Lady Elizabeth hears about this!"

Carolyn watched the hostess dash after the Persian, too amused to be appalled. She loved cats, but some guests might well be put off at seeing one try to steal honey from a table in the dining room.

Watch out for the gray, huh? Still grinning, Carolyn gathered up her dishes and the upended honey jar, dabbing at the small spill on the once-immaculate floor with her linen napkin. She was halfway to the kitchen door when Lucy returned, puffing. Apparently, the cat had won the chase.

"Oh, Miss Carolyn, you can't do that!"

The hostess was beside her, snatching the sticky jar out of her hands before the dining room door had swung shut. She reached for the dishes as well, nodding toward the hall. "You just go on and have a look around the place, luv, and never mind this."

Carolyn held on to her plate with the tenacity of a terrier. Aunt Elizabeth might have refused to accept any money for her stay here, but Carolyn wouldn't be a freeloader if she could help it. "I'm sure you could use some help cleaning up," she began her perfectly sound argument, only to be interrupted by a new voice.

"Why, good morning, dearest! I hadn't thought to see you before lunch. Whatever are you doing up so early, and after such an exhausting trip?"

"Aunt Beth—good morning—" Carolyn turned toward Lady Elizabeth, coming across the dining room, only to have the dishes snatched out of her hands in the moment of distraction.

34

Exasperated, she snapped her gaze back to the Irishwoman. "Lucy—!"

The hostess was already halfway into the kitchen, *tsk*ing, ignoring her plea. Still frowning vaguely, Carolyn faced her aunt with a helpless shrug that slowly turned into a smile.

Lady Elizabeth looked like royalty.

The tiny woman with silver-gray hair and blue-veined skin too pale to have ever been touched by the harmful rays of the sun was the very picture of blue-blooded nobility, a delicate vision of Victorian elegance in a white day dress and shawl. For a moment Carolyn almost felt awkward in her plain jeans, mauve sweater, and black suede boots, but Aunt Beth's bright, cheerful countenance dispelled any unease.

Lady Elizabeth, too, was trying to make her feel better about imitating a bear in hibernation.

"I really do appreciate everyone's tact, Aunt Beth," Carolyn finally offered somewhat sheepishly after accepting a welcoming hug. "But I know it's not morning. When I left my room half an hour ago it was already noon."

The smile on her aunt's delicate, animated features wavered for an instant before brightening again.

"The clock must have stopped, dear," she explained, twining Carolyn's arm with her own and leading her toward the doors to the hall. "It's very old, and it does that sometimes. Why, it can't be more than a quarter to nine! Are you sure you don't want to sleep a bit longer?"

Carolyn managed not to grimace. "Thanks, but

I'm wide awake, Aunt Beth. Really."

"Oh. Very well, then. I might as well show you around a bit, so you won't get lost in the place when you're by yourself. Now, did you have a nice breakfast? And did you sleep well? You must have, to be up this early. But do tell me if there's anything you need. . . ."

Walking arm in arm, they passed a middle-aged gentleman in an immaculately tailored gray suit on their way down the hall. At Carolyn's vague expression, Lady Elizabeth introduced Ben Masters once again and, before beginning "the tour," nodded toward the split staircase with a meaningful look at the butler.

"When you have a moment, could you please set the clock in Carolyn's room? *He's at it again.*"

The last sentence was spoken so quietly Carolyn barely heard it. She looked at Aunt Beth questioningly, but received only a brilliant smile in return.

"Well, let's be off, then, shall we? There's ever so much to show you at Thornwyck!"

Aunt Elizabeth had meant those words, Carolyn realized two hours later. And she apparently also meant to miss not a single detail about the place, regaling her along the way with tales of everything from the history of the castle's various architectural styles to her last winning bet at the track.

In relatively short order Carolyn found out all about the furniture from the time of Charles II, how old the Oriental rugs covering the tiled marble floors were, and how long it had taken to weave the 16th-century tapestries bedecking the stone walls of the great hall. Aunt Beth had made it a point to whisk her along "the gallery," that endless corridor of sea-blue cut velvet bearing the portraits of Warringtons from the past to the present in gilded frames. She'd also shown her around no few of the presently unoccupied chambers available for guests, all of which still contained porcelain washbowls and pitchers despite the modern facilities at the end of each hall, though dimmer-equipped electric candles had taken the place of wax and tallow ones in wall sconces and chandeliers.

"We don't mind progress, you understand," Aunt Beth pointed out as she ushered Carolyn into yet another of the second-story guest rooms. "We have washers, dryers, electric stoves, all such modern conveniences. But you will most certainly not find a satellite dish or a television set on the estate."

Aunt Elizabeth opened one of the room's windows and leaned out, waving. "Good morning, Cummings!"

Carolyn peered over her aunt's shoulder, feeling the cool air of what was definitely morning brush against her face. The chauffeur, a tall, aging man with thinning gray hair, was down in the cobblestone courtyard, by the looks of it just finished with waxing the Rolls. He waved to her, too, smiling broadly, and she waved back.

It had been Cummings who had picked her up at the airport last night, who had, despite her embarrassed protests that she was a fitness instructor and could haul her own luggage, carried her bags out into an older model, mint-condition black Rolls-Royce parked in the "No Parking" zone. After tipping the official-looking man who'd obviously kept watch over the car, he'd opened the back door for Carolyn and had waited patiently while she hinged her lower jaw again and scooted into the backseat. She didn't recall much of the drive through a fog-and-drizzle-shrouded landscape, but she did know Cummings had impeccable manners and unflappable poise.

Carolyn snapped herself back to the present just in time to see Aunt Beth closing the window and turning toward her.

" . . . used to be the stables, but it's the garage now," she was saying, guiding Carolyn back toward the door. "We even have remote controls for the doors—comes in ever so handy when the weather takes a turn for the worse. But come, there's something I want to show you downstairs, before we go out onto the grounds. And maybe you should take a sweater with you—it's rather chilly outside today. . . ."

Carolyn did as suggested, then slowed her usually quick, efficient stride to match her aunt's measured steps as they made their way down the split staircase to the ground floor again. At the far end of the marble hall Lady Elizabeth drew her into an open chamber wallpapered with pale blue velvet above the dark, satiny, gleaming wainscoting. The furniture was upholstered in patterns of blue, the carpet was beige and blue . . . and Carolyn wasn't in the least surprised at Aunt Beth's introduction.

"This is the Blue Room, dear. That cabinet, over there, is from the time of . . ."

But Carolyn wasn't looking at any cabinet. She was staring into one corner of the sun-drenched room, oblivious to her aunt's words. She had just fallen in love at first sight.

"Oh, you'll hear lots of this, never fear." Lady Elizabeth patted her arm reassuringly, apparently having noticed her utter preoccupation. "Well, go ahead and have a look."

Carolyn needed no urging to cross to the beautifully carved Irish folk harp that had captured her attention to the exclusion of all else.

"Maura plays it each afternoon, and often at night. You can try your hand at it, too, of course, anytime you like."

"I couldn't—I have no idea how to play it," Carolyn protested vaguely, yet her hand was already rising toward the elegant instrument nearly as tall as herself. Entranced, she ran her fingertips across the metal strings with something akin to reverence. Clear, bell-like sounds shimmered through the still air, shivering down her spine.

—she'd find solace in the strings, tonight, from his madness—

"Don't be afraid, dear. You can't hurt it. It's not very ancient—only a little over a hundred years old."

Carolyn blinked, staring at the hand she'd

snatched back as though it had been burned. Her thoughts were chasing madly after the foreign one, already long gone. She looked up at Aunt Elizabeth, who was smiling at her with definite smugness.

"I firmly believe that it is impossible, no matter how musically incompetent and untalented one might be, to wring an ugly note from a harp. You'll see, I'm right."

Carolyn smiled back wanly. Her fingertips seemed to be tingling where she'd touched the strings. And that thought—

"Come, now, you can spend hours on the harp later. There's still the gardens to show you, and the rest of the grounds. . . ."

Carolyn followed Lady Elizabeth out into the hall again, then through the back door of the mansion into the surprisingly warm September sun, letting her aunt's bright, running commentary chase away the disconcerting sensation that had touched her yet again.

"And—oh, look, there's Tippens. Over there, in the flower bed," Aunt Beth pointed out. "Lucy called him 'Twopence' when he first showed up here, because she figured that was about all he was worth. He never would earn his keep, you know, even when he was a kitten. The mice ran circles around him, and Serendipity would chase him something fierce, in those days. Goodness, but he must be almost fifteen, now. . . ."

Carolyn smiled at the sight of the grizzled old tabby sitting sphinxlike amid a patch of purple and yellow winter pansies. Even as she watched, the cat stretched, picked his way along the flowers, then sniffed the dark soil and, with untouchable dignity and unmistakable intent, began digging a hole. Beside Carolyn, Aunt Beth shook her head and broke into a conspiratory smile.

"Lyle will have a fit when he sees the tom digging around in the flower beds. But he's too good-hearted to do more than scold the old lad. Age should have its privileges, don't you think, dearest?"

Nodding to the rhetorical question, barely hiding a smile, Carolyn turned to follow her aunt on her tour around the outside of Thornwyck.

Lady Elizabeth loved this place. She could make the ancient stone walls come alive with their history, painting images of times long gone in Carolyn's mind, images so vivid she barely noticed the passage of hours or the chill, biting wind from the sea.

"Now that there," Lady Elizabeth pointed to the lone tower reaching into the sky over the southeast corner of the mansion, "is Rory's Tower, renamed after the youngest O'Rourke at the time, who lost his life defending it against Cromwell's soldiers."

Carolyn stared up at the round tower, reaching a good three stories above Thornwyck's roof. There was someone standing on the tower's parapet walkway, but the sun was in the sky behind it, making it impossible for her to see more than an outline of the person.

" . . . is the oldest part of Thornwyck," Lady Elizabeth was saying, "except for some of the foundations, and goes back all the way to the original 13th-century Anglo-Norman castle. The rest was razed during the invasion and, except for the curtain wall—you can see remnants of it toward the cliffs and by the whitethorn hedges, over there—was rebuilt later as a mansion. That dark masonry, and the light stone detail around the windows and corner parapets, is later work still. You don't care much for history, do you?"

Taken aback by the unexpected question, still staring intently at the round tower, Carolyn snapped around to face her aunt and shook her head.

"No. I mean, yes, I do—I love history, really—"

"Hmmph." Motioning for her to follow, Lady Elizabeth walked on across the cobblestone courtyard, past the garage and the brick courtyard wall that had long since been enveloped by a rising curtain of ivy, wine-red in the color of fall. After a last glance at the tower, bare now of the watching figure, Carolyn rushed after her, appalled to have been so misunderstood.

"Really, Aunt Beth. This place fascinates me. I—just don't know that much about local history. Yet," she added with a crooked grin.

Lady Elizabeth stopped to regale her with a brief, brilliant smile, and proceeded to lead the way through the perfectly tended, lush gardens some loving hand had coaxed from the shallow soil on the rocky headland, then across manicured lawns and up to the ancient, tiny, overgrown chapel on a rise north of the mansion.

From there, they followed the gigantic rhododendron hedge back along the northeasterly edge of the estate.

Delicious smells from the kitchen wafted on the wind by the time Lady Elizabeth and Carolyn returned to the mansion.

"Ah, look, there's Scathach."

Carolyn followed her aunt's gaze to a coal-black cat crouched on the top of a lattice that lead clematis up the castle wall. It was staring past them with slitted green eyes, the fur along its spine bristling and its long tail ramrod straight and puffed up.

Carolyn frowned and glanced behind them, wondering what the cat had seen. Aside from a handful of birds in a hazelnut tree, only leaves stirred in the rose garden beside the southern corner of the castle.

"I was wondering where she's been hiding out," Aunt Beth was saying, making her way down a white gravel path toward the terrace. Carolyn followed, still distractedly glancing about for whatever had spooked the cat.

"Going after birds, as usual. I don't know how to get her to stop that," Aunt Beth muttered good-naturedly. "Even a bell around her neck didn't do any good. We never could keep a collar on her, you know—she always managed to slip it over her head." Still shaking her head, but smiling, Aunt Beth looked at Carolyn. "Ah, well. Cats will be cats. How would you like to have lunch outside?"

Carolyn smiled at the sight of a white,

wrought-iron table on the terrace surrounded by rose trellises, giving up on her quest. "I'd love to. But does that mean the tour is over?"

"Well . . ." Lady Elizabeth shrugged, gesturing loosely. "There is so much more history and such that I've just skimmed over, of course, but most of the other rooms are the same as the ones you've seen, and we did cover all of the grounds. . . ."

"But you haven't shown me the ghost yet," Carolyn said jokingly as they sat down at the table. The back door of the mansion opened, drawing her attention for a moment to the emerging butler. When she glanced back at her aunt, a laugh bubbled forth at Lady Elizabeth's shocked expression.

"I'm just kidding, Aunt Beth. Honestly!"

Something changed in her aunt's face, almost as though a thought once visible had now become hidden. Then Lady Elizabeth smiled knowingly. "Ah. You don't believe in ghosts, dear?"

Carolyn chuckled. "No. But I thought it was a brilliant advertising scheme, all the same. Didn't work too well, though, huh?"

Lady Elizabeth met her gaze with raised brows. "What makes you say that?"

Carolyn shrugged. "Well, if it had been a success, you would have kept it up, right? But Mom only mentioned the ghost once—and that was a long time ago."

"I see." Aunt Beth nodded slowly. Then she glanced up past Carolyn. "Ah, Ben—could you have Lucy serve lunch out here? It's too nice a day to be indoors."

With a smile, Carolyn dropped the subject of Thornwyck's supposed ghost. Drenched in early afternoon sunshine and sheltered from the cold sea breeze by a somewhat more normal-sized hedge of rhodos, lunch amid the trellises of late-blooming, fragrant roses became her instant favorite.

Lucy, however, when she came to clear away the dishes and serve tea, didn't look at all pleased by the beautiful day. She looked, rather, as though she had swallowed something extremely distasteful.

Aunt Beth finally voiced the question Carolyn's concerned frown implied. "Is something wrong, Lucy?"

"Oh—no, not at all," the hostess replied quickly . . . a little too quickly. Aunt Beth sat back in her chair, a mildly resigned expression on her face, and Carolyn had the distinct impression that this sort of thing—whatever it was—occurred fairly frequently. Her aunt's next question confirmed her suspicion.

"What's happened *now*?"

There was a faint, barely noticeable stress on that last word, and Carolyn had to smile. Lucy looked up from stacking the dishes, then continued with her task for a moment longer before shaking her head.

"'Tis not something I should bother you with, Lady Elizabeth." Casting a quick look at Aunt Beth, she tilted her head aggrievedly. "But, you see, 'tis just—oh, he's made such a mess o' the room again this morning—all the bedding was on the floor, and the chair knocked over, too. And last night he opened the locked cupboard where I keep the honey, so that terrible cat could get into it again. And then he—"

"He's just looking for attention, Lucy, nothing more," Aunt Beth gently interrupted the hostess's increasingly agitated voice. "He'll settle down soon."

Carolyn glanced from her aunt to the hostess, wondering silently whose ill-mannered child they were discussing. Parents really should watch their youngsters more closely, especially in a place like this, where priceless antiques could be all too easily destroyed with one unthinking, rash action.

Lucy shut her mouth and glanced at Carolyn with something akin to guilt before nodding slowly. "Oh, I do hope so, Lady Elizabeth. I'd hate for something to happen again, like it did with Mr. Chandler—"

"That's most unlikely, Lucy, and you know it," Aunt Beth interrupted again. "But do be sure to remind me to give you a bonus for all that cleanup work. And thank you for keeping on top of these things, Lucy. You know I'd be at a loss without you."

"Oh, Lady Elizabeth, I didn't mean for you to . . ."

Aunt Beth smiled. "I know. But you deserve it, Lucy. And don't worry about it so much—he won't hurt anyone."

Finished with stacking the dishes, Lucy sent Lady Elizabeth a parting, somewhat shaky smile before heading off toward the back door.

"I hope you take a damage deposit when you rent a room," Carolyn muttered neutrally before taking a long sip of orange juice.

"Not usually, no, come to think of it," Aunt Beth replied brightly. "But then, I've never yet had anything valuable vanish, or get damaged by our guests."

Carolyn chuckled. "Better be careful. It sounds like that particular streak of luck is about to run out."

Lady Elizabeth smiled indulgently. "I'm not worried about that, dear. Boys will be boys, no matter what their age. Now, are you sure you won't have some tea? I don't suppose you drink as much of it over where you live. . . ."

Carolyn smiled, and eventually did agree to one cup, though she didn't need the extra sugar in her system that she invariably sweetened tea with. She was high enough on the vibrant energy that being in this place called forth in her. It was like a mild runner's high, all her senses alert, yet tempered by a sense of peace that was as foreign to her as it was welcome.

"I won't ask about your parents, dear, because I know how things have been for you," Aunt Beth ventured after some minutes of companionable silence. Carolyn's gaze snapped from a particularly large pink rose blossom on a trellis beside her to Aunt Beth's face.

Lady Elizabeth sipped at her raspberry tea,

delicate brows drawn into a frown. "I've not heard from your mother for many years. I used to think she named you after me because she still had some fondness in her heart for us in the old country, but that was a long time ago."

Carolyn took another mouthful of orange juice and gazed speculatively at her aunt. Just how much of the Masters family history did Aunt Beth know, or think she knew? That Carolyn's father had left without so much as a word one night, and never been heard from again? That life with a mother who was rarely sober had become a living hell? That, five years later, in a desperate attempt to find some affection in her life, Carolyn had made her only real mistake so far, ending up thoroughly disillusioned and having the boy she'd thought loved her bragging of his conquest of the "Ice Queen" every chance he got at the prom?

Carolyn shook her head impatiently, refusing to dwell in her past; there was little use in rehashing the ugly years other than to remind her occasionally of what a good life she had now. But something had to be set straight for Aunt Beth.

"I don't regret my past, you know—not anymore," Carolyn stated firmly, in a voice that left no room for uncertainty. "It made sure I learned my lesson early in life. And I was lucky to have learned it so cheaply, with only a silly teenager's misguided dreams of love as the price. Last year—" Carolyn cut herself off, shrugged, and took another sip of juice. Last year, Nicola, one of her colleagues, had paid for the same lesson with her life. But that was not for Aunt Beth to know, or worry about.

She glanced up from her glass and found Lady Elizabeth respecting her silence. Her aunt didn't prod, yet the frown still creased her delicate brows.

"I am glad that you've not grown up bitter, Carolyn. There is too much joy in life to have all your days tainted with that. But do tell me about yourself," she continued more brightly, not giving Carolyn the chance to ask if there was, perchance, a hint of sarcasm in her words. "Do you still work at the fitness club? We have a very nice gym in the cellar, you know, with a basement window opening up to the rose garden. And what about your work? I recall you mentioning in one of your letters that you're a 'systems analyst' now. . . ."

Carolyn couldn't help but grin at the way her aunt made that trade sound like something from outer space. Letting the past go, she sat back in the wrought-iron chair, made a mental note to check out Aunt Beth's "gym," and commenced filling Lady Elizabeth in on the high points of the previous decade or so of the life of Carolyn Elizabeth Masters.

"Well, it sounds like you've certainly made a life for yourself," Aunt Beth commented somewhat drily half an hour later.

"It's a living," Carolyn agreed with a shrug. "Keeps me busy enough." There had been something indefinable in her aunt's voice—something remotely wistful, mingled with surprise and pride that she had done so well for herself, and something else, still. . . .

Before Carolyn could ponder the enigma further, Lady Elizabeth rose. "Now, I have some business to attend to, dear, but you go ahead and explore, if you like." She smiled, indicating the grounds and castle with a sweep of her hand. "Just mind you don't go too close to the edge of the cliff. It's been crumbling a piece at a time for as long as this island has existed. One of these days, I'm sure, Thornwyck will end up washed by the waves."

Carolyn smiled involuntarily at her aunt's exaggeration. There were at least 200 yards of solid ground between the castle and the cliffs. "I'm sure that's not something the next ten generations or so will have to worry about, Aunt Beth."

Lady Elizabeth muttered something under her breath, but returned the smile. "I suppose so, dear. Well, I must run—but I'll see you at about two o'clock for a jaunt into town, if you like?"

"I'd love to." Likewise rising to her feet, Carolyn beamed at her aunt, who nodded, obviously pleased with herself, before making her way out of the rose garden to the back door of the mansion. Still smiling, Carolyn turned away from the castle and her aunt and cast a long, speculative gaze toward the cliffs.

The boisterous sea wind buffeted her as she made her way past the thicket of whitethorn and the crumbled, barely identifiable remains of the ancient curtain wall to the cliffs that brought the verdant seaward grounds to an abrupt end.

There was something about Thornwyck Castle that called to her senses, to her soul—an awareness of the very fabric of history, of time passing endlessly. But here, where the land met the wild, eternal sea . . . here it was close to a physical sensation, this presence of the past. It was as though soft, gossamer threads were folding around her soul, drawing her toward the end of the land, seducing her toward something she could not name but could not deny.

Carolyn ground to an abrupt halt five yards away from the cliff. Holding back the wind-tossed strands of her hair from her face, she stared down at the nearly vertical 300-foot drop extending along the shore.

Waves exploded into geysers of sea foam where they met the harsh rocks far below, rocks that once might have been part of this cliff, long since consigned to the sea. Spray rose on the wind, up the cliff, misting her face and hair and clothing.

—terrible man, to so delight in frightening her—

Carolyn backed away two steps, frowning as a third alien thought streaked through her mind, carrying with it a cold chill of fear and dread. Yet it vanished as abruptly as it had appeared, like a shadow passing when the sun emerges behind a cloud, and in its wake came elation. Carolyn felt, inexplicably, like dancing—spinning round and round on the short, hardy grass like a little girl, with the wind and the sky as her playmates. But she didn't indulge in such a childish display. She only straightened her spine exultantly in the face of the chill autumn wind hurling off the whitecapped ocean, thrust her hands skyward, and drew deep draughts of brine-tinted air into her lungs.

It was, Carolyn marveled silently, quite the strangest feeling. Never before had she felt so truly alive.

Lady Elizabeth let the sheer white curtain slide through her fingers and leaned back against the window frame of her second-story chamber. A tiny furrow creased her brows and deepened for an instant before smoothing away.

The image had struck her to the core: Carolyn, standing out on the cliffs, like a figure from an age long past, a priestess of the elements, exuberant in her power—

—or a sacrifice, hovering at the edge of the world, giving herself to the wind and waves and sky. . . .

Lady Elizabeth shook her head. Out of the corner of her eye she could see the black-clad figure standing on the walkway of Rory's Tower once more, watching with the unfailing attention of a bird of prey the woman standing on the cliffs.

Mouth tightening, Lady Elizabeth stepped away from the window, out of the wide beam of sun streaming through it, and wondered what in the world she had done.

Chapter Three

Carolyn reluctantly retired early on her third evening at Thornwyck, swearing that this would be her last day of giving in to jet lag. Aunt Beth, a few of the guests, and most of the staff were still in the Blue Room, where Maura was playing folk songs on the harp, with most of her audience either singing or humming along. Carolyn wanted nothing more than to stay, but she didn't care to offend Maura by dozing off in the middle of a song.

Humming "Come By the Hills," Carolyn made her way up the huge split staircase to her room on the second floor. Two sunny days had flown by, between chauffeured trips around the Ring of Kerry and through the nearby towns, while Aunt Beth played tour guide, historian, and gossip columnist. The staff at Thornwyck was like a big, happy family, with Lady Elizabeth the mother hen. Carolyn got along famously with everyone, except when it came to helping out: They wouldn't let her.

And Aunt Beth . . . Well, she was everything Carolyn had expected, and then some. After only two days Carolyn began to suspect that few of the high-and-mighty relatives who termed Aunt Beth crazy for sinking millions into Thornwyck's restoration and upkeep had even an inkling of the real Lady Elizabeth.

The woman was a devil in disguise. Twice widowed, she had a score of "gentlemen friends," whom she frequently met for luncheons and trips—around the countryside and to the local pubs.

Biting back a grin, Carolyn closed the door of her room. She gazed around the chamber and, as always, felt her smile grow wistful. The sensation of familiarity had not diminished over the last days. It was as though she'd been here forever . . . as though she had known this place forever. Even pouring water from the pitcher into the old-fashioned washbasin was an inexplicably familiar task.

Just as the land was familiar—and growing more so with each day. Perhaps it was only that she'd seen enough pictures of the Kerry countryside in movies and magazines. Yet, somehow, that explanation wasn't nearly as satisfactory as Carolyn would have liked it to be.

She let her mind replay yesterday's horse-drawn carriage ride from Killarney to Muckross

House, through the forested grounds overlooking Lough Leane and past the overgrown ruins of Muckross Abbey, thought of today's walk along Inch Strand, ankle-deep in the icy ocean, gazing out over the windswept sea as though she had done so a hundred times before. . . .

Carolyn finished scrubbing her face, erasing the frown, then wrung out the washcloth and hung it over the basin's edge. Slowly, she looked up and stared at herself in the wood-framed mirror on the dresser, seeing not her face but the reflection of the room behind her.

It would be hard to leave this place.

—and he could not send her away! It was her home, too, a home she had grown to love—

Carolyn shook her head, stared at her face in the mirror, a face framed by shadowed blond hair, a face frowning in puzzlement that bordered on alarm at another of the alien thoughts intruding into her mind.

She needed to get out and move. That was all that ailed her—too few workouts in the past few days. Tomorrow morning, before breakfast, she'd go for a half-hour run along the coast. And if that didn't cure what ailed her, there was always the surprisingly well-stocked gym in the vaulted cellar.

Deliberately summoning a smile, Carolyn gathered up the small stack of postcards that would go out in tomorrow's mail and sat down at the blackened-mahogany writing desk, armed with her favorite fountain pen. The first card, an aerial photograph of Thornwyck Castle—Aunt

Beth knew more advertising tricks, after all—was for Iris, her best friend back home. The card didn't leave much room for writing, between the address space and an almost complete history of Thornwyck in illegibly small print. Another bonus point for the card, Carolyn smiled to herself, jotting down a brief hello to her friend.

The mail quickly done, she retrieved her diary from the top drawer of the bedside table, leafing through yesterday's entry, pausing to add some more ink strokes to her amateur rendition of the ruins of Muckross Abbey. A chill whispered down her spine again at the thought of Thornwyck's walls torn down like the old abbey's, razed almost to the ground by the invading army. . . .

But what man could build, man could destroy. History had proven that often enough.

Turning her thoughts to brighter things, Carolyn chronicled the day's adventures, finishing off with a sketch of one of the tiny beehive stone huts that dotted the hills of the Dingle peninsula. Hearing the clear tones of Maura's voice echoing faintly from below, she added yet another item: A verse from one of the folk songs Maura had sung tonight in both English and Irish, lines that had struck so deep a chord in Carolyn that she'd not had to hear them twice to know them by heart.

Come by the hills to the land
where legend remains

Where stories of old stir the heart
  and may yet come again.
Where the past has been lost and the future
  is still to be won.
And cares of tomorrow must wait
  till this day is done.

She stared at the last lines for an instant, then shut the cloth-bound diary and rose, returning it to its drawer before climbing under the covers. Words to live by. Words she intended to take to heart.

Long before dawn, Carolyn woke, disoriented. She tossed and turned for some minutes, trying to remember the time difference between Ireland and the Pacific Northwest. Eight hours, wasn't it? Or nine? Seven? Were they still on daylight savings time?

She shook her head. Seven or nine, it was still enough to explain her highly irregular sleeping patterns since arriving here.

The antique clock showed midnight by the pale glow of the outside lamps filtering through the parted drapes, but the green digits of her radio alarm read 3:12 a.m. Belatedly, Carolyn realized the wall clock was no longer ticking. It had stopped again.

She frowned at it, making a mental note to ask Aunt Beth to let her tinker with that clock. She'd always had a knack for fixing things.

With a shrug, she resumed tossing for a while longer. When sleep remained elusive she finally drew on her robe over her flannel nightie and padded to the window. Slipping between the curtains, she scooted up onto the wide windowsill, and instantly began to shiver from the chill wood beneath her and the night cold radiating through the windowpanes.

Fog had moved in from the icy Atlantic Ocean, veiling what she could see of the courtyard in pale, twin-lantern lit mist. Carolyn felt as though she were staring out of the British Airlines jet as they'd approached Shannon. It had been the same view: white.

Well, perhaps not quite the same. The end of the ivy-shrouded courtyard wall was visible as a darker shadow through the fog, as was the part of the garage she could see from her room.

Carolyn let her gaze wander past the courtyard to the seaward grounds and smiled. There was a good reason why Ireland was in forty shades of green, and that reason wasn't constant sunshine—it was exceptional irrigation by Mother Nature. She'd heard somewhere that, on average, it rained here four days a week—

The creak of floorboards directly behind her sent Carolyn whirling around. She slid off the windowsill, got momentarily tangled in the curtains and drapes, and finally fought her way clear.

There was nobody there, of course. The room was dark compared to the lighted mist outside, but obviously empty.

Carolyn sighed raggedly, shaking her head at her own skittishness. This was an old building;

its wood creaked all the time. There was no reason for her to be so bloody high-strung.

Shrugging out of the robe, Carolyn slipped under the still-warm covers again and drew them tightly around herself. She'd make that an hour-long run, she grimly amended her earlier plans for the morning. Perhaps, for good measure, even an hour and a half.

He watched her burrow under the coverlet, draw it up until her face was hidden. She had not seen him, standing motionless in the darkness by the door. Had not, for but an instant, suspected that she might not be alone in her chamber.

The darkness that bore him ebbed for a moment, sharpening his senses. The faint scent of wild rose touched him like a questing flame, the exquisite pleasure and pain of memory. So long, he had waited . . .

Now, at last, she had returned.

And nothing in the world of the living or the dead would keep him from doing what he'd waited nearly three centuries to do.

But time had meant nothing. Endless were the hours he had prayed for this chance, endless the hours he had spent in vigil in this room, or on Rory's Tower, waiting . . .

And now, she was here.

Slowly, with heavy steps that made no sound upon the thick carpets, he crossed the chamber to stand beside the bed and watch her sleep, as he had done so often in days long gone. Tendrils of her hair lay like corn silk against the pristine linen of the pillow, swirled in childlike disarray.

He reached out his hand toward her, imagining that he could feel the warmth of her skin should he care to lay his fingers against the one high cheekbone exposed to the touch of the night. . . .

Yet the darkness rushed closer again, mingling with that colorless light. The bridal chamber was snatched from his senses, his awareness, until once again only the rushing of the ocean against the cliffs of Thornwyck remained. . . .

"Goodness, Miss Carolyn, are you sure that's such a good thing you're doing?"

Interrupted in her deliberate cool-down pacing of the courtyard, Carolyn pivoted sharply at the skeptical inquiry. Seeing Lucy peering out of the kitchen window, she smiled and waved at the hostess. "Best thing in the world for you!" she called back confidently, though she could see how the picture she presented might raise some doubt.

She was soaked, from sweat as much as what was called fog in this corner of the world but would pass for heavy drizzle anywhere else. Still, she wouldn't have traded the last hour for anything. The Irish coast in fog was something everyone should experience on a one-on-one basis.

"I'll have a cup o' char waiting for you when you get in!"

Lucy's voice followed Carolyn on her way to the front door. She waved again, then padded through the imposing two-story front hall, beneath the gigantic blackened antlers of an Irish elk of mythical proportions, and down the main hall. Before she could reach the split staircase, Aunt Beth emerged from her drawing room.

"Good morning, dear! Why, you look absolutely radiant today," Aunt Beth commented with a straight face that couldn't hide the gleam in her eyes.

Carolyn smiled and gave her aunt the now customary peck on the cheek. "If you mean to tell me that my face is beet red, I agree," she quipped good-naturedly. There were two things she always got teased about: her fondness for sleep, and the healthy color of her face when exercising. Since she spent five days a week teaching aerobics and step classes, the latter was by far the more common.

"Ah, but that is a sign of good health, dear. But before you disappear into the bath, do tell me if you'd like to come along to the races today. It's Cummings's day off, so you'd be treated to my humble driving skills."

"Does this mean it's my one and only chance to escape from this place today?" Carolyn asked, laughing. She was surprised to see a hint of uncertainty in Lady Elizabeth's eyes. "I'm joking, Aunt Beth. I love this place! And I'd love to go to the races someday. But," she continued carefully, "not today. If that's okay with you?"

Aunt Beth gave her a severe look. Two seconds before Carolyn would have cringed, Lady Elizabeth shook her head. "Of course it's all right with me! I should hope that you'll never think you must do something simply to humor me—or because you're afraid you'll hurt my feelings! Never, do you hear?"

Carolyn nodded, taken aback by her aunt's vehemence. "I won't."

"Good." Lady Elizabeth nodded vigorously, quite calm again, then patted Carolyn on the back. "Now you go have your bath, and do whatever you like with your day. And if you need transportation, just ask Lucy—she'll look after that for you."

"All right." Before Carolyn could manage more than that, Aunt Beth had turned smartly and disappeared back down the hall into the study that served as her office. Brows high, Carolyn shrugged, then turned and headed up the stairs.

Half an hour later, over a shared cup of tea, Carolyn came face-to-face with a previously unknown aspect of the gregarious Irish hostess: stubbornness.

"But, Lucy, it's *your* car—and I've never driven on the wrong side of the road before!"

Lucy waved her hand dismissively. "That's nothing to worry about, luv! My son, Iain, he's been to Europe many times—and he's never had any trouble sticking to his side o' the road. By the time you make it out onto the coast road you'll be doing just fine! And look, the fog's nearly gone—it will be a beautiful day today, just perfect for sightseeing. Besides, 'tis not polite to refuse hospitality, you know."

Carolyn, in the end, did the polite thing. The

somewhat aged, pine-green Renault had the stick shift and the steering wheel and the driver's seat—not to mention the driver's door—all on the wrong side, but Lucy showed no qualms whatsoever in sending Carolyn off in the car. Apparently the hostess had a great deal more faith in her ability to drive on the wrong side of the road than Carolyn did herself.

As usual, her worries were unfounded. By early evening Carolyn was on her way home from another day of wandering through Killarney, without even once coming close to the feared head-on collision or causing a pileup in one of the dreaded roundabouts. The occasional embarrassment of getting in on the wrong side of the car was quite bearable, especially considering the good time she'd had. And on the seat beside her was a treasure she'd eyed on her first trip to Killarney and had since decided not to do without: a forest-green, hooded cloak of cashmere wool, at a cost that was outrageous only if one hadn't actually seen the garment. As far as Carolyn was concerned, that cloak was the perfect complement to anyone staying at a place as historically authentic as Thornwyck.

The sun was setting amid wind-torn clouds, dripping red-gold fire into the ocean by the time Carolyn passed through Dingle—or *An Daingean*, according to the Irish sign. Some distance outside town, halfway to Thornwyck, the ancient church on the hillside caught her attention.

St. Mary's, Aunt Beth had called it as they'd driven by on the first day. Lady Elizabeth hadn't suggested they go see it, and Carolyn hadn't asked—out of deference to her aunt. The poor woman would surely have been bored to tears within the first day if she'd had to accompany her on every tour through every historical site Carolyn wanted to see. To Aunt Beth and most people here, St. Mary's was probably only another old church.

To Carolyn, it was a piece of history.

Giving in to curiosity, she turned off the coast road and followed the narrow gravel path to a tiny dirt parking lot.

Biting wind tossed her loose hair around her face as she climbed out of the car and walked past the old cemetery toward the church. Most of the profusion of Celtic stone crosses that marked the graves were tinged green, courtesy of moss or lichen. Some stood at odd angles; others were chipped, or had corners missing. The cemetery had a look of disuse, of abandonment about it, as though many decades had passed since anyone had been interred here or had cared for the grounds.

Not so the church.

Carolyn stared up at the tiny whitewashed building with a sense of awe and wonder. She was not a religious person, never had been. Blame it on her parents, who hadn't cared either way, on her own headstrong decision not to go to church when there were so many other exciting things to be done on Sundays. Whatever the reason, she had grown up outside the religious community.

Yet she loved these ancient buildings, perhaps

all the more so because there was nothing like them in the New World. She had seen more castles, ruins, round towers, and other ancient monuments in the last few days than in all of her life.

And each one had left her with that humbling certainty of utter insignificance such centuries-old monuments invariably inspired. It was far from comforting, being reminded so bluntly of one's own mortality, and yet there was an exultation of sorts in the knowledge that something created many hundred, sometimes thousand years ago, could endure to touch others.

Reverently, Carolyn pulled open one of the double-leaf doors and stepped into the church. Dark wooden pews filled the spotless stone-tiled floor, scores of candles flickered in the dim interior. More were being lit by a tall, gaunt man in a hooded brown robe. Carolyn remained silent, not wanting to disturb him, and continued her awed perusal of the church.

Paintings arced along the vaulted ceiling. Within a trim of gold, angels and devils and mere mortals looked down upon the worshippers still bound to earth. Slanting in through tall, stained-glass windows, rays from the setting sun highlighted streams of dust motes in a multitude of vibrant colors.

Something unfathomable made Carolyn turn toward the priest—pastor? cleric?—again, to find him measuring her out of deep-set, black eyes shadowed by the hood of his robe.

"Peace be with ye, daughter," he finally intoned softly, before turning again to lighting the candles, as though Carolyn did not exist.

"Um . . . good evening." Her words seemed utterly inadequate. But *peace be with you, daughter?* Did people actually still say that? Carolyn shook her head, brows furrowed, and after a moment returned her attention to the church.

Along the walls, even beneath the floor, graves of those long dead were marked by simple inscriptions, or effigies carved in mirror-images of life.

It was daunting. Magnificent, awe-inspiring, and daunting.

No. Haunting.

Carolyn's breath caught in her throat as a wave of hatred, of overwhelming anguish and fear broke over her, washing through her, scouring away all the wonder.

Turning too quickly, she strode back toward the entrance of the hushed church, suddenly chilled by the intangible breath of centuries gone by as a single instant of time.

The echo of her footsteps was deafening. An inexplicable web of panic tightened about her chest as she glanced around this house of eternity, with its rows of faces peering from their places in the walls, likenesses of those once living, cast in stone. She felt the weight of their blind stares, shuddered with the sudden longing for clean sunshine. Frescoes and gargoyles watched her flight dispassionately.

Outside, ten paces from the church, Carolyn slowed. The back of her neck prickled and she whirled around, half expecting to find one of the small, monstrous stone faces carved below the eaves leering down at her animatedly.

They were only stone. Cold, gray, pockmarked stone, brittle from centuries of exposure to the unrelenting elements.

And still, the chill would not leave her. Neither the fading warmth of the setting sun, nor the appearance of a carload of camera-laden tourists who had just pulled up, could drive away the shadow that had stolen into her soul within the walls of that house of God.

Chapter Four

Carolyn drove too fast in her hurry to get back to Thornwyck. It was almost as though she were racing the coming storm, a storm that had been born within the stone walls of St. Mary's.

Dark clouds were closing in to veil any remainders of blue sky, casting leaden shadows on the sunset sea. The wind had risen since she'd left the small church. It was tearing into the fuchsia hedges that flanked the winding road, was whipping the sea into foaming swells and dashing them house-high against the cliffs and strands. The single-lane *bohareen* that left Route 559 and led across the mosaic of stone-fenced fields to Thornwyck Castle was devoid of shelter, leaving the old Renault to the merciless buffeting of the wind.

There was only a handful of cars parked outside

the mansion as Carolyn pulled into the gravel parking lot on the road side of the castle. The sight roused a faint scowl on her face; Thornwyck was too big to be a mere bed-and-breakfast place. With the costs of upkeep, it should have been turned into a four-star hotel. That way, at least, it would have had more of a margin of profit.

Carolyn had to smile at the thought of trying to explain the logic of that to her aunt. Even after the mountain of money already sunk into the castle, Lady Patricia Elizabeth Warrington was still wealthy enough to have her own way—and would probably remain so until the day she died, if her confessed knack for betting on horseflesh didn't dry up.

Besides, Aunt Beth seemed as resistant to change as the eternal land itself. For one thing, she obviously still hadn't given up on that crazy advertising scheme. Two of the castle's rooms were still off-limits to regular guests—because they belonged to the ghost. Aunt Beth hadn't mentioned them to her, of course, but Lucy had dropped a hint or two after dinner last night. Carolyn hadn't had the heart to argue the point too much, though, because Lucy was either a wonderfully convincing actress, or else she really, truly believed that there was a ghost resident at Thornwyck.

Carolyn's scoff was not quite as vigorous as it might have been before her visit to St. Mary's. But then, nothing had really happened there. It had likely just been her own overactive imagination, coupled with the latent stress inherent in traveling across too many time zones and hours spent driving on the wrong side of the road.

She shook her head, automatically locking the doors of the Renault before heading for the front entrance of Thornwyck, a thank-you bouquet for Lucy half hidden in the bag containing her cloak. Perhaps, just for the hell of it, she would ask Lucy to show her those "haunted rooms" one day. . . .

But then, they were probably only a couple of empty chambers somewhere in the vaulted cellar, two rooms full of cobwebs and the dust of silent years. She could skip that dubitable entertainment. There was far too much else to see in her brief two weeks at Thornwyck.

"Don't you worry none about Lady Elizabeth," Lucy insisted yet again, gently but firmly urging Carolyn out of the doorway to the kitchen while thunder rumbled in the skies above Thornwyck. "She's often late coming home from the races, and I'll keep some supper warm for her."

"I'm not *worried* about her," Carolyn countered with a smile. She'd had a late dinner with the staff and, once again, found herself shooed out when it came to cleaning up. "But I do wish you'd—"

"No, no, none o' that, now." Lucy shook her head in that no-nonsense way of hers, still smiling but adamant. "You might go play the harp, if you wish to do something. Just because Lady Elizabeth isn't here doesn't mean she'd not have our hides if we put you to work. And while those flowers were absolutely grand, and quite unnecessary, they won't change my mind, either."

"All right, I'm going." Throwing up her hands in mock defeat, Carolyn strolled out of the dining room, a smile still on her face. Yet instead of succumbing to the temptation of the harp, she retrieved an extra sweater from her room and headed out the back door onto the seaward grounds.

Rolling thunder and the roar of surf and wind met her as an almost tangible force the instant she stepped out of the lee of the mansion and courtyard wall. The northern hedge of rhododendrons whipped about in the darkness like monstrous, grasping hands, shifting and reaching into the storm, starkly lit in instances of lightning. Carolyn pulled on the oversized wool sweater and smoothed it down her jean-clad thighs as she hurried past the rustling wall and toward the edge of the land that still drew her like a lodestone.

The air was thick with the taste of brine. Lightning flared over distant Mount Eagle, and thunder came again. In the darkness between bolts Carolyn could see the plumes of foam exploding high up on the cliff face of a bay farther along the jagged shore. Whitecaps glowed eerily on the water, shifting in a mesmerizing dance as the clouds brightened with yet another white-hot bolt of electricity.

She turned around to stare at the looming shape of the castle, giving the wind her back. Ben had closed all the wooden window shutters before dinner, and now only dim, uncertain lights flickered into the night from the massive block of darkness that was Thornwyck.

Carolyn's gaze wandered into the distance, along the hills where, somewhere beyond her sight, a tiny whitewashed church stood in the path of the wind.

You saw him, luv? Oh, he's an odd one, Miss Carolyn. I wouldn't want to cross paths with him. Looks after the church, he does, but 'tis said he lives in the crypt!

Memory of Lucy's words about the strange old man in St. Mary's returned to Carolyn, bringing an indulgent smile. And she'd always thought *she* had a vivid imagination! No wonder the Irish saw ghosts everywhere.

But there was nothing wrong with a healthy dose of imagination. Life would be dreadfully dull if people saw only the things that truly existed.

The lightning was growing more distant, receding over the mountains. Thunder rumbled again, more quietly, farther away. Soon, the rain would come.

Carolyn sighed; time to go in. But before she could take the first step back toward the castle, a hint of motion over by the rose garden caught her eye. She grew still, staring.

Something was moving between her and the mansion. A shadow . . .

She peered hard into the biting wind, blinking rapidly to keep it from blurring her vision.

There was someone else outside the castle. Out of the storm, out of the darkness of the autumn night, a man in a black suit came striding toward her.

Utterly unlike herself, Carolyn stared. It seemed almost as though he had been no more than a shadow at first, a shadow that had grown more solid as he drew near.

Who was he? A new guest at Thornwyck Castle? Was he perhaps restless tonight, out for a walk in the storm, like herself? Odd, that she'd not seen him before. She would have remembered . . .

The nearer he came to her, the more her certainty of that fact grew. This man she could not have forgotten if she'd spent a lifetime trying.

Perhaps he had just arrived tonight, seeking shelter from the storm.

Something deep down inside of her came vibrantly alive at the thought. As he came closer still an inexplicable sense of familiarity washed over her again. Just as she had known the castle and the land, she knew this stranger. . . .

He stopped two paces in front of her, this man out of every woman's secret dream, tall and powerful and oblivious to the buffeting wind, in a black suit recalling the grandeur and elegance of ages past. Yet he did not smile. His eyes, when distant lightning exposed his features, were the haunted eyes of a caged bird of prey.

Strains of a melody echoed through the storm, though Carolyn could think of no origin for the sounds. But then, she wasn't thinking so clearly anymore. Her gaze was locked with that of the stranger, lost in it.

He held out his hand, and she placed her own in it without thought, without question. As though it were the most natural thing in the world, she let him draw her close and into the dance.

He led flawlessly, without missing a step over the uneven ground of the cliff top. Soft layers of skirt whirled around her legs, tangling in the wind, and an odd constriction tightened around her chest, stifling her breathing. The hand holding hers grew tighter, warmer, drew her closer—

She never knew what would have happened if she hadn't glanced away at that moment. Ahead, in their path, lay not the carpet of hardy, springy grass but the edge of the cliff. The thunder of waves crashing ashore far below rose rebelliously to meet the howling wind.

With a cry of warning, Carolyn threw herself backward, with force enough to draw the man with her. His hold gave, and she stumbled back, nearly falling, her balance lost. Heedless of her absence, the stranger carried on through the steps of the dance—

—and straight over the edge of the cliff. Carolyn could have sworn he moved another four steps on thin air before a deafening thunderclap rent the night and he disappeared into the storm.

A small, lost cry broke from Carolyn's too-tight throat. She sank to her knees, arms wrapped around herself as shivers tore through her. The cold dew and sea mist on the grass soaked into her jeans, chilled her even more, until she couldn't stop shaking.

He hadn't fallen. *He had not fallen!* He'd simply vanished, and with him the haunting melody that should never have been audible over the roaring voice of the storm.

Carolyn pushed to her feet. Her legs were carrying her closer to the edge, closer to the mystery of the man who had disappeared. After only two steps she wrenched herself to a halt.

She'd never been afraid of heights, and wasn't now. But she knew suddenly, with absolute certainty, that she would fall over that edge should she venture near. That her body would be found on the harsh rocks far below the next day—

—and laid to rest in the vault of St. Mary's, alone for eternity, while her beloved roamed the storm-swept cliffs—

"No—!"

The hoarse sound of her voice was lost in the wailing of the wind, yet it drowned out the alien thought in her mind. Carolyn staggered backward, away from the lure of the cliff, away from the emptiness of that abyss that drew her like a magnet—

She bit her knuckles to keep from crying out, whirled away, and broke into a dead run for the mansion. A terrible litany droned through her mind, pounded through her head with every footfall: the ghost of Thornwyck Castle was not an advertising scheme of her aunt's, or a figment of Lucy's imagination. He was real. And he was trying to kill her.

Chapter Five

Carolyn jerked open the back door and scrambled into the hall, intending to make a dash for her room, preferably without encountering anybody on the way. She didn't trust herself not to start babbling some idiocy about a ghost trying to waltz her over the edge of the cliff.

She should have known better than to harbor such high hopes. She'd never been particularly lucky.

"Did you have a pleasant stroll, Miss Carolyn?" Ben Masters inquired solicitously as she passed through the front hall on her way to the stairs. He looked as though he'd been waiting, probably to take her coat, had she worn one. "Quite a blustery night out there, isn't it?"

Carolyn gulped, slowing her pace to something less than blind flight. God, had he seen her out there, dancing on the cliff? And if so, what else had he seen? The ghost, dancing with her . . . ?

She twisted her face into a smile, choking out, "Quite." Perhaps, in the golden light of the hall's electric candles, her face didn't look as ashen as she thought it must.

Masters nodded, apparently satisfied that he could be of no service here. If he noticed her state, he politely refrained from mentioning it. "A good night to you, then, Miss Carolyn."

"Good night."

As soon as Masters turned away to make a last round of the doors before retiring, Carolyn flew up the right-hand side of the split staircase with more gusto than she'd displayed during her aerobics instructor evaluation.

Some of the cold, blind panic was gradually giving way to reason, to rationale. Still, she fumbled to turn on the light in her room before entering it, then shut the door firmly behind her. The soft glow of a coal fire in the black fireplace across the room greeted her with its warming orange tones, and more of the tension eased out of her.

It had begun to rain in the time since she'd come inside. The shutters over her windows were closed, changing the sound of the rain to a more ancient melody.

Carolyn kicked off her wet boots, stripped out of the damp jeans and the two sweaters, and fumbled into her nightie, pausing now and again to warm herself by the fire, which shed as much, if not more, heat than the modern radiator beside the dresser. By the time she'd finished her evening routine and had slipped into bed, drawing the down duvet almost up over her head, she felt marginally more sane . . . and safe.

Yet the man's image would not leave her. It burned there, behind her closed lids, until she poked her head out from beneath suffocating covers and lay staring up at the bed's canopy, gilded with the glow from the coals.

Though it had been too dark to see clearly, those shadowed, sharp features were etched into her memory. She couldn't say what color his eyes had been, but they'd been cold, so very cold. And his mien . . . so harsh, so set, almost as if in anger, or utter despair. She could still see the ruffled lace of his white shirt gleaming beneath the tailored black waistcoat and jacket, could still smell the fragrance of the white rose on his lapel, still feel the wire-taut strength of his hand holding hers, drawing her close . . .

. . . could still feel the skirt and tightly laced bodice of her dress. . . .

But she hadn't been wearing a dress.

Shivering violently, Carolyn buried herself deeper under the duvet, squeezing her eyes shut against the fire-lit shadows in the room. This was insanity. Her imagination was working overtime. Perhaps there had been something in the food at dinner that—

The wooden floorboards in the hall creaked under slow, rhythmic footsteps. The sound startled Carolyn so much that her rigid body nearly cleared the bed. Before she could draw a deep breath, her heart had leaped into her throat, pounding so wildly it threatened to choke her.

Almost instantly she recognized the sounds. A flush stole into her cheeks. She shook her head, groaning softly in frustration and disbelief. Good God, she'd heard those same footsteps every night since coming to Thornwyck. It was only Aunt Beth returning to her room, probably exhausted after such a long day. Hot-water pipes ticked and gurgled; more floorboards creaked.

Determined to relax, Carolyn rolled over onto her side, schooling her breathing and heart rate back to normal. For a few minutes she toyed with the idea of visiting her aunt in her chamber two doors down, then shook her head, frowning. What in the world was she going to tell her? "Auntie, Auntie, I've seen the ghost!"?

With another sound of disgust, Carolyn pulled the covers up to her neck and curled up again.

But the storm denied her rest.

The wind was still howling in the chimneys. Wooden shutters groaned and cracked under the force of the gale as the storm hurled itself against the seaward side of Thornwyck. Lightning flared, cutting through the vertical gap between the shutters, through the half-drawn drapes, bright enough to shine through Carolyn's closed eyelids.

And amid the wail and thunder of the storm floated a faint, distant melody, a haunting echo carried upon the wind.

Morning came too soon. Still feeling somewhat groggy from a night of little sleep, yet determined to join Aunt Elizabeth for breakfast, Carolyn decided to skip her morning run and instead made her way down to her customary window table in the dining room.

A group of five tourists dressed for hiking occupied one of the center tables, but Aunt Beth wasn't present. With uncanny promptness, Lucy appeared from the kitchen the moment Carolyn had taken a seat.

"Good morning, Miss Carolyn! Quite the storm last night, wasn't it? 'Twas lashing out. But beautiful as you please today!"

"'Morning, Lucy." Carolyn blinked up at her with a bleary smile to acknowledge the sunshine streaming in through the mullioned windows and the aroma of the raspberry tea being poured. "Don't tell me I missed Aunt Beth already?"

"Oh, no," Lucy proclaimed, black hair bouncing as she shook her head. "Lady Elizabeth's not come back from town yet."

The spoon fell from Carolyn's suddenly nerveless fingers to clatter onto her saucer, then slip down to the floor. Carolyn bent down to retrieve it, her thoughts reeling madly.

"Goodness, are you all right, luv?"

Lucy had set the teapot down when Carolyn straightened. The Irishwoman peered into her face with brows furrowed in that motherly way of hers. "You're pale as a sheet! Oh, don't you worry," she smiled abruptly, patting Carolyn's icy hand. "Lady Elizabeth is perfectly all right. She rang late last night to say she'd be staying over at Darby's—one o' her gentleman friends, you know. She didn't want to make the drive out here in the dark, with the storm getting so bad—"

Carolyn stared up at Lucy's concerned face and tried valiantly to cling to reason. There was something cold crawling up her spine, a nameless, faceless demon: utterly unreasonable fear. She had to swallow twice before her voice would work.

"Did you—were you upstairs in Aunt Beth's room last night, Lucy? Was anybody? Making up the bed or something . . . ?"

The dark-haired woman shook her head emphatically, picking up the teapot again. "Not that I know, Miss Carolyn. All the staff's quarters are on the main floor, and there's no guests staying in that wing just now. Was there something that needed fixing? Did—did the clock stop again?"

Carolyn shook her head wanly. "Ah—no, everything's fine. I just . . . I thought I heard . . ." Catching her irrational thoughts, she snapped her mouth shut and mustered a wavery smile. "It was nothing, I'm sure. Just the storm. Can I have the usual for breakfast, Lucy?"

"Certainly, luv. French toast and orange juice coming up."

Armed with the teapot, Lucy flashed her a cheerful smile and headed for the other early risers in the dining room to offer refills before disappearing into the kitchen again.

Carolyn stared blindly into space, feeling as though the floor had been snatched out from under her.

She'd just spent a mostly sleepless night trying to forget last evening. Had, in fact, almost succeeded in convincing herself that she'd become so caught up in the storm and the ancient feel of this place that she'd simply imagined the whole thing.

Now her newly found complacency lay shattered all around her.

The sounds she'd heard last night had not been Aunt Elizabeth retiring to her room.

Carolyn bit her lip and refused to follow that thought to its utterly illogical conclusion.

Chapter Six

A knock on the open library door startled Carolyn so badly that she bumped her head on the third rung of the track ladder beneath which she'd been sitting. She scrambled to her feet only to find Ben Masters politely waiting for her attention just inside the doorway.

Face burning with embarrassment, Carolyn snapped shut the book in which she'd become so engrossed. "Um—yes?"

"Miss Carolyn, Lady Elizabeth will be taking tea shortly. She's wondering if you would care to join her in the rose garden."

"Of course!" That bit of news got her attention. "I—I didn't know she was back yet."

The gray-haired butler nodded once. "She just returned a half hour ago. I shall tell her you'll be down, then."

Carolyn nodded. "Yes, please do."

The butler turned smartly and disappeared down the hall. With a long sigh, Carolyn sank back down onto the floor. God, but this was becoming ridiculous. She was supposed to be relaxing, and here she was, more high-strung than a racetrack thoroughbred. And while this morning's run had left her lungs burning and her muscles shaking with exhaustion, it hadn't done a damned thing to purge the image of Thornwyck's ghost from her mind.

Frowning, Carolyn stared at the large coffee-table book still in her hand: *Haunted Castles of Britain*. Not a week ago she would have laughed at such a title, never deigning to turn even the first page. But, really, it wasn't nearly as sensationalistic as it sounded. Especially now that she'd seen a ghost—had been *touched* by one—

Carolyn sprang to her feet, heedless of the book slipping from her hands and thumping to the floor. She glanced around wildly, but no one else had entered the library.

Blast it all! She could have sworn she'd heard laughter. Faint, muffled, low male laughter . . .

She didn't pick up the book, didn't scale the ladder to return it to its slot. She spun and fled from the library.

By the time Carolyn reached the red-brick garden terrace the prickling fear dancing along her spine had turned to anger. Dressed in lavender and lace, Aunt Elizabeth sat with her back to the sun at the white wrought-iron table, leafing through a *Victoria* magazine. Tea had not yet been served; considering the amount of honey with which Carolyn usually enriched hers, it was probably a good thing. Right now the last thing she needed was more sugar in her system.

"Aunt Beth, we have to talk about this!"

Lady Elizabeth looked up in surprise, white brows arching delicately. "Of course, dear. Whatever is it that has you so upset?"

"I'm not upset," Carolyn retorted just sharply enough to belie her words. She plopped down on a chair across from her aunt and leaned very unladylike elbows onto the starched, pristine white tablecloth.

"Very well, then, you're not upset." Aunt Beth's smile was somewhat careful, a bit too sweet, the kind of solicitous gesture one would use with a slightly addled relative. "By the way, that was a charming thing you did, with the flowers. Lucy is still carrying on about it. But, please, do tell me what it is we have to discuss."

Carolyn took a deep, bracing breath. "That ghost. That—" She took another breath, trying to get her voice to stop shaking and drop half an octave to near-normal. "That—*man* who thinks he can do whatever he pleases in this place, and—"

"Ghost!" Aunt Elizabeth's brows shot up again, this time in obvious alarm—very much the way she'd looked when Carolyn had first asked about the ghost, the day after her arrival. Carolyn watched warily as she sat up a bit straighter, something that should have been physically impossible, and reached out hands marked with age spots to enfold her own.

"Dearest, are you sure you're feeling quite well? Perhaps the storm last night left you a bit overwrought—?"

"Don't start on me with that!" Snatching her hands out of the cool, smooth hold of her aunt's, Carolyn shot to her feet, pacing up and down the pebbled walkway for a few steps and casting a short, disturbed look toward the cliffs. "I'm perfectly all right. Never better."

She stoically refused to meet her aunt's gaze, unwilling to see ridicule on her face. God knew, *she*'d given that kind of look often enough, whenever people spoke of ghosts, of the supernatural. But this was different. This was real! She had *seen* it!

And besides, Aunt Beth *had* written of a ghost in this castle. And if it really hadn't been a publicity stunt . . .

Folding her arms across her chest, staring at a trellis of climbing pink roses, Carolyn ground out, "I'm telling you, there's someone—some*thing!*—in this house."

There was a moment of silence behind her. Then: "Of course, dear. There are seven staff members and eight guests currently staying at Thorn—"

"No." Carolyn spun around, crossed to the table in three angry strides, and braced her palms onto its top. "That's *not* what I mean, and you know it! Don't tell me you've lived here all these years and never come across anything strange, and don't tell me Lucy's very good at trying to make your ad work. I remember what Mom used to say about you, talking about this place being haunted." Carolyn ran an agitated hand through her hair, shook her head. "I was so sure it was a publicity stunt—and you never bothered to deny it! But I've been here less than a week, and God knows I've never believed in ghosts, but I'm getting close to it!"

Aunt Beth leaned back in her chair and folded her hands in her lap, an exquisitely smug, satisfied expression settling on her fine-boned features. The last time Carolyn had seen that kind of look it had been on Serendipity, after the successful purloining of a mouthful of honey.

"Good."

Carolyn blinked, then scowled, bewildered. Finally she found her voice, but the word she thought might come out as a yell was a mere whisper instead. "What?"

Aunt Elizabeth rose, took Carolyn's hand, and drew her down the white stone path among the roses. "I said, *good*, dear. Come, let us go for a little walk. I think you'll find it most enlightening."

Carolyn was so stunned, it never occurred to her to resist. Out of the corner of her eye she saw Ben appear on the terrace with a loaded silver tray to serve tea, then saw him turn around and disappear into the mansion again at her aunt's dismissing gesture.

"You can't image how glad I am that this happened," Lady Elizabeth commented with all the glee and elation of a child receiving a long-wished-for present. "Oh, it makes everything ever so much easier."

"Easier!" Carolyn stopped and stared down at her aunt, appalled. "Aunt Beth, I don't think we're talking about quite the same thing here—"

"But of course we are, dearest." The brilliant smile lifted a dozen years from Lady Elizabeth's time-lined features. She tucked Carolyn's hand over her arm and continued down the path. "I'm ever so glad that you've met him."

"Met him." The echo was toneless, less than a whisper. Carolyn scowled. *Met him?*

"Why, his lordship, Tiernan O'Rourke, Ninth Earl of Thornwyck, of course."

Carolyn ground to a dead halt while her heart doubled its beat in her chest. Tiernan. "The ghost."

Aunt Beth glanced at her pensively, then nodded. "Yes, I suppose he is that, now."

"But—you said—" Carolyn shook her head and shot her aunt a suspicious glare. "You just made it seem as though there is no ghost, and I was just—just imagining things!"

An enigmatic smile turned up the corners of Lady Elizabeth's mouth as she resumed walking, drawing Carolyn onward.

"There's never been an advertising scheme, has there?" Carolyn demanded after a second. "And—the other day—Lucy wasn't complaining about someone's misbehaving child." She swallowed hard, because suddenly there was a lump in her throat. "Was she?"

Aunt Beth's smile brightened a fraction. "No,

to both of your questions. But you see, had I told you about his lordship along with Rory's Tower and the cats, you would have laughed," Lady Elizabeth confided smugly. "Oh, perhaps not to my face," she continued before Carolyn could deny it, "but you'd not have believed me. I've grown tired over the years of having people think his lordship the figment of an old woman's imagination. It's ever so much easier to let him do the convincing—and much more effective, don't you think?"

Carolyn only stared, dumbstruck. Aunt Beth, glancing up at her, chuckled. "Oh, come now. He can't have scared you too much—he's really not a bad sort, as far as ghosts go, you know. He's never actually harmed anyone, or tried to frighten away our guests, so long as they don't intrude. Actually, I quite think people like the idea of staying at a place haunted like this. Not with some tormented spirit knocking over things and going on a rampage after dark and driving people mad with just one look at him . . . but with that dashingly handsome earl wandering out by the cliff on stormy nights."

That last bit restored Carolyn's power of speech and tightened her hand on her aunt's arm. "How did you know? That he was out on the cliff last night? And what makes you think he's not tormented? Or that he's harmless?"

Aunt Beth laughed delightedly at the rapid-fire questions.

"This isn't funny, you know!" Carolyn shot

back, humiliation rising where anger had receded.

Lady Elizabeth only shook her head, smiling. "Ah, but it is, my dear. There's not been a single woman staying here that's seen him and not wanted to know more, and never mind if she's six or sixty."

Carolyn's spine stiffened as though it had been lashed to a broomstick. "I don't care about *that*, Aunt Beth," she retorted primly. "It's just that I've never seen a real ghost before, and I want to investigate—"

"Investigate!" Lady Elizabeth hooted, clapping her hands together delightedly. "Oh, dearest, they all say that!" She waggled a finger at Carolyn. "You can't tell me which way the wind blows, dear. I've seen the old chap, and if I didn't know him better, I'd be wanting to *investigate* him myself!"

After the first second Carolyn managed to overlook the teasing in her aunt's voice and replay her words instead. Brows furrowing, she stared down at her. "What do you mean, 'know him better'?"

Lady Elizabeth smiled enigmatically, then smugly. "You don't think he's just appeared out of nowhere, do you? Why, his lordship has resided here all his life . . . *and* all his death! He doesn't show himself too often, but I've seen him plenty of times in my fifty years."

Carolyn smiled involuntarily, biting her tongue not to reply "seventy." It was more like seventy-five, anyway. And, God help her, it suddenly didn't seem at all ridiculous that Aunt Beth had been sharing Thornwyck with a ghost all her life.

"Tell me, dear, how much do you know of this area's history?"

Lady Elizabeth had directed their steps toward the fountain, and now she gracefully sat down on the carved black marble rim. Carolyn plopped down beside her, eyeing her warily . . . and, admittedly, eagerly. "I've a feeling I'm about to learn more," she hazarded a guess.

With a beatific smile, Aunt Beth nodded, warming to her subject. "That you are, my dear. But I'll keep this brief—after all, there are some seven centuries to cover." She folded her hands in her lap and closed her eyes serenely, as if better to see the past. Carolyn stole a deep breath and concentrated on listening.

"You see, way back in the 13th century, King Edward I granted the land of a 'conquered' Ireland to his lords. They came, evicted the locals, built their castles, and laid down Anglo-Norman rule upon the Irish. Thornwyck, a true castle then, had barely been completed by the invaders when it was besieged and won back by the local O'Rourkes. In the 16th century, Queen Mary made Connor O'Rourke the first Earl of Thornwyck. The castle more or less quietly remained in the family until all hell broke loose again in the country with Cromwell, and came to stay with the Penal Laws in the late 1600s."

Carolyn nodded faintly in agreement to her

aunt's last sentence. One of her history teachers had described the Penal Laws as a system of rules laid down to break the Irish. Hell was a mild word for it.

Lady Elizabeth shook her head, frowning. "It was a dark time for the land, that was, and I'll be the first to admit it, English or not. A Catholic had fewer rights than a slave under those laws." She glanced at Carolyn, who said nothing, then shrugged philosophically. "But back to Thornwyck. It was partially razed by the Commonwealth, and the seventh earl went into exile in Connaught while his estate was given to one of Cromwell's soldiers. When Charles II gained the throne Thornwyck was restored to the seventh earl, with permission to complete rebuilding it as a castellated mansion, so long as his peaceful intentions were never in doubt. The seventh earl died just as the Penal Laws came into effect, and his son, becoming the eighth earl at the tender age of thirteen, turned Protestant to inherit the whole estate before the Crown could confiscate it again.

"A few decades later Ireland was still under English rule, and none too happy about it. Rebellions were brewing, the Irish Catholics had fewer rights than ever, and the eighth earl decided to reinforce the family's ties with the ruling class further, through marriage. And yet, within less than a year, the O'Rourkes of the area were gone, and Thornwyck again passed into the hands of the English—the Warrington family, this time."

Carolyn's gaze had sunk to the groomed lawn

beside the pool as her aunt's words had led her into the past. She looked up expectantly as Lady Elizabeth's abrupt silence grew longer.

"Oh, would you like to hear more?"

Carolyn bit her lip not to smile and shrugged casually. "Well, only if you don't mind. . . ."

Aunt Beth beamed. "Why, not at all, dear. I just didn't want to bore you with ancient history and such."

Carolyn shook her head, suddenly serious. "You couldn't. Please, do go on."

Looking inordinately pleased with herself, Lady Elizabeth nodded.

"Well, Tiernan O'Rourke was the ninth Earl of Thornwyck for all of about two months." Her smile turned a bit wistful, as if remembering a fond acquaintance of somewhat tainted reputation. "He was nothing at all like his shrewd, pragmatic father. He was the youngest of five children, two of which had died in infancy, and had the reputation of being a hothead and a troublemaker, a dashingly handsome rogue with a devilish side to him, as rash and impetuous as The O'Donoghue is said to be wise. Apparently he had several scandalous affairs, and was even found duelling some wronged husband or enraged father. He got at least one public whipping for that, since Catholics weren't allowed to bear arms under the Penal Laws.

"Still, he managed to survive to his twenty-third birthday, to be faced with a forced conversion to the Protestant faith and an English bride, both courtesy of his father. The eldest brother had died just before he could wed the lady in question, and his lordship was suddenly the only surviving male heir of the O'Rourkes. His mother was beyond childbearing age, and his father was determined that the line of Thornwyck earls would continue into history."

Carolyn shivered, the past hauntingly alive in her thoughts. "But something went wrong."

Aunt Elizabeth waggled a finger at her. "I'll tell you, if you'll let me finish, dear. Now, you see," she continued, with the smile of a storyteller who knows her audience to be well and truly captivated, "the Warrington bride was brought to stay at the mansion, so that his lordship might properly court her. Rumor had it that he wanted nothing to do with the girl, that his father was trying to get him used to the idea of marrying one of the hated *Sasanaigh*. But the period of grace he gave his son apparently backfired.

"One night, the girl ran screaming from the house, into a storm much like yesterday's, and nearly fell off the cliffs. She was a sheltered, fragile, gently raised creature, you see, and apparently his lordship had near scared her to death with one of his tales. In any case, it was quickly decided that if the wedding didn't take place soon, it likely would not take place at all."

Hands curled into fists, Carolyn stared at her aunt. "Did she run away? Did he?"

Aunt Beth shook her head. "Nothing of the sort, though I am sure the thought crossed both their minds. The wedding took place on a beautiful summer day. Some weeks later, the eighth earl and his wife died in a coach accident. And, one evening not long after that, his lordship took his lady wife for a stroll on the seaward grounds. Nobody stopped them, despite the storm brewing in the night. They were last seen dancing along the seaside, far too near the cliff's edge."

Carolyn grew utterly still. Something like ice was starting to trickle down her spine, along her nerves, a certainty of disaster, the chill of witnessing a prophesy come true. She found herself holding her breath, waiting for her aunt's next words.

Lady Elizabeth sighed, brows furrowed, all but oblivious to Carolyn's tension. "Ah, 'tis just the thing he would have done, always tempting the devil," she muttered almost angrily, shaking her head. "A section at the edge of the cliff gave way beneath them, and they both fell to their deaths."

Dumbstruck, Carolyn stared at her aunt. She half expected her to take back the words just spoken and admit it was just a joke. Yet Lady Elizabeth did no such thing.

Dancing along the seaside . . .

. . . and falling off the cliff's edge.

Carolyn shivered again, goose bumps rising all along her arms and back.

God help her, but now it made sense. So that was why she had seen him moving out over the edge of the cliff, apparently on thin air. Because, in his day, there had still been ground there, before—

"Carolyn? Are you quite all right, dear?"

She looked up to find Aunt Beth chafing her chilled hands between her delicate, slender ones, frowning in concern. "Perhaps you—"

Carolyn caught her aunt's hands abruptly, stilling them, her grip more than a little too tight. "Is she ever seen? The . . . bride?"

Lady Elizabeth slowly shook her head. "No."

"Then why him?" Carolyn demanded. "Why Tiernan?" *And what happened last night on the cliff?* But she didn't speak those words aloud.

Aunt Beth replied with a philosophical shrug, smoothing out the skirt of her dress. "Who knows? Perhaps it is guilt—perhaps the rakehell did have a conscience. But I doubt that. He probably stayed simply to do more mischief. I'd believe that before I'd believe him to be searching for atonement for the murder of his wife."

"Murder!" Carolyn shot to her feet, eyes wide in shock.

"Well, of course." Lady Elizabeth nodded emphatically, though there was no judgment, no condemnation in her voice. "He would have known full well what he was courting there, on the edge of the cliff! It's dangerous out there. Poor thing must have been frightened out of her mind that something like that might happen— and it did!"

Carolyn stared at her aunt, speechless, shivering, while her thoughts whirled in stunned, horrified circles.

The ninth Earl of Thornwyck had killed his wife on the seaward cliffs. And last night . . . last night, he'd almost killed her.

Chapter Seven

The terrified glint in her eyes didn't escape Aunt Beth, though it did appear to surprise her. Carolyn looked away, feeling cowardly and foolish. Lady Elizabeth took her hand and started them back toward the terrace.

"Ah, dearest, you needn't be afraid of him. Truly." She smiled encouragingly, until Carolyn managed to curve her lips up in a faint echo of that gesture.

"I was five years old the first time I saw him," Aunt Beth went on, reminiscing. "Or, I should say, the first time I can recall seeing him."

Her smile changed, became more serene, wistful. "I was out in the rose garden, just over there. Josephine, my nanny, had spied me picking one of Mother's special roses. She had chased me down to the fountain and was scolding me fiercely when his lordship appeared and tripped her by tangling her skirts. And off she went into the fountain, wailing like a banshee. Then he picked another one of Mother's favorites, and gave it to me on bended knee, as though I were a real lady, not some spoiled little brat."

Lady Elizabeth laughed softly. "I think I adored him from that day onward. It didn't matter to me that Josephine hadn't even be able to see him, or that he was supposed to have died two hundred years earlier. I think I decided even then that I'd spend my life here, and not move back to London like the rest of the family."

Carolyn searched her aunt's face, struggling to make sense of what Lady Elizabeth knew of the ghost, and what she, herself, had experienced. "He likes you, then. Even though you are . . . a Warrington."

Aunt Beth shrugged, and her smile grew somewhat misty. "I don't know what his reasons are, dear. He loves mischief, but I've never known him to do real harm to anyone."

At this, Carolyn looked away. She couldn't meet her aunt's eyes and lie about last night. He hadn't actually harmed her, true . . . but there was no telling what would have happened if she hadn't pulled away.

They walked the rest of the way back to the terrace in silence. Carolyn was floundering amid too many disconcerting thoughts to stay for tea with Aunt Beth. She excused herself, cast a look of mixed longing and wariness toward the cliffs, and then made her way back to the library, instead, to find more on the history of the Earls of Thornwyck.

An hour later, Carolyn gave up her research and resignedly relaxed back into one of the old leather chairs to stare at the walls filled with shelves and books. There was no single volume on Thornwyck's history. There were, however, at least a hundred other tomes, in any of which there might be a tidbit of information.

A door close by slammed, sending Carolyn straight up and out of the chair, her heart pounding fiercely.

With a groan, she sank back into the chair. A draft! There was a draft somewhere in the house, and she was ready to scream bloody murder.

Carolyn let her head fall back, eyes closing. Perhaps she just wasn't cut out to live in a place that had a ghost in residence. So she wasn't as gutsy as she'd always thought herself to be—she could live with that. Sure, Aunt Beth had been coexisting happily with the earl's ghost for over seventy years. But then, Aunt Beth hadn't been out there on the cliff, nearly being waltzed off it!

Carolyn's head came up when the mahogany shelving on the far wall shuddered as though some heavy object had rammed against it. Several books tumbled off the shelves and thumped to the floor.

Startled, she scanned the library. There was no one here. Had something heavy fallen over somewhere in the mansion? Perhaps there had been an earthquake . . . ?

Carolyn rose to her feet, warily crossing over

to where the books lay scattered on the floor. Frowning, she bent down to collect them, intending to reshelve them—

—and leapt back three feet, instead, cursing a very unladylike blue streak under her breath.

There were no books on the floor. They had vanished beneath her fingertips before she could touch them. Not a single title was out of place on the wall shelf.

It was too much.

For the second time that day Carolyn fled the library.

By dinner time she had managed to regain most of her fraying composure. A very cautious walk on the cliffs had helped—especially since nothing strange whatsoever had occurred in its course. So Carolyn didn't even flinch when Aunt Beth returned to the topic of the ninth Earl of Thornwyck just as soon as the table was cleared.

"You know, I've often wondered if his lordship hated his father for that shrewd diplomacy of his," Lady Elizabeth mused, gesturing lightly with her teacup. "Hothead that he was, he'd likely have preferred taking on an entire English army to forging an alliance with their nobility."

Unable to help herself, Carolyn listened up, tilting her head slightly in thought. "Would he perhaps have chosen to kill himself and his bride rather than—but that doesn't make any sense, either!" She shook her head, abandoning her theory in midthought. "Even married to her, he would still have been the head of the family, and his heirs would have inherited Thornwyck."

Aunt Beth nodded. "Very true. I used to spend much time trying to solve the riddle of his past, but I've come to the conclusion that there must be something we don't know, some key part that's missing. History is written by the winners, dear— or the survivors. Never forget that. In this case, I'm afraid the Warringtons were the ones who wrote history. And even if it had been his lordship's intent to keep Thornwyck from English hands, it sadly misfired, because he was the last of the O'Rourkes here, and the castle went to his wife's family—the Warringtons."

"Of course!" Carolyn burst out, then bit her lip, frowning. "That might explain why he's still here—all he'd done was in vain, in the end, because the estate did fall into English hands."

Lady Elizabeth tilted her head from side to side, then resolutely shook it. "I used to think so. But he's not violent against myself or the staff. He pulls the occasional prank, yes—but usually they are harmless ones, and more often than not on some guest he takes a dislike to."

Carolyn sighed, nodding reluctantly. "And it still doesn't explain why he killed her in the first place. It doesn't make sense! What about the ghost's rooms? Is there anything in them to . . . ?" She let her voice trail off, recalling only too clearly her thoughts on "the ghost's rooms" only a day ago. But Aunt Beth seemed not to notice her chagrin.

"No, dear. There are only two rooms I've shut to the general public. One is his lordship's old chamber, at the far end of the north wing. He occasionally musses it up a bit, on nights when he's feeling restless. And he got—upset, once, when Mr. Chandler stayed in it. The other room . . ." Lady Elizabeth smiled, rising to her feet. "The other chamber is his wife's, where he sometimes tinkers with the clock."

Carolyn stared up at her aunt in disbelief. "My—*my room?*"

"The very one." The smile faded somewhat from wrinkled gray eyes, changing to concern and something else Carolyn couldn't put a name to. "It is still one of the nicest chambers, but I'll certainly give you another, if—"

"No." Carolyn shook her head without a second thought. "No, this one's fine." She paused, staring out the night-darkened windows for an instant, wondering if a solitary figure roamed the cliffs while they sat indoors. "I only wish I knew . . ." She shrugged helplessly.

"So do I, dearest," Aunt Beth agreed. "But the family annals only tell one story. Perhaps you could ask his lordship, if you see him again. In any case, I'm for bed. Good night, dear."

Lady Elizabeth headed out of the dining room, leaving Carolyn to ponder the chances of questioning a ghost . . . and of receiving an answer.

And the insanity in considering either one of those possibilities.

With a sigh, Carolyn quit chewing on the end of her pen and leaned back against the headboard of the bed. Then she straightened, staring down at the blank page of the diary on her lap. The quest of putting into words the turmoil of emotions and thoughts the last two days had unleashed within her was not going well at all.

Fear of the unknown was still in constant battle with the rational part of her mind that insisted that none of this was really happening. But Aunt Beth had taken quite a chunk of confidence out of that rational voice, had managed to replace it with a growing sense of . . . pity? Not quite. Something akin to it, perhaps. Empathy. Something that wanted to find all the answers, and help that wandering soul—

" . . . ssahh . . ."

Carolyn's head flew up at the sibilant, unintelligible whisper. Her breath came in softly as she saw the man standing at the foot of her bed, gazing down at her with the motionless intent of a bird of prey.

No, not man, Carolyn corrected herself sharply, though she refused to pick a word more appropriate. This man had been dead for over two centuries.

Her first impulse was to run, to dash out of bed and flee to the safety of the hall, the dining room, any place where there were people present to keep her from this madness.

Yet she remained beneath her covers, motionless as he, staring at him. Waiting for him to disappear again, as he had before.

He did not. He simply stood there, in the shadows, looking exactly as he had that night on the cliff, with his dark, unholy beauty and those cold, cold eyes. Green eyes.

Carolyn did not know how long they remained like that, in still, silent stalemate, with the bedside lamp shedding golden light and shadows. Did not know when the icy fear churning in her gut finally ebbed, to be replaced by cautious curiosity.

She wanted to know why he was here. Why he came to her, always to her . . . and why he had tried to kill her on the cliffs the other night.

Yet the words were frozen in her mind. The earl suddenly reached out his hand toward her, palm up.

And spoke that word again.

The soft whisper was lost in the silence of the room even as the one who had spoken vanished yet again.

Carolyn stared at the empty spot for a long time, wondering what would have happened if she had placed her hand in his. Then she calmly put aside her diary, turned off the light, and waited in the silence of the darkened room.

Waited, until the first pale light of dawn touched the sky. But he did not return.

Carolyn spent her fifth day in Ireland driving around Kerry in Lucy's Renault, sightseeing, walking village streets, and gazing out over the verdant Irish countryside.

She returned to Thornwyck in the early evening, to roam the ancient halls some more. Cummings still had not returned from Killarney with Lady Elizabeth; apparently her day's "business" was taking longer than expected.

As for herself, Carolyn couldn't have cited a single memorable thing she'd done all day. While she should have been relaxing and enjoying her vacation, she was instead mulling over the past.

The Earl of Thornwyck would not leave her thoughts. It did not matter whether she was having a solitary lunch in one of the Dingle pubs or trying her hand at the harp, that angelic instrument which, true to Aunt Beth's words, produced no discordant sounds even in her musically ignorant hands. Tiernan was there always, a shadow in the back of her mind, an awareness, a silent presence that would not be denied.

Near sunset, Carolyn bundled up in her new cloak and went outside again to wander along the seashore, well back from the edge of the cliffs. Shivering not from the cold, she stopped at the place she had encountered the earl's ghost that stormy night . . . was it only two days ago? It seemed like a lifetime.

But today, again, she was alone. No shadow, no man dressed in the elegant clothing of another age, appeared on the seaward grounds.

Wrapping her arms around herself beneath the cloak, she gazed out over the sunset sea, drinking in the brine-tinted air, wondering what it had been like here, near three hundred years ago. Had, perhaps, someone stood on this very spot while the sun set? Had Tiernan ever stood here, watching the burning sun sink into the mountains of cloud that shadowed the sea, thinking about what the future might bring?

"Carolyn, dear!"

She glanced around, torn out of her reverie. Aunt Elizabeth waved to her from some distance away yet, smiling, as always.

"Ah, beautiful view, isn't it," she offered a moment later, stopping beside Carolyn to scan the cloud-torn sunset horizon. "I shouldn't care to live anywhere else." After a pause she added, "Well, I've just returned from town, and I am positively starved. Will you join me for supper?"

"Love to." Linking her arm with her aunt's, Carolyn matched her stride to the old woman's shorter one. "Did you have a good day, Aunt Beth?"

A brilliant smile met her query. "I certainly did, dear. Everything went just splendidly. And you're not suffering from boredom out here in the country, are you?"

"Never." Carolyn's own smile stopped somewhat short of carefree, shadowed by the ever-present specter in her thoughts, by the knowledge that time was passing much too quickly. The bittersweet tilt to her lips must have been more pronounced than she'd thought, for Lady Elizabeth slowed their steps further.

"Does he bother you?"

Carolyn glanced at her aunt, then shook her head. "No, not—not really." There was never any question in her mind who *he* was. "But—" She shrugged helplessly, sighing. "I can't forget about him. It's rather like a sore tooth, I guess—always on your mind."

Aunt Beth chuckled delightedly. "Oh, wait till his lordship hears that. I don't think he has ever encountered that particular comparison before."

They had almost reached the house. Heavy golden light bathed the mansion, gilded the grass and trees. Carolyn frowned at her aunt's words.

"Does he speak to you, then? Tell you things?"

"Speak?" Lady Elizabeth shook her head, seeming pensive. "No. He joins us, sometimes, when Maura's at the harp, singing the old songs, and new ones. He likes 'Wild Mountain Thyme' a great deal. I could swear, sometimes, that he's humming along." She shook her head again. "But he doesn't talk to me—though he can make himself understood, certainly, if he so wishes. He's spoken to you, has he?"

Carolyn shrugged. "Not really, no. But the times I've seen him—in my room, at night—he seems to whisper something. I can't make out the word, but—"

"Why, that's extraordinary!"

Carolyn shrugged again, offering up a crooked smile. "I just wish I knew—"

"Ah, yes." Aunt Elizabeth nodded sagely. "He is our own mystery, the last Earl of Thornwyck. And everybody likes mysteries, don't they?"

Carolyn didn't reply to her aunt's rhetorical question. She, for one, did not like mysteries. She liked answers, immediate if possible, to her questions.

They reached the back entrance by the rose garden in companionable silence. Carolyn held open the door for her aunt, and followed her inside only to nearly trip over Serendipity, stretched out full-length on the rug.

Lady Elizabeth automatically stepped over the Persian, then paused in the hall to gesture up the split staircase.

"You go on and get changed, dear. I'll meet you for supper in a few minutes."

Carolyn nodded, a preoccupied frown lightly creasing her brows. It still hadn't disappeared when she returned to join Aunt Beth for dinner ten minutes later.

"There are several volumes in the library that deal with the period during which he lived," Lady Elizabeth suggested, accurately interpreting the distant look about her. "He's not mentioned much in them, and I'd not call them light bedtime reading, but . . ." Meeting Carolyn's gaze, she shrugged, then nonchalantly unfolded her napkin.

"I'll have a look at them tomorrow," Carolyn decided, nodding absently. The shadow of a frown was still there, as though watchful for any tidbit of information that would fit into the puzzle. "I don't suppose there would be a painting of him, somewhere?"

"No, dear." Aunt Beth shook her head regretfully. "I'm afraid not. The Warringtons did not keep any of the O'Rourke portraits."

Carolyn's mouth tightened faintly. So much for her plan to take home a photo of the ninth Earl of Thornwyck.

"But, if you really want to get a closer look at him . . ."

Her head snapped up at that, all attention focused on a hedging Lady Elizabeth. "Yes?"

"Well . . . there's always his tomb," Aunt Beth continued drily. "The effigy is quite exceptional—made by William Kidwell, no less, one of the most famous sculptors of the time. The eighth earl had made arrangements with Kidwell to have him carve the effigies of the O'Rourkes for as long as he could ply his craft."

Carolyn stiffened. A tomb. Of course—no mere grave plots for the nobility. There would be a slab of stone, like in St. Mary's, carved with the likeness of the man or woman whose bones rested beneath it. . . .

A shiver coursed over her. But if the only starting point for this ghost-hunting was to be the tomb of the ninth earl, so be it.

"Where . . ." Carolyn drew another breath, stiffening her spine. "Where was he buried?"

"Ah." Lady Elizabeth pursed her lips and tapped one slender, ringed forefinger against them. "Well, originally they had him in the crypt of St. Mary's, where the rest of the family lies. But they moved him shortly after his death because he gave them too much trouble in the church."

Carolyn didn't even ask. She didn't really want to know what her aunt classified as "trouble."

"He's been much better behaved since he was placed in the chapel vault, though," Aunt Beth continued, inclining her head pensively. "He probably didn't much care for the close company of the rest of the family, especially since they'd laid his wife down beside him."

A lump was rising in Carolyn's throat, and she swallowed hard, remembering her visit to the church only too well. That strange old man, and the inexplicable emotions that had assaulted her, the fear, anguish, hatred . . .

She shook her head to dispel the sensations even now trickling through her mind. "So which chapel vault is he in now, then?"

Aunt Elizabeth gestured loosely northward, smiling as she glanced out the windows. "Why, in the Thornwyck chapel, of course."

Chapter Eight

In the Thornwyck chapel. Just a three-minute walk from the castle's front door. Out there, by the huge rhododendron hedge, overlooking the mansion and the untamed sea . . . Alone for eternity.

Carolyn swallowed hard, any taste for the delicious Irish stew presently being served gone. She got through the meal anyway, even managed to keep up her end of the casual dinner conversation that ensued.

But Aunt Beth, usually so perceptive, did not offer to accompany Carolyn to the old chapel after supper. In fact, she conveniently excused herself from the dinner table to tend to some paperwork, just as Carolyn was about to ask her to play tour guide yet again.

By the time Carolyn had worked up the nerve

to make the trip to the chapel alone, a rising north wind was prowling around Thornwyck. Still, determined to get to work on solving the mystery of the ninth earl, Carolyn sought out Lucy in the kitchen to inquire about the possibility of borrowing a flashlight. She hadn't thought to pack one, and the prospect of making her way along the gigantic rhododendron hedge in the dark, with only an easily extinguished candle to light the tiny chapel, was quite enough to scare off her resolve.

Fortunately—or unfortunately, Carolyn thought, depending on which way one looked at it—Lucy procured the asked-for flashlight with the efficiency of an organized housewife.

"Here you be, luv. It hardly ever gets used, so the batteries should be good as new. Did you lose something on your walk?"

Testing the flashlight, Carolyn distractedly shook her head. "No. I'm going up to see the chapel."

"Surely you're not!"

Taken aback by the hostess's shocked exclamation, Carolyn looked up from the satisfactory beam of light. Lucy was staring at her, wide-eyed, shaking her head.

"Oh, 'tis not at all wise to be going out there after dark, Miss Carolyn. *He* haunts the cliffs at night, you see. And the chapel—!"

Carolyn suddenly found herself grinning, though her spine was crawling with a chill. "Well, with a bit of luck I might find him on the cliffs again. And, if not there, then perhaps I'll see him in the chapel."

Before she could turn around Lucy had caught her by the sleeve of her windbreaker. *"Again*, luv? You mean you've seen . . . ?"

Carolyn nodded once. "Yes, I've seen him. Out on the cliffs, the night Aunt Beth was away." Amazed that her voice held so steady, she caught Lucy's hands, squeezing them reassuringly. "I'll be careful; I promise. And I won't—" She smiled, cutting herself off. *Won't dance with him again*, she'd almost said. "Won't do anything you wouldn't do," she finished instead. "Besides, he's never harmed anyone before, right?"

Lucy's eyes grew even rounder. She was nodding, Carolyn realized after a moment.

"'Twas not for his lack o' trying that he didn't," the Irishwoman whispered scornfully in a hushed voice. "First time Mr. Chandler came into the place, the antlers in the front hall came crashing down on him!"

Carolyn's face froze in the act of smiling indulgently. One of the tips of those antlers was broken off—her memory supplied that fact without difficulty. She'd been amazed that something so old could last that well in the first place. But now . . .

A man could be gored by those antlers falling from that height. Killed.

And Aunt Beth called that harmless?

Carolyn exhaled sharply, impatient with herself for believing Lucy's superstitions so readily.

There were, of course, numerous perfectly natural explanations for those antlers falling from the wall. They'd probably been hanging from the same peg for three centuries, and, if anything, it was a miracle they hadn't fallen down sooner.

"Was—was he all right?" Carolyn finally asked, frowning distractedly. Aunt Beth had said no one had ever been hurt by the ghost, but this accident could hardly be blamed on supernatural happenings.

Lucy tilted her head from side to side. "He wasn't injured, if that's what you're meaning. Gave him quite the scare, though—Lord, I would have dropped dead o' fright, if it had been me!"

"No, you wouldn't have. You're made of tougher stuff than that," Carolyn decided aloud, giving the hostess's arm a companionable squeeze before turning toward the door. "Besides, you have lots of guests here that aren't bothered by the ghost, right?"

Lucy hedged. "Well, yes. . . ."

"So there," Carolyn argued logically. "Perhaps he just didn't like Mr. Chandler."

Lucy's face didn't lighten up in the least. "Oh, Miss Carolyn, I don't know. . . ."

Truth to tell, Carolyn didn't know, either, that she really wanted to do this. But she took her leave with a bright smile, forcing aside the uneasiness, the fear fanned to life by Lucy's reaction to her planned outing. Perhaps she should wait until morning . . .

But then memories of last night rose in her mind, of dark, aristocratic features too proud to ask for anything, even in death. Of a hand reaching out to her, from beyond the grave . . .

She shivered, with the image as much as with the brisk night wind that greeted her at the door. She had to know—now, before another night of finding a ghost at her bedside could come to pass. Had to find out what he wanted of her, why he came to her. And his death was the only starting place she had.

Putting her nervous energy into her strides, Carolyn reached the rise that held the ancient chapel in no more than two minutes. Yet the beam of light that had seemed so bright even in the well-lit kitchen was faint and thin now, not at all comforting in the inky night. Carolyn already rued the fact that she hadn't taken a spare set of batteries. Or another flashlight. What if the bulb in this one burned out while she was down in the vault . . . ?

Shuddering at the thought, Carolyn stared up at the chapel rising eerily out of the darkness. The towering rhododendrons formed a black, rustling wall around the back of the tiny building, as if waiting to snatch up any mortal foolish enough to come into their reach.

Carolyn inhaled deeply of the cold night air and with a determined stride crossed the last few yards to the closed wooden door. Its handle gave easily beneath her touch, but after opening only a few inches the door caught. Carolyn shoved harder. Rusted hinges gave with a spine-chilling wail.

A curtain of cobwebs met her as she stepped

into the chapel. With a choked sound of disgust, Carolyn swiped her hands wildly across her face and hair, until the last traces of sticky thread were gone and she suddenly realized she was standing in the doorway to the chapel with her eyes closed.

She snapped them open, wide, and stared into the shadowed interior of the building.

Blood was pounding hard and fast through her veins. She was afraid—of course she was afraid; she was the most devoted coward she knew. But she'd sworn to herself many years ago never to let her fears stop her. Because right after falling prey to one's fears one became dependant on someone else for strength. And that was the beginning of the end of independence and control.

Carolyn tightened her hand around the flashlight, mildly surprised at how the anger flaring up from years long past could shove tendrils of fear out of the way. With a steady hand she wove a web of light through the chapel, chasing shadows.

The place smelled musty, of dust and time and slowly rotting wood. Except for faded paintings on the whitewashed walls and ceiling, the chapel was empty. No pews, no altar—nothing. Yet if this forgotten hall was bare of its clerical trappings, it was also mercifully free of the living shadows that had sent her fleeing from St. Mary's.

Drawing her resolve around herself like an ancient cloak, Carolyn crossed the marble-tiled, dusty floor and descended a narrow stone staircase into the vault. Her footsteps echoed off the bare, close walls, breaking through the silence that had rested here for . . . how long? Weeks, months, years? Centuries?

There was only one dais in the low-ceilinged limestone chamber below the chapel. It stood on the far side from the stairs, by the seaward wall.

Halting steps took Carolyn across the vault, toward the tomb. The air was close, stuffy, dry enough to tickle her throat. She swallowed hard, refusing to cough, gripped by the ridiculous fear that any sound she might make would awaken the ghost sleeping in that tomb.

Her offhand retort to Lucy's worries returned to taunt her: *And, if not there, then perhaps I'll see him in the chapel.*

Please, God, not tonight! was the only thought that careened wildly through her brain now. Tomorrow—tomorrow she'd be ready to face Thornwyck's ghost. But not tonight—not in this place, so far from the light and warmth and human company at the castle. Not now, *not yet . . .*

Carolyn clenched her jaw, gripped the flashlight tighter, and grimly shone its watery beam onto the tomb less than two yards before her.

The words *Tiernan Padráig O'Rourke, Ninth Earl of Thornwyck*, were inscribed in large, graceful script at the foot of the horizontal slab from which rose the supine, life-size image of the earl. Below the intertwined letters, carved in Roman numerals, were two dates: 29.03.1709 and 10.10.1732.

Hands shaking, Carolyn raised the flashlight until its beam scoured the last remnants of darkness from the marble effigy resting in its flowing robes of stone on top of the tomb—

—and took an instinctive step backward, nearly dropping the flashlight from nerveless fingers. The carving looked so much like the specter who had visited her room, the man with whom she had danced out on the cliff, that her breath caught in her throat. It seemed as though he might rise at any moment, dust off the whiteness of the marble and the lacy shroud of cobwebs, and face her again with those cold, piercing emerald eyes.

Knuckles bloodless around the flashlight, Carolyn stepped closer again, forcing herself to reach out with a trembling hand and touch the cold, smooth, ancient stone of his face.

It seemed to burn her, in that instant of contact. Her hand jerked back and came to her mouth to stifle a breathless cry. Yet she made no sound, could not even take her gaze from the ghostly white marble carved with such exquisite, lifelike detail it bordered on obscenity that it should portray a man in death, not life. The high cheekbones and arched brows were just so, the full, generous lips set in somber lines, the bright eyes, green as his beloved country, closed for eternity.

Carolyn stared at the finely chiseled features until illogical tears rose to her eyes and the effigy blurred in the glittering light. She wasn't afraid anymore—couldn't, at that instant, even conceive

120

of the concept of fear. Her heart and soul were too full of other emotions to spare a thought to something as trivial as fear.

The man whose death mask graced the tomb before her had been dead and buried for over two and a half centuries. A week ago she hadn't even known that he'd ever existed. And now . . .

Now she could only stand there before his cold stone effigy and mourn the loss of something that had been taken away by time and chance long before she had ever found it.

Ever-faithful Ben Masters intercepted her just inside the door and took her windbreaker from her before wishing her a good night. Carolyn managed to mumble something in reply, wandering zombielike through the front hall. Her gaze caught on the blackened elk antlers far above the open doorway to the main hall, and her steps slowed.

She could still feel the presence of the earl's ghost. It was something she'd not left behind in the chapel vault, something that surrounded her, permeated the very stone of the castle. His presence had been there always, from the day she'd first set foot in Thornwyck—she'd only been too close-minded, and then too afraid, to understand it.

A tiny smile curved her lips as she passed beneath the antlers into the hallway. They wouldn't fall on her. She couldn't have said how she'd known that, but know it she did. Whatever had happened on the cliff that night . . .

it was different from the presence of the ghost somehow. Carolyn couldn't explain it, couldn't rationalize it, couldn't even speak of it to anyone else—but she was certain that the ninth Earl of Thornwyck did not mean her harm.

All the questions still remained . . . but from now on, she would be seeking the answers without the shadow of fear to haunt her.

As she passed through the hall on her way to the stairs, Carolyn noticed the sliver of light coming from Lady Elizabeth's study, beside the Blue Room. She hesitated in front of the door for only an instant before reluctance to disturb her aunt gave way to the longing for a few cheerful words to lighten the melancholy mood that would not leave her.

"Aunt Beth?" Carolyn tapped her fingers against the polished wood of the door. "You in there?"

"Come in, come in," came the bright reply from the other side of the door. Carolyn slipped into the room, summoning a tenuous smile. Cascades of bright, clear notes greeted her, the sound of wind and string instruments and perhaps a hammer dulcimer issuing softly from the stereo concealed in a wall cabinet.

"Hello, dear." Aunt Beth gestured to an armchair across from her desk, eyeing Carolyn expectantly. "I thought you might stop in. Did you find any answers?"

Sinking into the chair with a long sigh, Carolyn shook her head. "No." None that she could explain, anyway. "I only found the date of his death, which I'm sure you already know."

Aunt Beth nodded, idly straightening the papers on the desk in front of her. "Yes, that isn't much of a secret." She shrugged, smiled resignedly. "And I suppose the rest of it will remain as such, until . . ."

Carolyn stopped toying with the flashlight in her lap, meeting her aunt's gaze. "Until?"

Lady Elizabeth shrugged faintly. "Why, until the earl decides to tell someone, of course. He is the only eyewitness left, you know."

Chapter Nine

"But he—"

An abrupt knock on the half-open door interrupted Carolyn's wide-eyed retort.

"Ah—excuse me, but I wonder if I could interest you in taking in two orphans. . . ."

The head, shoulders, and then the body of a blond, bearded man in perhaps his early thirties appeared around the door. Two piteously mewling kittens clung to the front of his thick, white wool sweater, supported there by one large hand while the other still remained on the doorknob.

Carolyn was the first on her feet. She rushed across the room and, with no more than a distracted smile for the tall man, disentangled first one sharp-clawed burr, and then the other.

"Come here, you little darlings. God, but they're

so tiny!" Especially when compared to Serendipity. Carolyn's smile warmed a little more, letting care for the kittens take away some of her sorrow for Tiernan. As a little girl she'd always wanted a kitten. Glancing up at the man standing so close, she almost dropped the two fluffy creatures as a sharp, unexpected jolt of fear twined with hatred shot through her. It was gone in the next instant, leaving her heart beating wildly on a rush of adrenaline—fight or flight, a visceral reaction over which she had no control.

The sandy-haired stranger was nodding in agreement to her words, stroking the kittens' downy fur with his fingertips, oblivious to her inexplicable shock.

"Can't be more than a month old, if that," he offered in a pleasant, mellow voice. "They were crawling all over the road, just before the turnoff. I was nearly on top of them before I saw them, what with the mist rising and the sun gone down. Their mama and one other kitten weren't so lucky. They were already dead when I found them."

Carolyn found the man's sky-blue eyes meeting hers, and caught her breath softly as another of the alien thoughts shot through her mind.

—horrid, despicable man—

She glanced away uneasily, over her shoulder, at Aunt Beth standing just behind them. "Can— can we keep them?"

Lady Elizabeth's eyes rolled heavenward as she stepped closer to peer at the kittens. Carolyn snatched a deep breath, feeling shaken still,

126

drained. The surge of alien emotions had vanished as abruptly as it had appeared, yet her hands were still trembling ever so slightly. She busied them with stroking the fluffy, soft, squirming kittens.

"Well, why ever not?" Aunt Beth finally replied. "Thornwyck is big enough, and, Lord knows, three cats can't possibly be enough." But she was smiling, and Carolyn saw it and smiled in return.

"You won't be sorry," she said, beaming at Aunt Beth. "I'll take care of them; I promise. I'll take them to the vet and make sure they get their shots, and get the right food—"

Lady Elizabeth nodded firmly. "Yes, you certainly will. And they're not going to be living in the kitchen cabinets, either. You can take them up to your room, if you get a litter box and plenty of newspapers from Maura."

Carolyn shot her the look of a child who has just found the long-wished-for pet under the Christmas tree. Confining the kittens to one hand, she gave her aunt a hug. "Thank you!"

Then, with a polite if nervous smile, Carolyn turned to the dazzlingly attractive stranger. "And thank you, too, for bringing them home."

He returned the smile, blue eyes sparkling with pleasure. "No thanks necessary, I assure you. Name's Erik Chandler."

He took her free hand and bowed over it.

"When in Rome, do as the Romans do," Erik stage-whispered to her as he straightened with a wink. Carolyn, clinging to the kittens, promptly blushed.

So this was Lucy's American businessman. Yes, she could see why the hostess spoke of him so often—and perhaps had a bit of a crush on him. For sheer charisma and flamboyance, Carolyn had yet to meet his equal.

"It's a pleasure to have you back, Mr. Chandler," Aunt Beth offered from beside Carolyn, coming to her rescue and receiving the same bow, minus the wink and the whisper. "And this young lady is Carolyn Masters—"

"Masters!" Chandler cut off Lady Elizabeth's words.

Carolyn, now fully occupied in trying to keep the two kittens from crawling off in different directions on her body, heard the surprise in his voice. She glanced at him, seeing arched blond brows and widened blue eyes.

"You're not related to the butler . . . ?"

"—my niece, Mr. Chandler," Aunt Beth finished with a smile. "From Canada. A neighbor of yours, you might say, geographically speaking."

"Oh, somebody help, please!" Before Carolyn could spend more time wondering about this odd first meeting one of the kittens escaped over her shoulder. She bent forward at the waist, still holding on to the second furball, while its twin attempted to walk down her back, its tiny, needle-sharp claws digging through her sweater into her skin.

"Ah, well, that's a relief." Erik Chandler's voice came from just beside her, rich with amusement.

"I was afraid we'd be depriving this place of hired help when we elope."

Deceptively strong hands gently disengaged twenty claws from Carolyn's back, then handed the little terror over to her as she straightened. Realizing what the man had just said, she glanced up at him with a mixture of shock and uncertainty, but his disarming smile fostered one of her own.

How could she have felt any animosity toward this charming man? What in the world was playing havoc with her emotions these days?

Some of her melancholy returned at the thought. The answer to that question, as she knew only too well, lay precisely two minutes' walk northward of the front door.

It was the unceasing mewling from the kittens that hauled Carolyn out of her thoughts and urged her into motion. "I'd better feed these two," she excused herself, heading for the door with a smile at Aunt Beth and a quick nod to the blond man.

She wasn't even halfway down the hall when Erik Chandler caught up to her, now carrying a black briefcase.

"I'm hoping Lucy has some dinner left over for me too," he explained as he matched his stride to hers.

"You just got in?" Carolyn asked conversationally, pleased in spite of herself to hear a familiar accent.

He nodded. "Yeah. I've spent the last day and a half on the road—or in the air, rather. And I

129

could sure do with some real food for a change. Like a nice hot bowl of Lucy's Irish stew."

Carolyn sent him a sidelong glance, remembering her own exhaustion after arriving, noting again the perfect fit of his obviously hand-tailored clothing. The man had money, and wasn't shy about showing it. "You're in luck, then. There was stew for dinner tonight, and I'm sure Lucy won't turn you away if you beg humbly enough."

Erik laughed at her teasing and flashed her a dazzling smile.

Lucy was still tidying up when they reached the kitchen, humming to a tune playing on the radio. She looked up, saw the kittens in Carolyn's grasp, and clapped her hands to her head with a wail that would have done a banshee proud.

"Saints preserve us, not another pair! Oh, Miss Carolyn, we've—"

"Already got three cats, I know. Four, if you count Serendipity as two." Smile unfazed, Carolyn left Erik to charm dinner off a now welcoming Lucy, and warmed some milk for her charges. "Is Maura still up?"

Lucy sent her a baleful glance, busy ladling some stew into a smaller pot. She plunked it down on the stove, still frowning. "Last I saw, she was playing cards with Cummings and Lyle in the library. Oh, but Miss Carolyn, why did you have to—"

"Thanks, Lucy." Smiling at the Irishwoman's plaintive look, Carolyn collected milk bowl and kittens and headed for the hall. "'Night."

"See you tomorrow?"

Carolyn grinned over her shoulder at Thornwyck's latest guest. "Breakfast's at seven."

Amid the clattering of dishes, Lucy's muttering and Erik's chuckles followed her down the hall.

He stared down at Thornwyck from the lofty height of Rory's Tower, torn by unease.

He was back again.

And his arrival was timed perfectly to the return of Elyssa.

The darkness around him flickered, threatening to swallow him up and whisk him from the world of the living, as it so often did. But then it retreated, leaving to him what would once have been hate. Rage, dread even, of what he might not be able to prevent.

Aye, his prayers had been answered. And so had his worst fears.

Gazing up toward the mountains, he watched the clouds sweep across a midnight sky and listened to the thunder of the surf against the cliffs. He could almost taste the brine in the air, could almost feel the chill bite of the wind. The darkness was far away, so far that, were he in the bridal chamber, he would be able to smell the rose perfume of the woman playing with two red kittens, the same scent Elyssa used to wear. Perchance she would even be able to hear his voice. . . .

He turned away from the castle, toward the sea.

In truth, she did not look very much like Elyssa. Beyond the kerry-blue eyes and spun-gold hair, there was little resemblance. Where Elyssa had been gently raised, with soft hands and a soft, feminine

131

body, the woman Carolyn was . . . quite different.

In his time, she might have been thought to come from a poor family, with never quite enough food to eat and a body worn and toughened by hard labor. Yet she glowed with health and vitality, and there was a compelling quality to her every movement, a lithe grace that made him think of a sleek, alert cat.

But no matter her strength of body, her heart was as great and tender as that of Elyssa.

He had watched her last night, as she struggled with the fear that so easily chained the mortal soul. Had watched her descend into the vault, bringing light where none had been for over two centuries. He had felt the walls of her fear crumble, leaving her a little less blind to him, to his presence. . . .

And he had watched as her eyes had filled with tears—tears for him.

Tears for what the rational part of her would never understand, or admit. Tears for a life that was cut short in its brightest days, for a love that was treacherously murdered.

Ah, but her tears had not spilled. She had not given in to the despair, the grief. Aye, she was strong.

And he could only pray that she would be strong enough to face the storm clouds building on the horizon, for the arrival of Chandler heralded no good.

Twice he had tried to frighten the man away; both times Chandler had shown more pluck than Marshall ever had.

It did not bode well. The battle, should it come to that, would not be easy to win—perhaps it would be impossible. . . .

Nay, that did not bear thinking upon.

And he, who could no longer touch the living, could do naught but pray that a merciful God would not let the past come to pass again.

"Why, dearest, you look tired this morning. Didn't you sleep well?"

"Good morning, Aunt Beth." Carolyn blinked over her teacup at Lady Elizabeth, then yawned into her hands and rubbed her burning eyes. "I'm sure if I had actually managed to sleep I would have done so very well."

Eyes crinkling, Aunt Beth took a seat across from Carolyn. Lucy appeared immediately with the teapot.

"Ah, thank you, Lucy." Tilting her head slightly, Lady Elizabeth glanced at Carolyn. "Mr. Chandler was here two hours ago, apparently expecting you to join him for breakfast before he left on business." Her brows furrowed in concern at Carolyn's obvious exhaustion. "Was *he* visiting you again?"

"Huh? Oh, no." Vaguely embarrassed about her missed appointment, Carolyn shook her head. There had been no trace of the earl last night. But she almost wished there had been; he might have intimidated the kittens enough for them to stop trying to tear her chamber apart. "My new roommates were up exploring all night."

That wasn't the whole truth, unfortunately,

but Carolyn was afraid her aunt might evict her *and* the kittens if she were to hear all the unsavory details. The little tom, especially, had been hell–bent on determining what the top of the curtain rods looked like.

"Oh." A moment of silence followed Aunt Beth's voice. "Well, perhaps you should take them down into the garden for a while."

Carolyn's smile turned sheepish as she let her gaze follow Lady Elizabeth's out the windows. "Actually, they're already out there." Where, exactly, she couldn't have said. Scathach had decided to start an argument the instant she'd spotted the newcomers in Carolyn's arms outside the back door. In a matter of seconds the kittens had been flying off in two different directions, with utter disregard for flower beds. Tippens had joined the chase with remarkable enthusiasm for his age, while Scathach had sat hissing and spitting on the top step of the terrace before streaking up a hazelnut tree after a flock of sparrows.

"It's been—an interesting morning," Carolyn summed up, then strategically changed the subject to one guaranteed to get Lady Elizabeth's attention. "You're going to the races today, Aunt Beth?"

A hopeful smile lit time-lined features. "Don't tell me you'd care to come along?"

Grinning, Carolyn shook her head. "I'm heading for the library. All those history books, remember?"

"Ah, yes, indeed." Aunt Beth sipped at her tea. "But you really should consider tagging along one day. I'd never have thought I'd like the races when I was little, you know. But Father, well, he loved them. And he took me along. And before you knew it . . ."

Carolyn smiled. "Thanks, but I still think I'll stay here. I'm investigating a mystery, don't you know?"

Aunt Beth beamed back at her, then gave her a conspiratory wink. "Well, I can only hope you have as much luck with books as I do with those fillies."

Carolyn didn't. For four hours she leafed through volume upon volume of Kerry history, in vain.

Not that there wasn't any information in those books. There was—just not the particulars that Carolyn was looking for. But at least the library was quiet today, free of shuddering shelves and falling books.

Carolyn didn't realize how late it was until the clear, airy notes of the harp filtered in through the open door of the library from the Blue Room, two doors down. Maura usually spent an hour or so practicing each afternoon, though as far as Carolyn was concerned, it wasn't practice so much as pure enjoyment.

She sighed, glancing at her watch. Her stomach gave a faint complaint about the missed lunch, but she ignored it, leaning back in her chair and stretching. Then, closing the thick book in front of her with a solid *thump*, she added it to the two-foot-high stack on her right and chose another volume from the equally massive stack on her left.

Next door, Maura had finished her customary warm–up and began a song. It sounded like Heather was there, too, singing along as she sometimes did, harmonizing with Maura's high, clear voice.

Carolyn sighed again, pushed the "finished" stack farther away on the huge round table, and opened the next book, a promising biographical volume on Munster families. She paused once while leafing through the index, her attention diverted by a refrain echoing softly from next door.

"I dreamed it last night that my true love came in,
So softly she entered, her feet made no din;
She came close beside me, and this she did say
'It will not be long, love, till our wedding day.' "

The haunting melody, the wistful words, restored in Carolyn's mind's eye once again the specter of Tiernan as he'd stood at the foot of her bed, reaching out to her. . . .

Shaking her head, she returned her attention to the book before her. Gazing off into space wouldn't bring her any answers. But her eyes were burning, and her stomach had resumed its complaints with a vengeance.

With yet another sigh, Carolyn pushed to her

feet. She picked out another two books from the stack on her left, added them to the volume before her, then reshelved everything else. She'd scrounge a couple of biscuits from the huge cookie jar in the kitchen, get some fresh air to wake herself up, put in a half hour in the gym, and then take the books up to her room for, as Aunt Beth had called it, "bedtime reading."

Humming along to "Come by the Hills," Carolyn headed for the kitchen.

He had been watching her all day.

And he watched her now, as she wrapped the green cloak around her and strode out toward the cliffs. The wind tore at her short flaxen hair, sending it streaming like a flame behind her as she faced the whitecapped sea.

He stopped by the remains of the curtain wall, the sensations rising in his soul becoming unbearable. Had he had a body, it would have trembled, torn between the sweetly soaring joy and the piercing sorrow that was his.

It could have been Elyssa, standing there. She had had a cloak of forest green, lined with silk and trimmed with fur. Often she had stood at the cliffs like this, staring into the distance as storm clouds darkened the colors of the sunset sea into cooling lead.

And, sometimes, a very few times, he had stood there beside her—sharing a cloak, arm in arm, looking into a common future. . . .

Ah, damn Marshall. Damn Lord Warrington, that greedy, unscrupulous—

He moved aside abruptly. The woman who had been Elyssa and now was Carolyn had turned and was striding back toward Thornwyck with that lithe, long-legged gait of hers. And she had nearly walked through him.

"Tiger, no!"

Horrified, dumping her armload of books on the dresser, Carolyn shut the door and rushed across the room to scoop up the red tom—too late, for the damage had already been done. Claw marks crisscrossed the finishing of the ancient oak chest, and a small piece of the delicate, ornate carving lay on the floor, chewed or broken off.

"Oh, look what you've done! I should have told Maura to leave you outside, and let Scathach eat you! Aunt Beth will have your hide, you nitwit, and mine, too! That chest is over three hundred years old!"

Groaning, Carolyn tossed a nonplussed Tiger onto the duvet and knelt down to examine the damage more closely. Lily shot out from underneath the bed with all the enthusiasm and uncoordinated grace of a kitten, attacking Carolyn's hair and startling her into a yelp before leaping clumsily up on the bed to join her brother. Carolyn glared at the two tail-twitching little dervishes, trying hard not to succumb to a smile.

"From tomorrow on, you're outdoor cats! Both of you!" It was an empty threat, and both kittens seemed to know it. Catching sight of his sister's tail, Tiger launched himself onto the unsuspecting kitten. Another very vocal wrestling match ensued, with intimidating, if baby-sized, growls and snarls.

Carolyn lost the fight and broke into a smile. Still, she should find Aunt Beth, who must be back from the races by now. Perhaps there was some way to polish up the finish of that chest, at least, to reduce some of the damage done.

She was about to rise when the piece of ribbon caught her eye. It was just a tiny end of pink, peeking out from the bottom of the chest—where there should have been a solid joint, and no possibility of anything peeking out.

Frowning, Carolyn scuttled closer, until she was lying on her back beside the chest, trying to peer at it from underneath wherever the ribbon stuck out. Since that proved impossible, she explored the section with her fingertips. There was a definite edge there, and something that felt cool to the touch, like metal—

The edge gave under her probing fingers. A small, previously hidden and obviously spring-loaded drawer at the foot of the chest popped open, stopping only upon connecting with Carolyn's forehead.

She scrambled back with a squeak, rubbing her face, then sat up and examined the open drawer. The pink ribbon was attached to a tiny, ancient-looking key. Underneath it lay a black, gold-engraved, leather-bound book.

Breath surged into Carolyn's lungs in a long, slow gasp as she stared at her discovery.

A diary.

"Time for supper, dear!"

The unexpected call, combined with three quick raps on her door, sent Carolyn half a foot into the air. It took her a good five seconds before she'd caught her breath and processed her aunt's words. Then she was up and running, flying out the door.

"Aunt Beth! Wait! I've found something—!"

Lady Elizabeth, dressed for dinner and halfway down to the first landing of the staircase, halted and looked up at her questioningly. Carolyn's hands clenched around the railing.

"I—" Then she broke off and shook her head impatiently. "Oh, just come up; I'll show you."

A scarce moment later Lady Elizabeth stopped beside Carolyn in front of the dresser. She didn't comment on the mess the room was in, with litter box in the corner, kitty litter scattered by the overanxious digging of little paws, and several scrunched up paper balls on the floor, waiting for attack. She only gazed down at the secret drawer.

"Look at that, Aunt Beth."

Carolyn's words were superfluous. Her aunt was already looking—was staring, actually, at the once-hidden drawer and its contents.

"My goodness." Sinking down, Lady Elizabeth took the diary out of the drawer and gingerly, almost reverently, brushed her fingertips across its surface. Then, pursing her lips and exhaling softly, she looked up at Carolyn. "This is hers."

Swallowing hard, Carolyn bent closer to her aunt's hands, still gently cradling the diary, trying to decipher the ornate calligraphy on the cover. She knew, but still she asked. "Whose?"

"Why, Elyssa Warrington's," Aunt Beth replied softly. "Or, I should say, Elyssa O'Rourke, Countess of Thornwyck."

An icy finger stroked down Carolyn's spine and lingered low between her shoulder blades, then disappeared.

Answers. There, before her, in that ancient, leather-bound book, could be all the answers she had quested for these last days.

"Can I—may I please—read it?" The hand she held out trembled.

Lady Elizabeth scrutinized her for a moment, then briskly handed her the diary. "Of course you may. I couldn't think of anyone more fit to read it than you."

Carolyn didn't have time to frown at the odd choice of words. Aunt Beth was looking down at the key still in the secret drawer, brows furrowing. Recalling the damage done, Carolyn winced, set aside the diary, and scrunched down to examine her kitten's work yet again.

"Oh, blast—I'm sorry, Aunt Beth! Tiger—he found the end of the ribbon sticking out from that drawer and scratched up the finish—there's even a small piece he's chewed off—" She held up the item in question, meeting her aunt's eyes miserably.

Lady Elizabeth waved off her concern, still frowning. "It's quite all right, dear."

Carolyn cursed again, this time silently. "Are you sure? I know it's an antique, and probably worth a fortune, and—"

Aunt Beth's gaze met hers with unaccustomed brightness. "I am quite sure, dearest. As a matter of fact, I'm willing to bet this diary is ten times more valuable than the chest. You can give that red devil an extra dish of cream, as far as I'm concerned."

Dumbstruck, Carolyn watched her aunt turn toward the door and pause with one hand on the frame. "I'll have supper sent up to your room, if you wish," she offered, smiling. "And I'll even send your regrets to Mr. Chandler."

Carolyn had the manners to wince at the mention of Thornwyck's new guest; she'd totally forgotten about him again. But then a smile lit up her face, a smile meant exclusively for Aunt Beth. How in the world could this wise old woman whom she'd never even seen before last week know her so well?

"Thanks, Aunt Beth. You're the best."

A muttered "I knew that" from halfway out the door brightened Carolyn's smile even more, and almost brought tears to her eyes.

Blinking rapidly, Carolyn watched the door close behind Lady Elizabeth. Then, with unsteady hands, she retrieved the ancient key and the diary.

Carolyn never even touched the covered tray of roast beef placed safely out of the kittens' reach on the desk some time ago by Lucy. She sat against the headboard of her bed, down duvet tucked in around her, while Tiger and Lily cavorted on the carpet,

chasing one of her knitted ponytail hold-
ers.

The closed diary lay before her on the covers,
looking utterly out of place . . . and yet belonging
perfectly.

Carolyn really hadn't any hope of being able
to read much of the writing inside it. To judge
by the intertwined script on the cover, she'd be
able to read nothing at all. . . .

But before she could even worry about the
reading part, she'd have to hope that the lock
mechanism hadn't seized up.

The pink ribbon, faded and slightly yellowed
by time, whispered across the duvet cover as she
slid the key into the lock and, as though it were
made of spun glass, gingerly turned it.

The mechanism gave obediently, with only a
slight catch. That simply, the private thoughts of
a woman long dead lay unlocked before her.

Carolyn's hands were suddenly shaking. The
prospect of unraveling the past of the ninth earl
shortened her breath, pumping adrenaline into
her bloodstream.

With a deep breath, she carefully opened the
diary partway through. Pages brittle and yellowed
by the passage of centuries stared up at her. She
focused on the first lines of the left-hand page,
read them—

—*read them*, without any difficulty at all, as
though the beautiful, intertwined script were her
own handwriting, not that of a woman who had
lived and died at Thornwyck over two centuries ago.

I rode along the Shore with Caitlin this day. She is visiting Thornwyck from the North with her husband, and has done much to Welcome me here. Though she is of the Catholic Faith, as is her husband, she has shown me nothing but Kindness. She seems not at all like her brother, my Betrothed. I have been here four Days, and have never yet seen him smile. It is almost as though he does not wish me here.

The entry was marked June 16, 1732.

Chapter Ten

June 26
*The Wedding is a fortnight hence. His Lord-
ship, the Earl, is in good Cheer, though he
still misses his eldest Son dreadfully. Caitlin
took me to St. Mary's today, where Bryce lies
now. I did not know him, yet I cannot help
but think he would have been a kinder man
than my Betrothed.*

July 2
*I do not wish to marry him! God help me,
but he hates me. I know it, though all others
deny it out of pity. Just this Night, when he
came to sit with me by the fire in the great
Hall, I thought he would finally give some
kind Words to me. Instead he spoke of horrid
things, until I begged him to stay his tongue,*

yet he would not. I fled from the House, and nearly came to grief upon the Cliffs.

July 12

The Wedding was beautiful. My lord Husband is the most handsome man I have ever Seen, and had I been granted but one Wish today, I would have had even a single smile from him. 'Tis our wedding night, and I am alone in this Chamber.

The ink was blurred in places. Carolyn could see her far too clearly—the new bride, sitting alone, lonely, with her diary, tears spilling from her eyes. A single white rose petal lay pressed between the pages. It cracked and crumbled into tiny fragments as Carolyn carefully turned the page.

July 15

We have been wed for three Days. He is not as Cruel as I had feared, though he gives more Kindness to his horse than to his Wife. He has not made ours a marriage in Truth, and makes it no secret that he will have nothing to do With me. Lady Catherine is the kindest of Souls, for she does not let me feel too Sharply the shame of being so spurned. I do not even know where he spends the Nights, nor does he speak to me on his wishes, or any other Matter. God give me the strength to be a good wife to this man who Hates me so.

Mouth tight, Carolyn turned the next page and softly caught her breath.

Sketched in exquisite, loving detail, with the title "Our Wedding Day" inscribed above, the image of Tiernan and Elyssa stared back at her from the yellowed paper. The bride was in a gown of white, seated on a chair in what might have been the library. Tiernan, in a suit of black, with a white rose in the lapel, stood slightly behind and to the side of her, one arm placed on the back of the chair. His countenance was somber, even grim, yet Elyssa's fragile smile was enough to capture anyone's heart.

With a long sigh, Carolyn looked up from the diary, and stared at the empty space at the end of her bed.

Where was he now, the ghost of Thornwyck? Could he see her, delving into the past, reading the words of his bride, his wife? Did he know of the anguish he had caused her, the sorrow and loneliness?

She pressed her lips together and glanced at the ink drawing again, critically. Elyssa was a beautiful woman—not in the modern-day, anorexic image, but with a more classical, feminine beauty. Her sensuous, soft curves stood in stark contrast to the harsh lines of Tiernan's face. His stance reminded her of a man facing a firing squad—defiant, proud, and fully aware of his doom.

There was a short entry below the sketch, confirming Carolyn's suspicions.

July 17
Our portrait was begun Yesterday. My lord
Husband loathed the sitting almost as Much
as he loathed the wedding. If not for his Lady
Mother's insistence, I do not think he would
have stood for it at all. Yet the Portrait is
turning out Magnificently. I have attempted
to draw it in this Book, but my Skill at such
is much lacking.

Carolyn smiled at Elyssa's modesty, then leafed
on, slipping all too easily into her somber mood
again.

It was becoming frighteningly real, the life of
this woman. Her emotions, her fears and simple joys, all lived so vividly between the pages
of her diary, a legacy that lent her immortality. Carolyn found herself skimming some of the
entries, impatient to find the answers she had
been seeking, almost certain that she would find
them in Elyssa's elegant script.

August 14
A terrible tragedy has struck this House.
His Lordship the Earl and Lady Catherine
were killed when their carriage overturned on
the coast Road on their way back from Town.
My husband is in a dreadful State. God have
Mercy on their Souls, and on his.

August 16
He had gone mad. God forgive my words,

but 'tis the Truth. He blames Mother and Father for the death of his Parents, even of Bryce, calls it murder. He has been in a terrible Rage since the accident, cursing all within his Reach, myself included. He calls me a ban-draoi, a sorceress. He does not eat, nor Sleep, and goes about like a wild man. Even the servants are Afraid of him. He said Today that he wants a divorce. Perhaps that will be for the best. I am glad now that he does not visit my Chamber.

August 22
My lord Husband has finally come to himself again. He has said no more of a Divorce, and even spoke of attending Mother's birthday Ball. I do not know if he jests to torment me, or means it truly.

September 6
This day has not seen its end. We attended Mother's ball, and a beautiful Celebration it was. Yet his lordship Winston Marshall attended also, and behaved quite improperly toward myself. 'Twas terribly embarrassing, and Frightening, for my lord Husband immediately challenged the Earl to a duel. Father managed to halt them before my lord could Kill the Earl. I know it is wrong of me to be proud of my Husband, but that I am. He fought for my honor Tonight, and for my Safety. I do not understand why he did not simply turn his Back, as he might have done,

but I am glad he did not. Winston Marshall is a horrid, Despicable man, and, God forgive me, I wish Father had not interfered.

September 7
A storm has broken this Eve, fierce winds and Lashing rain. The voice of the Thunder is so loud in my chamber, it frightens me. Yet I have consolation this Day, for something has changed in my Lord Husband. His eyes, I think. They are haunted still, but no longer so cold and full of Rage.

September 8
It has been near two months since our Wedding. He came to me late last Night, reluctantly, perhaps. Lonely, like myself. I had not Dreamed he could be so very gentle.

Carolyn stared at the haunting words, at the date, then stared blindly toward the end of the bed while a cascade of shivers tumbled down her spine. She knew, suddenly, what the ninth earl's ghost had whispered that first night she'd seen him, that night she'd arrived, September 7.
Elyssa.
Blinking back tears, Carolyn exhaled a ragged breath and shut her eyes for a moment. A tiny questing nose nudged against her hand, bringing her back to reality. She glanced down to see Lily investigating the diary.

"No, love, you can't eat that." Scooping up the kitten, Carolyn placed it on the covers beside her legs, where it immediately curled up, purring mightily.

With a bittersweet smile, Carolyn lowered her gaze to the diary again, and read on.

> *September 10*
> *Tiernan no longer remains absent at Night. He is a restless sleeper. I cry for him, for his Pain. He is so Tormented, so torn inside, I wonder how he bears it. I can only Pray that the love I hold for him will be enough to heal the Hatred and anger in him, but I fear his Irish blood has known too much pain and Betrayal at the hands of my People.*

Carolyn skimmed on, and came to an entry on the bottom of a right-hand page, perhaps three-quarters through the journal. She swallowed hard, drew a bracing breath, and then focused on the entry again to read it, knowing there would be only blank pages after this.

> *I am quite certain now that I carry my Beloved's babe. I told him this Morn, and it seemed he was Pleased. I do not think he hates me so very Much anymore—he calls me* grá mo Chroí, *his darling. Pray to God that our trials are over.*

Lips compressed into a pale line, Carolyn gently shut the diary. Her hands were cold as she placed the book on the bedside table and turned out the light. Then she curled up under the duvet, burning eyes squeezed shut.

With an inquisitive grumble, Lily came padding across the covers to curl up in the hollow of Carolyn's shoulder. Tears suddenly began to slip, hot and silent, from beneath her closed lashes, tears for Elyssa and tears for the apparently instinctive understanding of that silly little kitten that someone needed comforting. She turned her head into the bundle of fluffy, rumbling content-ment and inhaled deeply the warm, soothing scent of cat fur. And still the tears continued welling from her eyes.

It could have marked a fairy-tale ending, that last passage in the diary. It certainly read like one, so full of hope for a brighter tomorrow.

Except Carolyn knew there were no such things as happily-ever-afters. She had seen the date of the entry before, chiseled in white marble.

October 10, 1732.

Chapter Eleven

Carolyn dreamed. She knew she was dreaming because she was in her bedroom at Thornwyck, but not in the bed. She was floating weightlessly in the chamber, an invisible observer staring down at the young woman in the frilly, lacy white nightgown and nightcap who sat in bed beneath white coverlets. A candelabra on the bedside table shed flickering light onto the diary in her lap.

Carolyn frowned. She knew that diary. Knew, as well as she knew herself, the woman in the room that was now hers.

The dream changed, smoothly and unquestionably, as dreams do. She was no longer observing from some indefinite point in the room, but was becoming the woman on the bed . . . becoming Elyssa.

She shrank back into the pillows as the door crashed open without the courtesy of a knock. Her heart caught for an instant, then quickened, leaping into her throat. With widened eyes she watched the fearful, shadowy figure of the man who brashly strode into her room and stopped in front of the bed.

Narrowed, fierce green eyes glowered at her in the candlelight, eyes glinting with tendrils of madness. Two days' growth of beard shadowed his jaw and cheeks, removed all pretense of civilization from his cold countenance.

"I think, wife, that I shall divorce ye."

Her hand flew up to her throat, to stay her heart from choking her with its beat. She stared up at the implacable face of her husband and knew why even the servants feared him now. He truly must have gone mad, to suggest such a thing.

Her voice, when she found it, trembled as much as her hands. "But—Thornwyck—"

The new earl laughed, a cold and cruel sound that lashed her with mockery.

"Thornwyck!" he scoffed, mouth twisting into something only the devil would have called a smile. "Dinna ye know it, sweet wife? Have ye not realized yet that I dinna give a tinker's damn about this estate? I am the O'Rourke now, the last Earl o' Thornwyck. There's none *left* t' inherit but bloody *Sasanach* invaders!"

Elyssa lowered her gaze, escaping his scalding anger, feeling suddenly as though the pungent smell of the slow-burning peat would choke her.

154

He had misunderstood, as he so often did, eager to think only the worst of her. She'd meant only to say that Thornwyck was her home now, too. Would be the home of their children, if he ever decided to be husband in truth to her, to fulfill the marriage vows he had spoken.

She dared look up at him again. "But—your heirs—our—"

"Heirs!" The hiss cut off her words, widened her eyes with fear. He saw it, and his lips drew back in a wolf's feral smile as he crouched down beside the bed, better to glare at her, frighten her, as he so loved to do.

Breath growing tight in her throat, Elyssa stiffened her spine and tried not to cower, praying silently that she had not provoked him with her words, that he would not come to her in such a rage to remedy the husbandly duties he'd so far foregone.

His face only inches from hers, he laughed again, more hatefully than before.

"Little fool! Did ye think I'd have it go that far? Or stay in this trap, when yer bloody wonderful Protestant faith allows a way out? I'll not let yer high-and-mighty noble *English* family be manipulatin' everything I do through ye! Nor will I watch them murder me kin, and no' raise a hand t'—"

"They did no such thing!" She jerked back, away from him, blood draining from her face in shock at his words. Truly, he was going mad! "'Twas an accident, my lord! They would never—"

"But they did, the bloody murderin' *Sasanach* dogs!"

He shoved away from the bed and surged to his feet, flaying her with his icy, scornful gaze— punishing her for the crimes he imagined of her family.

"'Tis what they do best, after all!" he ground out harshly. "They've been at it long enough. Their adored Cromwell slaughtered women and children and monks, and then bragged o' his great *victory*. Compared t' such, what's one more Irish family quietly done away wi'?"

"My lord—I beg you, please—"

He turned away sharply and strode out of the room, into the candlelit hall, giving her not so much as a backward glance or word of parting. The door slammed shut like the gates of Hell closing behind him, and the chamber suddenly dipped into inky night.

Floating weightlessly, bodiless again, Carolyn watched in her dream as the darkness shaped itself into a storm-filled night. A cold, pale moon stood high above the sea, dancing out of sight behind torn fragments of clouds. Winds howled across the seaward grounds with the voices of the damned, calling the living to death.

Again, her sight took on perspective, and she was no longer observing, but part of the scene. She was dancing with Tiernan, there on the cliffs, lost to the rushing of the sea wind and the warmth of her husband's embrace. She smiled up at him, tremulously, only to lose some of her courage at his brooding, coldly set features.

"My lord. Are you not happy with the news?"

Her too-soft whisper caught his attention even over the sound of the storm. The beginning of a smile softened his features, warmed her soul like the brightest ray of summer sun.

Yet before he could speak the sharp report of a shot shattered the night. What might have been an endearment burst as a short, shocked cry from Tiernan's lips. He jerked in her arms, stumbled, blood welling on his temple and forehead, dripping, flowing down into his eyes.

"Tiernan!"

She clutched at him, cried his name again and again as he reeled backward, toward the gaping emptiness behind them, his weight too great for her to bear. The wind snatched away the sound of his name, hurled it out over the abyss and into the sea. Suddenly the once solid ground beneath their feet began to crumble, falling away into the emptiness, leaving them weightless for an eternal instant of terror before the pounding surf rose up with blinding speed to engulf them—

"No—!"

Carolyn jerked awake, a scream caught in her throat. Blankets entangled her, clinging to her, pulling her down into that endless fall. . . .

Breath rushed from her lungs sharply, on a hoarse, ragged sound. It had been a dream. No more than a dream, nothing more than an overworked imagination fired by too many history books and the all too real passages from a dead woman's diary—

"Oh . . . God. . . ."

Carolyn hugged the covers against herself with hands that were shaking and buried her face in them. Then she lunged across the bed and switched on the lamp on the nightstand to banish the world of shadows that was threatening to suffocate her.

The light helped, somewhat. By its golden glow memories of the dream faded mercifully into the vague, indistinct images that were the remains of half-forgotten nightmares. Even when she grew bold and snatched at the fragments they slipped from her mind's grasp, into the shadows beyond consciousness.

Shivering, Carolyn lay back and drew the covers up to her chin again. She was alone in the bed; Lily had disappeared sometime in the night. A quick glance around the room showed the two kittens shamelessly yet innocently intertwined in a tangle of limbs and tails on the armchair by the window.

She shoved out of bed, selfishly scooping up the unprotesting kittens and depositing them on the duvet. They never woke up, never stirred, simply continued sleeping.

God bless all kittens, Carolyn thought gratefully as she curled up beneath the covers again, one hand lightly stroking the feather-soft fur of her companions.

Still, it was almost dawn before she turned off the lamp and resigned herself once more to the perilous realm of dreams.

*   *   *

He shifted away from the wainscoting by the door and crossed toward the window. The darkness was far away again, this night. He'd been able to watch her sleep, watch her dream—and watch her wake in mortal terror.

He knew what she had seen, knew why she had cried his name in her sleep, as another had cried it in the last instant of life. He could see it all, as vividly as though it had been but yesterday, that darkest night upon the cliffs. He could almost feel the sweet weight of her body pressed against him as they moved as one in the dance, round and round, ever closer to the roaring of the surf far below, while rage had burned in his mind, desire in his veins, despair in his heart.

God above, he'd never meant to let himself care for her, to—love her. Yet how could he have helped it? She'd been nothing like he'd expected, nothing like the cold, greedy, hated English he had known. She'd given of herself so freely—given, without reserve, without judgment, in a world where everyone knew only how to take. . . . Everyone, including the man she'd called husband.

The corners of his lips tugged up with the remembered elusive scent of the white rose she had put on his lapel as they'd passed through the gardens earlier that night. He stared down at the pale form of the flower that was with him still, and his expression sobered. It reminded her of their wedding, she'd said as she'd plucked it, smiling shyly. And he, coward that he'd ever been, hadn't replied.

Merciful God, what could she have found pleasant about their wedding? Or the weeks that followed it? He'd given her nothing but scorn, hatred, and callous disregard.

And she had borne up under his anger and had returned it with love.

Fury rose again, sharply, directed only at himself. He'd not believed her to be real, this angelic wife of his. So much easier to think the worst of her, than to believe such saintliness. Certainly he'd never meant to make a marriage in truth of that mockery. But it had taken preciously little, in the end, to lose his heart to her. When he thought of her sleep-tousled, radiant face only that fateful morn, telling him what every man should be exultant to hear, that she wished their babe to be a son . . .

Nay, he'd not thought of her as a hated Sasanach, *then. He'd been irrationally joyous, thinking only of a boy-child with his raven hair and her kerry-blue eyes. . . .*

Jesu, but the cruelty of fate, the terrible price they'd all paid for his self-righteous mistrust! By nightfall that same day, he'd convinced himself once more that he could not believe her professed innocence, her love, that he could not believe her to be aught but a pawn of her parents, to be used against him when he least expected it. Ah, ever had he turned his hatred of the Warringtons against her, because she had been the one within his reach—and ever had she deserved nothing but kindness, gentleness from him, far more of it that he could give.

160

He turned away from the bed and stared out through the gap in the window curtains behind him. There was no mist over the land tonight, nothing to bar the sight of the cliffs from him. With a silent oath he spun back to gaze at the woman curled up under the covers. It had been his fault, as much as that of their cursed assassin. Had he not been so blinded by his suspicion of Elyssa, had he searched elsewhere for betrayal . . .

Ah, too late. Far too late, now.

Dizziness surrounded him, the darkness that never left for long swirling closer again. It was like that night on the cliffs, his vision dimming, his senses confused, hands clutching at him in vain. Yet instead of the sickening sensation of falling and the terrible rage and fear and denial, there was only weary resignation.

Slowly, inexorably, night coalesced around him, taking him into itself. Yet his gaze remained fixed on the woman, now peacefully asleep, until the darkness grew complete and the world ceased to exist.

Chapter Twelve

Carolyn wearily laid the cool washcloth across her eyes, resting her elbows on the smooth wood of the dresser. The room was silent, for once, lacking the sound of the kittens' boisterous play. Carolyn hadn't been able to track them down again after the morning trip to the vet, but she wasn't worried about them; they knew the place well enough by now to find their way to the garden-facing kitty door and the communal food dishes and litter box downstairs. And they'd certainly make their presence known outside her door if they wanted in.

She sighed, rubbed her eyes through the wet cloth, still not straightening from the commode. A full day of poring over accounts of eighteenth-century Ireland and leafing through Warrington family records while Aunt Beth had read Elyssa's diary had left her only marginally closer to solving the mystery of the last Earl of Thornwyck. But she had found one tidbit of new information.

She never had gotten around to the volumes she'd brought up to her room, not after the discovery of the diary. Instead, she'd taken them down to the library again in the morning, where, after a brief breakfast with Erik and Aunt Beth, she had resumed her research with renewed vigor.

And, finally, just about when she'd been ready to give up and head down to the gym to work off her frustration, there, on page 572 of one of the largest tomes, she had found the paragraph that even Aunt Beth had not seen before.

It was a brief biographical sketch of one Thomas Ambrose Warrington, born in 1628, a soldier in Cromwell's army who had been given vast landholdings following the invasion. It was a sentence mentioning one of his sons that had made Carolyn sit up and read aloud the words that hit like a blow. She could see the paragraph even now, hovering in her memory like glaring neon script against the darkness of her closed eyes.

. . . was in 1691 that William Oliver Warrington (1667-1734) became the sole inheritor to the Warrington estates. However, in his last years, said William sold much of the family lands to Robert Lancaster, having gained through the untimely death of his daughter and son-in-law, the 9th Earl of Thornwyck, that neighboring estate.

Another piece of the puzzle. She had many pieces now, too many, even. And still she couldn't fit them all together. She didn't know why Tiernan yet roamed the halls and cliffs of Thornwyck.

The tiny creak of the floorboards behind her betrayed his presence in her room and snapped her out of her memories.

Think of the devil . . .

Heart in her throat, Carolyn straightened away from the commode and lowered the washcloth slowly, because suddenly she didn't want to see—and it seemed that, perhaps, if she did not look at him, he would not really be there. Reading history texts and facing a real-life ghost were two vastly different ways of seeing the past. But she opened her eyes and stared into the mirror before her. Her own eyes, widened in alarm, stared back at her.

There was a shadow against the wall beside the mirror, a shadow cast by the electric candles on the wall behind her. With a wet plop the washcloth splashed into the half-full china bowl.

Summoning all her courage, all the bravery she'd thought she didn't possess, Carolyn slowly turned around. Her heart hesitated for an instant before resuming its beating triple time.

Somehow, she should not have been surprised. After all, she had seen the serene beauty of his face carved in marble, had danced with him once, had seen him in her room. But his effigy had been cold and lifeless, and in the darkness of the storm she hadn't seen him clearly. She'd had only glimpses of his unholy beauty, lightning-revealed instances in which to see a face that would have been a mask of male perfection if not for the merciless severity of his mien.

The soft candlelight reflected in the mirror stole the edge from the harsh set of his features. It painted gold and shadow across high cheekbones and a wide, stubborn jaw, gilded the full lips closed into an uncompromising line.

He was watching her—utterly motionless, standing not two steps away from her. His eyes, bright and hard like cut gems, kept her frozen in place and time, like the shining needle that pins a butterfly against black velvet.

Then, suddenly, his gaze left her to wander across the room. Carolyn sucked in air, as though the weight of his stare had suspended her ability to breathe. She watched him scan the old furniture, the half-drawn velvet curtains, finally letting his gaze come to rest on the four-poster bed. His eyes widened as he saw the diary she'd taken back to her bedside table. Already tight lips compressed even further, and his hard stare fell upon her once more.

She imagined accusation in his eyes, fury in the taut line of his jaw. Betrayal . . .

"I read her diary. She loved you."

Carolyn never knew what made her say that, so defiantly, almost accusingly. He did not stalk toward her to punish her for that intrusion, for her transgression. He remained unmoving for long seconds, then slowly looked away.

"Aye."

It was a real voice, not the hollow whisper of a ghost in the night. It was the voice of a bard, a poet, reciting the death song of kings, deep and rich and velvety in its Irish lilt, and full of unspeakable pain.

"Then why did you do it?"

His unreadable gaze returned to her, and his voice grew harsh. "I?" he demanded of her angrily. "I did nothin' save waltz along the seashore wi' me wife." He stepped closer, one stride, two. "'Twas I who was murdered, just as me kin!"

Carolyn backed up, felt her hip touch the edge of the commode. She could understand him easily, despite the heavy brogue, the different words and sentence inflection. But he was too close.

Breath caught in her throat as the images of last night's chilling dream returned to her . . . the dream that had held more truth than the Warrington family annals.

Impossible . . .

"What—what do you mean, murdered?" Her voice came out squeaky, breathless, frightened. Carolyn clenched her fists, her jaw, and stiffened her spine, hoping not to appear a complete coward to the ghost of Thornwyck.

"I would think the word is plain enough." His voice was soft again, lilting. His hand rose to touch his right temple, as if in remembered pain. "I was shot. The bastard aimed for me head, so the wound wouldna be noticed when they found me body down below, on the rocks. Elyssa . . .

167

she tried t' keep hold o' me, but the ground at the edge gave way 'neath us."

Carolyn shuddered with reaction to his words, to how easily he gave her all the missing pieces of the puzzle . . . and how utterly unemotional were his eyes and voice as he spoke of that day.

So this was the coldness Elyssa's diary had spoken of, part of the ghost as it had been part of the man. Yet he did not look like a ghost. He looked far too much like a man, flesh and blood, bone and sinew—

She shivered again, this time purely from the implications of his plain, factual words. So precisely he had described her dream, so simply explained the rage, the anger still lingering in St. Mary's. To have her love snatched away from her so shortly after it had blossomed . . .

Carolyn shook her head to clear it. "Who—?"

"Marshall." His narrowed eyes bored into her, livid with rage, and his accent grew thicker. "That bloody *Sasanach* bastard Winston Marshall! She didna know—didna even guess that her own da would have married her t' that coward as payment for killing the last o' the O'Rourkes here. 'Twas Marshall who killed Bryce, Marshall who arranged the coach accident. Marshall who shot me. She wasna supposed t' die. That bastard wanted her, just as he wanted Thornwyck. God's blood, he knew she was wi' child! He'd have taken our unborn son from her womb, for fear o' the vengeance of an O'Rourke—!"

He spun around, giving her his back. Carolyn could see his fists clenched white, his wide, black-clad shoulders trembling with uncontrol-lable rage. No lack of emotion in him now, but a storm tide of it.

"He killed her all the same, though he didna intend it. Killed her, and our unborn babe—"

Carolyn let her gaze sink to the floor. She wanted to move forward, wrap her arms around his shoulders and hold him close, give him comfort. But she only swallowed hard, clearing her throat. "Aunt Beth was right again."

Her voice was a whisper, filled with shock and pain for him, no longer with fear of him. A tiny laugh trickled from her throat, a broken sound. "I never realized how much the victors would alter the truth. I mean, we always think of history as being true, don't we, and—"

She looked up, as though to seek agreement from him, only to find that merciless, shattered-emerald gaze piercing her once more. The intensity of his regard took her voice away, her very breath. Finally she shook her head faintly.

"Why—why are you here? Why can you—talk to me, now?"

Something dimmed the brilliance of his eyes, as though a shadow had passed over him. Emotions flickered behind that momentary veil, things too fragile to be held, before he turned away again. Carolyn instinctively moved forward the step he had retreated, drawn by the glimpse of his torment, the hope to give solace.

"Do you—is it the lies? You want your inno-cence known?" There had to be something she could do, something to—

His harsh laugh sent more shivers down her spine. She backed up that step again, past the dresser this time, until the wall stopped her retreat. Her hands pressed against the wood paneling, as though in silent plea to make it yield another inch.

Slowly the earl turned to face her.

"Milady, I may no' have been the bastard the Warringtons would have me be, but I dinna believe *innocence*"—he spat the word, as though it were something filthy—"is somethin' I've ever laid claim t'." Apparently noticing her attempt to merge with the wall for the first time, he shook his head.

"Nay, *a ghrá*, I've ever cared little for what others thought o' me." His voice was bitter still, yet calmer. Almost soothing. Slow steps took him closer to her again.

"Ye read the diary, milady. Ye believed—and more. As for the other . . ." He shook his head slowly, advancing toward her. "Marshall didna live t' reap the rewards o' his foul deeds. Vengeance was mine . . . yet it gave me no peace. Ah, milady, I never realized in life the truth I learned only after 'twas too late."

He closed the final step between them, until there was but a hair's breadth of space separating their bodies. A harsh tremor ran through Carolyn; tears suddenly, inexplicably burned in her throat, her eyes.

"'Tis said that if the little bright-headed one calls on the ground behind ye, yer wife will be taken from ye by force. And if the raven calls from a high tree, then 'tis death tidings o' a young lord. Grandda wouldna have doubted the signs, but I was too blind t' see them. And I lost both, milady, in one stroke o' the sword."

She could feel the heat radiating from his body, could feel the rhythmic, gentle warmth of his breath stirring her wispy bangs. Her gaze was fixed straight ahead, on the white lace at his throat. She did not remember that he was so tall. Did not remember wanting so very much to reach out and touch the fine wool of his coat, the warm skin beneath it. . . .

"But I knew ye would return, someday."

Her gaze snapped up, met his, and skittered away again in an uneasy mixture of fear and embarrassment and longing and sorrow.

"*Na gabh eagal, mo rún,*" he entreated softly. "Dinna be afraid, no' o' me. Pray God, no' anymore. I have spent an eternity waiting. For ye. T' beg yer forgiveness . . . and t' tell ye that I love ye, *grá mo chroí.*"

Carolyn's mouth dropped open at his huskily whispered words. Her heart picked up its beat at the sound of that endearment—

—*spoken to her just the way he'd always spoken it*—

She shook her head at the impossible thought even as it skittered away again. "But you—you don't know me."

The tremor in her body had invaded her voice. She was still pressed against the wall, still struggling with the desire to reach out and touch him.

"Ah, but I do," he contradicted. "And ye know

171

me. 'Tis why ye can hear me voice. Ye've—" A slow smile stole over his features, and Carolyn suddenly knew why his bride would have wished for but that one gesture on her wedding day. The cold mask of severity became the countenance of a fallen angel when he smiled.

"Ye've but forgotten, *mo rún*," he continued. The words were honey-sweet, a velvety rasp like a lover's caress, drawing her closer, toward him.

Carolyn's stiff body relaxed of its own accord. Her hands strayed from the wood paneling, rose toward his face, intent on touching that unholy beauty.

"Nay." He moved back, too quickly for her senses to follow. Carolyn snapped her hands back, curled them into fists. It was almost as though he had vanished, then appeared again two steps away.

The space between them returned a good part of the ability to reason to Carolyn's mind. She regarded him levelly, silently mourning the loss of warmth from his features even as she straightened.

"You would have killed me," she stated levelly, making the words a challenge by the way she spoke them. "That night on the cliff, when you danced with me."

A frown appeared on his face at her words, drew his brows together. He remained silent, not replying to the accusation in her voice.

"Aunt Elizabeth said you never hurt anybody. You said you love me. So why did you try to kill me?" It was her one defense, still, against that world of wanting, longing, rising up inside her. Carolyn shifted away from the wall, came toward him. The surge of rejection from when he'd shrunk away from her touch mingled with uncertainty, and with it came anger. "You near scared me to death half a dozen times! Why?"

At her last outburst a rakehell grin touched his lips, making his mouth softer, shockingly sensual.

"Ye've always been remarkably easy t' frighten, milady. And such a delight t' tease. Remember that night by the fire, afore we were wed? I'll admit, ye did take it a wee bit far, t' run screamin' from the house—"

"No!" Carolyn cut him off. "How could I remember that? Do I look like I'm over two hundred years old?"

She stalked closer, aggressively, remembering Elyssa's diary, remembering the poor girl's fright and torment, betrothed to a man she believed hated her.

"She was in love with you, damn you, and you never even showed her the kindness you showed your horse—!" Carolyn lashed out at him, then, an instinctive, simple, open-handed blow against his shoulder. Her hand passed through him as through empty, frosted air.

She lost her balance, recovered, sprang back with a cry. And stared at him, wide-eyed, hands clapped to her open mouth. "Oh—my—God."

The earl took another step back, frowning at her stark fear.

"Dinna forget, milady, I am no longer flesh

173

and blood. At times I can touch things o' this world, but I canna touch ye . . . or anyone. And none o' the livin' can touch me."

While Carolyn stood rooted to the spot, hands closing into fists, Tiernan glanced at the diary, then crossed over to the bed. "And yet . . ."

His fingertips lightly traced the calligraphy on its leather cover, caressingly. Reluctantly, it seemed, he abandoned the diary and faced Carolyn again, features pensive.

"I wonder, now. Perhaps there be a meetin' ground, between the world o' the livin' and that o' the dead. Perhaps there are crossroads, where the two can touch. . . ."

"What—" Carolyn swallowed hard. "What are you saying?"

The corners of his mouth turned up slightly, without humor.

"That night—the night ye say we danced upon the cliff . . . I followed ye onto the grounds, watched ye . . . but I canna remember aught past that, other than . . . leavin' again." He shrugged, frowning lightly. "Why, I suppose even a ghost may forget, but I do recall the last several centuries o' me appearances quite clearly. And I doubt I would let the memory o' dancin' with ye elude me. But I did dance wi' me wife the night we died."

Carolyn shook her head. She didn't understand what he was getting at, didn't want to understand, didn't dare—

"Ye came t' *me* that night, milady," Tiernan told her softly, giving voice to her own frantic thoughts. "Dinna ask me how, but for just a moment ye crossed into *me time!* Me life."

"No." She was shaking her head, refusing to believe what his words implied. "That's impossible; you know it is."

He shrugged. "I once thought meself quite knowledgeable in a great many things, milady. Yet now . . ." He sighed. "I find I am no longer so certain o' what is possible, and what isna."

Carolyn stared at him and bit her lip, then blurted out the words. "What would have happened if I'd gone over the edge with you?"

The earl seemed to consider the question, fixing her with his level regard. Finally, ruefully, he shook his head.

"In truth, I dinna know. I suspect ye would have died."

Even as he spoke the last words his shape began to waver, reminding Carolyn with cruel clarity that the one with whom she had been carrying on this conversation was as insubstantial as the air she breathed. Before she could reply to his dry admission, the ghost of the ninth earl dissolved, like shadows fading in brightening sunlight.

True, she had her answers. Had all the pieces of the puzzle, whether she chose to believe their truth or not. Yet the satisfaction that should have come from solving this mystery was hollow, empty.

With heavy steps, Carolyn crossed her beautiful chamber and sank down on the bed, feeling more alone than ever before in her life.

Chapter Thirteen

"Ah, will you look at that. I've found the elusive sprite again."

Startled, Carolyn looked up from the harp strings to find Erik standing in the doorframe to the Blue Room.

"Oh, good morning," she offered politely; then she smiled. "And, no, I haven't been trying to avoid you. I just haven't gotten around to breakfast yet."

With a tiny sigh she ran her fingertips along the metal strings once more, then rose from the stool. She still didn't know the first thing about playing the harp, but that didn't stop her from spending hours with it. And this morning plucking the ancient strings made her feel closer to the past, let her think, again, of what had happened last night, think of how she could tell Aunt Beth about it when she returned from town.

"Ah. And just what were you doing last night that made you sleep in this morning, hmm?" Erik asked, brows high in mock disapproval.

With a reluctant smile, Carolyn ambled toward the door and stopped three feet away from Erik to brace one hand against the wall. He was impeccably dressed, as usual, in designer sweater and dress slacks. The strange emotions that assaulted her the first time they met had never returned, and Carolyn couldn't imagine that they'd been anything more than an extension of her emotional turmoil that night. Erik was great company, easy to talk to and kid around with, and this morning he happened to be the perfect escape from her somber mood.

"I'll have you know that I've already spent two hours in the torture chamber this morning," she replied in her haughtiest, mightier-than-thou voice. Working out in the cellar gym had brought some reprieve from thinking about her encounter with Thornwyck's ghost last night. She met Erik's vivid blue eyes, then shrugged sheepishly. "I got carried away, I guess. Missed breakfast."

"Poor baby," Erik commiserated. "But I'm sure Lucy would fix you something if you—"

"Begged humbly enough; yes, I know," Carolyn finished for him, grinning, then shook her head. "Nah, I don't want to trouble her.

When I get hungry I'll just sneak something out of the kitchen. You know, like Serendipity does."

"Ah, yes, the Persian pasha," Erik nodded sagely. "By the way, how are the little tigers doing?"

Carolyn's face darkened in mock alarm. "You haven't a clue how often Lucy has cursed your name in the last few days," she replied in an ominous voice before lapsing into chuckles at Erik's horror-struck expression. "When the two little devils unraveled all the toilet paper in three of the bathrooms I thought she'd go after you with the meat cleaver."

Erik shuddered fittingly. Carolyn smiled and shook her head. "They're terrorizing the whole house, those two. I think they must know their way around it better than I do by now."

"Ah." Some of the humor faded from Erik's face. "You haven't been here before, have you?"

"No." Carolyn shook her head, a wistful smile touching her lips at the thought that it would probably be at least a year before she could come back again. "This is my first time."

"I thought so." Erik nodded. He turned where he stood in the doorframe, glancing down the hall to the huge split staircase before looking down at her again, the hint of a frown drawing his brows together. "Run into any odd things yet at night?"

"You mean—" Carolyn's eyes widened. "You know about—?"

"The earl?" A chilling smile crossed Erik's

features. "Yeah, I know about him." Then he sighed and shook his head, a frown of disapproval creasing his forehead. "I've never been able to figure out why Lady Warrington doesn't do something about that problem."

Carolyn's spine stiffened instinctively, and not because of the slighting way in which he'd referred to her aunt, as though she were the wife of a titled man, not titled in her own right. "Problem?" she echoed carefully, all laughter gone from inside her.

Erik nodded. "Yeah. You know, talk to a priest or something, get him to exorcise this ghost. Oh, there's Brian—gotta go. I'll see you at dinner. Six o'clock, say?"

Carolyn just stared, so lost in shock that the honk of a car horn outside hadn't even registered in her mind. But Erik was already striding down the hall toward the front door, waving once to her before disappearing outside.

She watched the main door close after him, then turned her back toward the wall and leaned against it, frowning at Erik's words . . . and at her own reaction to them.

Had he spoken those same words a few days ago, before she had ever read Elyssa's diary, before she had heard a tale of the past from the lips of a ghost, she would probably have agreed with Erik.

But now . . .

Carolyn shuddered, suddenly chilled despite the comfortable temperature of the room.

Now the thought of trying to harm Tiernan,

of trying to *exorcise* him from Thornwyck, was tantamount to murder.

After being the first one in the dining room for lunch, Carolyn spent the mild afternoon ambling through the grounds, warring with ghosts of her own making. Erik's words had unwittingly brought up an issue she had, incredibly, somehow overlooked in the general excitement of it all.

Tiernan's ghost. *Ghost,* for God's sake!

Carolyn realized that she'd very conveniently disregarded the fact that he must be a tormented soul, that he couldn't find the rest that was his right. That she should be thinking of some way to release him from this unnatural state, not take joy in his presence!

Perhaps . . . perhaps if she could go back, as she had the night when they'd danced on the cliff top, if she could stop Marshall from shooting at Tiernan—

But she'd already been in the past, according to the earl, and her refusal to continue over the cliff with him had only sent her back to her own time. Besides, she had no idea how the whole thing had happened, or how to make it happen again.

In any case, wasn't there an unwritten hypothetical rule against messing with history? Altering the past could snowball all sorts of changes into the present. But how was she to know that the past was *supposed* to have happened the way it had? And—

—and what in the world was she doing here, worrying about such outlandishly ridiculous impossibilities? If she wanted to help Tiernan find rest, perhaps talking to a priest or minister really would be the way to go. . . .

Carolyn was still trying to find a solution to that dilemma when Lady Elizabeth found her sitting cross-legged on the lawn by the fountain, staring blindly into the distance and picking apart blades of grass.

"I was beginning to think you're not enjoying yourself anymore, or that you might be getting bored." Aunt Beth smiled brightly, sitting down on the rim of the fountain. "But I see I was wrong. You seem to be having a splendid time ravaging the lawn."

Carolyn looked up, intending to brush off her aunt's concern, but the words died in her throat and the smile would not touch her lips. She gazed down at the bits of grass scattered all around, halfheartedly brushed them off her jeans and cream-colored sweater.

"I've been thinking about something, Aunt Beth. Erik sort of brought it up."

"Ah." Lady Elizabeth sighed. "I know he is wealthy and utterly charming, but you should not take everything Mr. Chandler says to heart, dear."

Surprised by the lack of humor in her aunt's voice, Carolyn looked up to find no trace at all of a smile on the pale, delicate features.

Brows furrowing, Carolyn got to her feet, covertly limbering muscles and joints stiff from too much time spent sitting in the same position. "What do you mean?"

Aunt Beth shrugged lightly. "Oh, I'm not saying he's a bad sort, mind you. But his lordship sure took an instant dislike to him, the first time the man ever set foot on the estate. It's the only time I've ever seen him come close to doing real harm."

Recalling Erik's casual reference to exorcising "the ghost," Carolyn frowned, pensively catching her bottom lip between her teeth. She could well imagine Tiernan taking exception to that attitude.

Another memory rose, and Carolyn stared at her aunt for an instant. "The elk antlers!"

A smile gradually brightened Lady Elizabeth's face. "Ah, yes, Lucy would have told you about those. She tells everyone, at some point," she remarked, rising from the fountain rim, "just as she repeats the rumors about the priest at St. Mary's. But there's more."

Seeing Aunt Beth start down the pebbled walkway, toward the sea, Carolyn fell into step beside her. "More?"

Lady Elizabeth nodded slowly. "Yes. The incident with the antlers was quite spectacular, of course, although they landed a fair distance from where Mr. Chandler was standing. But when he was coming down for dinner that first night he stayed here, about four years ago, one of the steps suddenly gave way under him," Lady Elizabeth recalled, a delicate frown marring her thin, arched brows. "He fell, and God knows how he managed to stay unhurt. I saw him tumble down that whole flight of stairs, and I thought he'd not rise again."

"But—" Carolyn shook her head, staring down at her aunt. "What makes you think the earl had a hand in that? He wasn't there, was he?"

Aunt Beth shot her an unreadable look. "Ah, dear, but a ghost will never be seen if he doesn't want to be seen. That staircase is strong enough to bear a team of horses. There was no rot, no decay in that wood. We were lucky Mr. Chandler was so understanding and polite about the whole matter. He could have tried to sue us."

Carolyn thought about that for a moment. "What else happened to him? Besides the thing with the antlers?"

"You'd better ask him that, dearest," Aunt Elizabeth suggested, expression neutral. "Or, perhaps, ask his lordship himself why he's so opposed to Mr. Chandler's presence."

Carolyn remembered the last time her aunt had suggested she talk to the ghost, and all that had happened since. She took a slow, deep breath. "Tiernan has told me a great many things already, Aunt Beth."

Lady Elizabeth came to an abrupt halt and turned to face Carolyn. Meeting her aunt's surprised gaze with a level one of her own, she asked, "Remember that paragraph I showed you in the library the other day? And remember how you told me history is written by the victors, and that we might never know the truth, until the earl decides to tell someone?"

"Why, yes, dear, of course I do. I'm still trying to understand all the implications of that new piece of our puzzle—"

Carolyn shook her head gently, silencing her aunt. "He came to my room again last night. And told me the original version of what happened."

Aunt Beth listened without interrupting even once while they ambled slowly across the grounds. But Carolyn found herself leaving out bits and pieces of the truth—her dream of the night previous to her encounter, and the sudden, inexplicable longing to reach out and touch this man who was more compelling to her than any man alive.

They had reached the edge of the land by the time Carolyn finished her tale with a disturbed frown. "He said . . . he said that he loves me. That he has been waiting for me, to tell me so. He said—"

Tears suddenly burned behind her eyes, tightening her throat and stealing her voice. She laughed shakily and shook her head again, and Aunt Beth's hands came around hers, surprisingly warm and strong.

"Said what, dear?"

Carolyn stared out over the endlessly rolling sea beneath a cloud-flecked sky, not meeting her aunt's gaze. "He . . . seems to think that I should know him. That I—"

She broke off again, looking down at her hands, at the hardy grass covering the ground. She couldn't say it, just couldn't. It was too outlandish, too ridiculous a notion to speak aloud. There was no such thing as reincarnation. No such thing as hearing the thoughts of a woman who had lived over two hundred years ago, no such thing as feeling the touch of death as she'd walked over what might have been her own grave in St. Mary's—

Carolyn turned away with a broken sound of panic. Behind her, Lady Elizabeth sighed, then placed a slender, wiry arm around her shoulders.

"I was worried for you, at first, you know," she admitted reluctantly, slowly urging Carolyn back toward the castle. "I know he's never harmed anyone, but I did not understand why he was so set on seeing you."

"Why he *what?*" Certain she'd heard wrong, Carolyn stopped dead, forcing her aunt to turn toward her. The frown drawing Lady Elizabeth's brows together was back, etching lines of concern into her pale, timeworn skin.

"He saw your picture, many years ago, when you were still a little girl," she informed Carolyn evenly. "I think he knew, even then. But when you sent that photo of your birthday party last year, he would not quit pestering me until I brought you here."

Carolyn drew back a step, staring incredulously at the tiny woman before her. "You mean it was *his* idea to invite me here?"

Aunt Beth shrugged, hedging. "Let's say it was an idea whose time had come. You see, I had already decided to bring you over for a visit. His lordship merely—hastened the matter."

Carolyn laughed, a thin, reedy sound. "So you believe—all this." Her hands gestured loosely, almost desperately. "Don't you?"

Her words weren't really a question, but Lady Elizabeth answered them, a faint, wistful smile curving her lips.

"Ah, but why should I not, dearest? Don't you know that the dead can tell no lies?"

Chapter Fourteen

"Since Crimthann's son was drowned
I will have no other love.
Many leaders fell at his hand
But his shield on the day of need was silent."

The last silvery glissando faded away, leaving silence in the Blue Room. There was no applause; appreciation of such a song in this house was expressed by pensive silence, and Thornwyck's guests seemed to sense that fact instinctively.

After a slow glance around the assembled group Maura flicked a number of the sharping levers on the harp, then launched into a lively melody.

Seeing her aunt rise from the armchair in the far corner and slip out the door after a nod to Maura, Carolyn followed suit. "Aunt Beth?"

"Yes, dear? Oh, don't mind me—I'm just turning in a bit early tonight," she offered when Carolyn frowned at the direction in which they were walking—toward the stairs.

"Are you feeling all right?"

"Oh, quite well, thank you, dear. Just a little tired. But do go back and enjoy the music, if you want."

Carolyn smiled but shook her head as she ascended the stairs beside her aunt. "That last song of Maura's—there's a story behind that, isn't there?"

Aunt Beth chuckled softly. " 'Créide's Lament for Cael.' Ah, yes, I thought you might like it. Maura put it to music herself."

She paused on the halfway landing of the split staircase to regard Carolyn with a tired smile. "It's one of the ancient stories about the Fianna—and a tale set in this area, too. A long time ago a young warrior named Cael won the heart of a king's daughter with his exquisite poetry. Créide, her name was. The two became inseparable; she even traveled to the wars with him, to be by his side. But on the last day of the battle of Fionn Trágha, Cael was drowned. Créide found his body washed up on the shore, and, dying of grief for him, recited his poetry until her life was spent. The two were buried in the same grave, and immortalized in bardic tradition."

Seeing Carolyn's somber expression, Lady Elizabeth shrugged easily. "It's a tragic tale, to be sure. But you know what they say about the Irish."

"No." Carolyn shook her head faintly, hardly having heard her aunt's words. There were altogether too many tragic endings abounding of late.

Lady Elizabeth started up the stairs again. "It's something like:

" 'The Great Gaels of Ireland
Are the men that God made mad
For all their wars are merry
And all their songs are sad.'

"G.K. Chesterton," she finished with a smile, looking quite smug. "Chap wasn't born till 1874, but the character of the Irish hasn't changed in the last millennia or two."

Carolyn offered up a distracted, wan smile, keeping pace with her aunt up the stairs. "There was something else I wanted to ask you," she began hesitantly.

"Ask away, dear," Aunt Beth encouraged her brightly, stopping in front of the door to her chamber. " 'You'll never learn anything unless you ask,' Father used to say."

"I think all fathers say that," Carolyn replied with a smile, but then she grew serious again. "It's about Erik."

"Ah."

"He's taking a day off from whatever it is he does here and wants to take me out," Carolyn ventured. "And I'm trying to be very rational in my decision about whether to agree to his proposal."

"Ah." Aunt Beth nodded sagely. "You mean you don't want to let the probably random occurrences that may or may not have been caused by the ghost of Thornwyck influence your thinking."

Carolyn frowned at her aunt's choice of words. "Not—quite like that," she disagreed, shaking her head. "It's not like I'm going to get involved with him or anything. I just wanted to know whether you had any serious reasons why I shouldn't be going off across the countryside in the same car with him."

Lady Elizabeth seemed to consider her words, then smiled indulgently. "No, I don't. In fact, I don't see any harm in it, dear. You're a grown woman, you can take care of yourself, and we all know what a charming chap Mr. Chandler is. I'm sure you'll have a wonderful time with him."

Carolyn scrutinized her aunt's face. "Really?"

Aunt Beth gave her a good-night hug, still smiling. "Really, dear."

Carolyn mirrored the smile. "Thanks, Aunt Beth."

"Anytime." She winked rakishly. "Now go tell Mr. Chandler the good news."

"All right."

Lady Elizabeth watched her niece trot down the stairs and disappear into the hall before turning to open the door to her bed chamber, a frown creasing her brows.

She'd lied to Carolyn.

It was only a little white lie, true—perhaps not even a real lie, at all. More a keeping of silence, when perhaps something should have been said.

But there was little good in burdening Carolyn with concerns that were likely unfounded and certainly without proof, in burdening her with the fears and worries of an old woman. Carolyn was young, vitally alive, and still as convinced of her own immortality as all young folk were. It was only the old ones, whether of years or mind, that looked to every day seeing black clouds on the horizon.

Perhaps, Lady Elizabeth mused with a smile as she folded back the covers on her ancient four-poster bed, the fact that she was starting to worry so much was a sign that, some day, she, too, would be getting old.

Remembering only too well the last time Thornwyck's ghost had become the topic of conversation between them, Carolyn had refrained from mentioning Tiernan again in Erik's presence. In the morning she'd left with Erik in his rented Mercedes, schooling herself in relaxing while someone other than herself drove. She was getting quite good, she congratulated herself when they stopped in Killarney for lunch, at giving up control in these little matters. Still, she was delighted when, the second time she poked fun at Erik's nearly getting in on the wrong side of the car, he nonchalantly handed her the keys as though he'd meant to get in on the passenger side, and let her drive to Bunratty Castle for the Medieval Banquet they would attend that evening.

Erik was just the sort of man she would call a friend back home—he was cheerful and charming, and he could make her laugh. So he was a bit headstrong, and lost his temper a touch too quickly when something unplanned came up—such as that herd of sweaters on the hoof trudging along, slowly southward on the coast road, forcing the Mercedes to crawl along behind them. Carolyn hadn't been able to decide whether to laugh or cringe at Erik's colorful curses. But the important thing was that he'd never tried to make any advances. Because, if he had, she would have had to reject them, and the easy camaraderie between them would have been destroyed.

As it was, she almost missed him over the next couple of days, when he was off on business again. But the real dark spot on Carolyn's happiness was Tiernan.

He hadn't returned since that night when he'd told her of the past, and she had no way of knowing if he ever would. There was still the trace of his presence, that inexplicable sensation that always remained with her, but no more appearances. Despite Erik's return the next day and his easy company, she missed Tiernan terribly. The man, she found to her dismay, couldn't take the place of the ghost.

And, suddenly, the days had passed too quickly. After a late candlelight dinner downstairs with Erik, Carolyn went to bed with the gut-wrenching realization that she was leaving in three days.

She lay awake for hours. At one point the kittens, who visited her only occasionally now, cried outside her door, and Carolyn let them in only too gladly. They curled up on the foot of the bed, Lily purring and Tiger yawning, and within minutes were deeply asleep. Carolyn stared at them for a long time, vaguely amazed that the very act of watching the little ones happily roaming the gardens of some dream world didn't put her to sleep too.

But it didn't. Though she was yawning at the rate of twice a minute, sleep would not come. Her thoughts wouldn't quiet down enough for that . . . thoughts that, come to think of it, hadn't been hers to control for some time now. They kept returning to Tiernan at any and all times of the day and night, even when she was with Erik.

But soon Thornwyck and its ghost would lie far behind her, across an ocean and a continent.

Carolyn tried to imagine returning to the world she'd called home up until two weeks ago, to the job that was waiting for her, the apartment, the people, but it seemed unreal to her—an old, bad dream that, happily, was nearly forgotten.

She tried placing herself back there with all the power of her imagination and promptly burst into tears. She drew the covers up over her head, ignoring the sleepy complaints from the kittens, and cried silently for half an hour.

Then, feeling utterly foolish, she crawled out from under her hiding place. The first thing she saw was the single white rose lying on the pillow beside her.

That sent her into another bout of tears, one which finally took her into exhausted sleep.

*   *   *

The light of day did nothing at all to help her state of mind. Especially not since that dawn heralded her second-to-last day at Thornwyck.

Carolyn lay awake, staring at the canopy of the bed, the shadows in the plasterwork of the painted ceiling, while listening to Tiger's claws on the wood floor and carpet as he chased his own tail. She wished Tiernan would return once more, before she had to leave.

Perhaps then she could ask him if there was a portrait of him hidden away somewhere, one she could take a picture of, or if there wasn't, if he'd mind terribly if she took the diary home, so she would have more than that ink sketch of him, something to read and gaze at and cry over at the odd time, something to remember him by. . . .

Tears were stinging her eyes again, burning in her throat. Carolyn thumped her fist on the covers, squeezing her eyes shut.

It just wasn't fair! She was so strong, so tough, so independent! She didn't need any shoulders to lean on. She didn't want the complication of a boyfriend or a lover or a husband! She'd always been happy to just have friends, and be able to run her own life.

And now . . .

Now she was falling apart at the prospect of leaving a house, an old aunt, two rambunctious kittens . . .

. . . and the ghost she had fallen in love with.

Carolyn scrambled out of bed and into her

clothes, fleeing that realization. Soon it would be time to pack.

The thought made her want to crawl under the covers all over again. She looked at the ancient diary on the bedside table, at the rose she'd placed on the leather cover only a few minutes ago, and realized that she would gladly have taken Elyssa's place.

That, if the Earl of Thornwyck were real, not a ghost, she would have wanted nothing more than to spend the rest of her life with him. She'd happily have altered all her schedules, gone when and where he wanted her to go, as long as it was with him.

But he was what he was: a man dead for nearly three hundred years, with only the shadow of his love now touching the world of the living.

Carolyn suddenly realized that it didn't matter. She thought of handsome, charming Erik Chandler, and came to a frightening conclusion.

She would rather sleep in an empty bed and find roses from a ghost on her pillow than live with any flesh-and-blood man who wasn't Tiernan.

Chapter Fifteen

"Miss Carolyn."

"Good morning, Ben." Carolyn managed a smile for the always impeccably dressed butler as she descended the last steps of the split staircase. After breakfast, which she'd eaten more from desire for company than desire for food, she'd begged a vase off Lucy. Over the suspiciously lengthy search for the object in question, the Irish hostess had enthusiastically carried on about Mr. Chandler, whom she obviously thought was the supplier of the white rose.

"Good morning, Miss Carolyn." Ben Masters smiled with just the proper amount of personable warmth as she stopped beside him at the foot of the stairs. "Lady Elizabeth will be gone overnight," he informed her in that perfectly polite way of his. "She asked me to tell you to have a nice day, and that she will see you for breakfast tomorrow morning. And she left this for you."

Brows drawing together in a faint frown, Carolyn accepted the proffered ivory envelope. "Thanks, Ben."

With a curt nod, the aging butler took one step back, then turned sharply and headed off in the direction of the front hall.

Carolyn wandered after him more slowly, gazing at the envelope in her hands. She turned off into the Blue Room and sat down at the harp before extracting Aunt Beth's note, a familiar piece of ivory vellum.

Smile, dear, it read. *I'll have a surprise for you when I get back.*

Carolyn did smile, wryly. Aunt Beth had left her a note to say that? Good God, how could she expect her to be cheerful when she was leaving the day after tomorrow?

Carolyn set the textured paper and envelope aside, and turned her attention to the harp. Rain was pattering in changing cadences against the garden-facing windows, filling the room with its muted drumming.

It was the perfect weather for her mood, Carolyn mused as she ran her fingertips lightly over the strings. She didn't want to go for a run or work out, didn't want to stroll around the estate, didn't want to drive into town or sightsee. She wanted to bury herself under the covers of her bed, stare at the white rose in its crystal vase on the bedside table, and pretend that time had no meaning and tomorrow would never come.

Instead, she closed her eyes and played, badly, any and all melodies she could think of on the metal strings. The sound of the harp wasn't as clear as when Maura played it, for Carolyn's nails were too short to pluck the strings, but it still soothed her thoughts. One tune in particular, an Irish song she'd picked up from Maura, suited her limited skills on the harp. Over and over, she played the simple melody, more slowly than Maura ever did, mournfully, sometimes softly singing along. Somewhere on her second or third time around, the whisper of a low, rich male voice accompanied her on the last line of the refrain.

" . . . heather, will ye go, lassie, go?"

Carolyn's hands jerked on the strings, sounding an ugly *twang*, but the voice continued unhesitatingly into the next verse, gaining in volume, growing deeper, more resonant with every pounding beat of her heart.

"If me true love she was gone . . ."

"Tiernan." She stared around wildly, but not even a shadow had entered the drawing room. "Let me see you."

" . . . I would surely find no other . . ."

"Tiernan, please!"

The beautiful voice fell silent. Carolyn stood, shaking inside. She'd not seen him for so many days. Was he angry with her? "Please let me see you."

But only silence met her plaintive whisper, silence and an empty room.

He likes "Wild Mountain Thyme" a great deal.

201

I could swear, sometimes, that he's humming along.

Carolyn remembered Aunt Beth's words, now. And she could see this room in his time, could imagine a beautiful woman, even Elyssa, sitting at a harp, playing the ancient songs, singing in clear, silvery tones, could see Tiernan standing by the fireplace, joining in, carrying the melody with his lilting, rich voice—

But those would have been rare and precious days, to judge by what she knew from Elyssa's diary. Rare and precious days not quite forever gone, for some part of Tiernan yet remained. . . .

Biting her lip, Carolyn sank down at the harp once more and resumed playing the simple melody, again and again, while tears slipped unheeded down her face.

"Determined to master that thing, aren't you?"

Startled, Carolyn glanced up, twisting her lips into a smile as she saw Erik in the doorway. Her tears had dried a long time ago, when her soul had ceased to think of tomorrow, had simply existed in the clear tones of the strings. She hadn't even heard him come in, had no idea how long he might have stood there, watching her.

With a heartfelt sigh, she stood up. "I don't think I'll make it in the time I have left."

A shadow marred Erik's grin for an instant. Rubbing his beard pensively, he crossed the room to stare out through the mullioned windows into the garden. "Ah. You're leaving shortly, then."

"Yes." Carolyn lightly drew her fingertips

along the strings in an artless glissando, again, then again.

"This place won't be the same without you, Cary."

And I won't be the same without it. But she didn't say the words, only crossed the room with slow steps and joined Erik by the windows. "It's stopped raining."

He laughed at her mild surprise. "You have been here a while, haven't you? Did you miss lunch too?"

She nodded, still staring through the glass. She should leave the harp alone pretty soon now; Maura would be coming in for her afternoon practice. Perhaps she'd get herself into gear and go for a run. . . .

"Come for a walk with me, Cary." Erik laid his hand on her shoulder, rubbing it lightly. "I'll be gone on business most of tomorrow. This may be the last chance we have to spend some time together."

"All right." It didn't really matter to her what she did. But perhaps Erik could distract her from the well of sadness growing ever deeper inside her, threatening to swallow her soul. He was so good at telling funny stories, entertaining with his bubbling charm.

Outside, Erik lit up a cigarette, silently striding along beside her until they reached the rose garden. A thin mist hung in the air and she shivered, although the temperature wasn't too low.

"Here."

Carolyn nodded her thanks as Erik wrapped

his suede jacket around her. They ambled down the white gravel paths and stopped beside the fountain.

Erik scooped up a handful of pebbles, tossing them one by one into the pool. "I've been coming to this place for years, Cary. But I don't think I'll want to return again, knowing you won't be here."

Carolyn watched the ripples shiver along the surface of the water, gently stirring lily leaves. "I'll miss you too."

Erik dropped the rocks and turned to face her, but remained silent until her gaze left the fountain and rose to meet his.

"Not nearly as much as I'll miss you, Cary. I know we've . . . barely had a week together, and this probably sounds insane, but . . . you've come to mean a lot to me."

Carolyn shifted away slightly, avoiding his eyes. She knew what he wanted to hear but couldn't bring herself to say words that weren't true.

"You've become a good friend to me, too, Erik."

It was the best she could do, and it wasn't good enough. She could see that in his eyes, in the slight slip of his charming smile. This was the moment she'd thought wouldn't happen between them, the end of even their friendship.

She almost shrugged, but stopped the motion halfway. Perhaps, if he just let it go . . .

But he didn't. He tossed his cigarette into the damp grass and ground it out with his shoe, then grasped her hands, holding them tightly—too tightly.

"I had thought—perhaps—that you felt a bit more than that for me."

Carolyn sighed, wishing futilely that he'd just tell one of his jokes, or at least respect her mourning, instead of presenting her with this problem. "Erik, I really don't think—"

"We fit so perfectly together, Cary," he continued, speaking over her, slowly drawing her against him, his smile intent. "You know we do, sweet. Everyone who sees us says we'd make a wonderful couple."

Couple? Appalled by his suggestion, Carolyn stiffened and gently but firmly disentangled herself from his grasp. The mists of her sorrow were definitely being dispelled.

"I know you think you know me pretty well, Erik," she allowed with a sigh and a somewhat forced smile, "but I am not in the market for a relationship—or a husband."

He stared at her for a moment, then broke into laughter. "You make it sound like a highly distasteful chore. Come on, Carolyn, relax a little. Let go. You remember the fun we've had together—that sort of thing doesn't stop because you make a commitment."

His face was close to hers, his vivid blue eyes persuasive, his mouth smiling that innocent, boyishly attractive, cajoling smile. Carolyn realized his intent, recognized the pattern, and pulled back violently.

"This is where the fun stops, Erik. I mean it."

Her voice wasn't raised, wasn't angry, only certain.

He stepped back, throwing his hands up defensively. "All right, all right. Fair enough, Cary. But tell me this—is it men in general you don't like, or just me?"

Carolyn looked away.

"Tell me, damn it!" He caught her arm, made her turn until she faced him. "I want to know exactly where I stand."

His voice was urgent, his hand tight on her arm. Her muscles beneath his hand flexed instinctively, ready to break away. But she didn't move, only refused to meet his eyes. After a moment he sighed, and his grip on her arm loosened, gentled.

"I've fallen for you in a real bad way, Cary, and I want to know the truth." He exhaled sharply. "Damn it, I deserve that much, don't I?"

"Yes." Carolyn straightened her spine and met his gaze. "You're a wonderful man, Erik, charming and funny and witty, but I don't intend to marry you. Or anyone else, for that matter."

His grip tightened again, a cold spark momentarily flashing in his eyes. "Ever?"

A small knot of something akin to fear formed in the pit of Carolyn's stomach at the touch of his gaze. "For as much of 'ever' as I can foresee," she replied truthfully, meeting his gaze levelly. The harsh glimmer was gone from his eyes, but the knot in her stomach hadn't disappeared. She took a deep breath, prepared to explain her reasoning to Erik. "Out of all my friends, and all

206

my colleagues at work, exactly three of them are happily married. The rest of them are divorced, separated, or, worse yet, unhappily married." She shook her head. "And, besides, I don't believe the man exists who could live with a woman like me, or whom I could live with."

"Cary—" His voice was hard, subtly angry.

She only smiled and shook her head, sadness welling up to disarm the tension. "In any case, this whole thing is impossible. I'm leaving in two days, and I'll be glad to write to you and such. But, quite honestly, I don't think we'll be bumping into each other again. It's a big world out there, you know."

Emotions shifted across Erik's face, like clouds torn by the wind. Finally he nodded curtly. "All right. Friends, then."

He held out his hand to her. Carolyn placed her own in his and shook it as a friend might. Yet Erik brought her hand up to his lips for a quick kiss, as he'd done the first night he'd met her, before releasing it and stepping back to light another cigarette.

"But I won't promise not to show up on your doorstep and pay you a visit someday, when you least expect it," he commented with a crooked grin, taking a long drag and exhaling slowly.

Carolyn smiled with him, but her heart wasn't in it. As he walked her back to the mansion the only face in her thoughts was that of a shadow dissolving into night, a shadow with raven hair and emerald eyes and a deep, rich, lilting voice that drew her into a past long dead.

Chapter Sixteen

Carolyn shut the door behind her, leaning against it wearily. The conversation with Erik had remained with her through dinner and the nightly music session, making for the perfect ending to a terrible day.

He had no right to try to make her feel guilty for refusing him! A week ago they hadn't even known each other. And she'd certainly never asked him to fall in love with her! She was fond of him, true, but she didn't love him.

And she could never forget his words on "exorcising" Tiernan.

Carolyn stalked across the room and sat down on the edge of the bed, body taut with the turmoil in her mind.

Perhaps what Erik had so crudely hinted at

was true. Perhaps she was incapable of loving a real, living man, of committing herself to that perilous journey. Perhaps that was why she had fallen in love with a ghost.

She sighed, letting her gaze come to rest on Tiger and Lily, curled up in the center of the bed, cuddled together in sleep. Maura must have taken pity on them and let them in, perhaps guessing that they'd wear the finish off the door if their wishes were ignored.

She would miss those two little furballs, as she would miss everything else about Thornwyck—even Serendipity, whom she'd managed to bribe into a semblance of friendship with the occasional lick of honey.

With movements slowed by the sadness in her thoughts, Carolyn undressed and slipped under the covers, taking care not to disturb the sleeping kittens. Maybe she should get up and go pay the cellar gym a visit, and work herself into oblivion. . . .

No; she didn't have the energy for that. There was no anger, aggression, frustration or stress to be worked off. There was only an odd kind of grief, a lethargy that made the thought of movement, energy, of anything representative of the living a thing far beyond her.

With a sigh Carolyn leaned forward to brush the fluffy kittens lightly with her fingertips. Rewarded with instant purring, she reached over to turn out the light and curled up under the covers, thoughts mercifully blank.

*   *   *

Shortly before midnight Carolyn woke to the caterwauling of the orange kittens. It took her a moment to realize what the bloodcurdling sound was, but the needle-sharp claws digging into her arm curved around them were all too clear.

"Hush, you two, or—"

Whatever she had planned to threaten Tiger and Lily with was forgotten as she squinted toward them in the darkness . . . and stared past them.

Tiernan was there, standing at the foot of her bed as he had so often, a shadow of black and white against the night, gazing down at her. Carolyn drew a deep, careful breath; she could have cried with happiness.

But the kittens didn't share her sentiments. Unlike the last time, when they'd slept right through Tiernan's bringing of the rose, they seemed determined to raise hell now, yowling as though they were being skinned alive. Carolyn scooped them up protectively, muttering soothing nonsense only to have her arms and hands clawed for her trouble. Hissing and spitting, Tiger and Lily sprang from her hold and disappeared under the huge oak dresser to yowl from relative safety.

Carolyn tilted her head at the earl, lips trembling uncertainly, wishing with all her soul that, this time, he would stay for more than a moment. She swallowed hard and painted a smile on her face. "You frighten the kittens."

He did not smile in return. His countenance

was as cold as the ancient stone of Rory's Tower.

"I dinna frighten ye?"

"No." Carolyn shook her head, a soft, genuine smile touching her lips at the rich, rolling brogue, so alien to her and yet so welcome. Once, perhaps, she would have fibbed her answer. Now it was only truth. Understated truth, at that.

Tiernan regarded her levelly a moment longer. Then he looked away, at the diary on the bedstand. The kittens had fallen silent.

"I've come t' warn ye, milady. The man—Erik Chandler—he is up t' no good."

Carolyn's brows rose at the unexpected topic. "Erik?"

The tone of her voice returned Tiernan's narrowed gaze to her.

"Aye. He wants the estate. And he wants ye, *a ghrá*. He'll take both by trickery, if he can. By force, if he must."

Carolyn frowned severely. True, Erik had made a royal pain of himself last night, but he was basically a nice guy. "That's ridiculous—"

"'Tis the truth!"

Such vehemence, such fury, in his voice! *Don't you know that the dead can tell no lies?* Aunt Beth's words echoed in Carolyn's thoughts. Still, she shook her head in disbelief. "But he—"

"He has forged a writ o' debt, from the late Lord Warrington t' his own deceased father. It shows Thornwyck as the stake in a horse race, never duly paid." The earl's eyes closed for a moment, on a drawn-out breath. When he spoke again his voice was angry once more, ominous,

212

his gaze fixed upon Carolyn.

"I have seen him leafin' through the annals, tracin' Lord Warrington's signature. Each time he has come here over the years he has put together another piece o' this plan. He is patient, milady, but only t' a point. And he is ruthless."

"But why—"

Forestalling her words, Tiernan crouched down beside the bed. The sudden closeness of him momentarily robbed Carolyn of rational thought. She could feel the intensity of his gaze, like a faint breath of wind against her skin. A tiny shiver coursed through her.

"He—is like Marshall," Tiernan intoned softly. "*Is* Marshall, the way ye are Elyssa." He rose to his feet to pace along the bed.

"No' a fortnight after our deaths Marshall arrived t' take possession in the name o' the Warrington family. There never were any bastard sons o' Da's t' contest their claim on the estate." He met her gaze grimly. "The next day, milady, they carted Marshall's bloody carcass back t' Dublin."

Carolyn gasped softly. "What—?"

"He had . . ." Tiernan hesitated. "Fallen from the cliffs."

"Fallen?"

Instead of replying, he turned away from her to stare at the curtained window, as though he could see into the past of which he spoke.

"Aye, fallen. After he fled from the ghost o' the one he'd murdered, milady." He shook his head, an angry gesture. "He was a coward then, as he is now. Strong only through deceit, strikin' always from behind, out o' the shadows. I followed him through the mansion. When he saw me he got up the courage t' raise his blade against me."

Carolyn saw the earl shake his head again, saw his shoulders lift ever so slightly, as though on a sigh.

"He had as much success in touchin' me as ye had that night, milady. After that he fled before me, all the way t' the edge o' the land . . . and beyond. 'Twas a fittin' end for him, t' share the death he had meted out."

Carolyn shivered at the grim satisfaction so evident in Tiernan's voice. He turned suddenly, to fix her with that somber emerald gaze again.

"Ye must stay away from him, *grá mo chroí*. Tell Lady Elizabeth o' me warnin,' and trade no more civil words wi' this man."

Carolyn sat up straighter in bed, brows furrowing. "I—I can't just have Aunt Beth evict him." She shrugged helplessly at the angry furrowing of Tiernan's brows. "He *is* a paying guest, you know. And Thornwyck *is* open to the general public. And as long as we have no proof of his plans, the police won't be able to do anything."

Tiernan came to the bed, grim smile speaking eloquently. Yet he said nothing, only backed away slowly.

"No—wait—!" Afraid he would leave again, Carolyn reached out toward him but stayed her hand short of touching him, remembering the last time she had tried that. "Don't go . . . yet."

Emerald eyes gazed down at her. Still, he said nothing.

"I will tell Aunt Beth about this when she comes back tomorrow," she offered pacifyingly, racking her brain for something that would keep him in her company a bit longer. For just another moment, another instant to lock the memory of his face into her heart . . .

Tiernan nodded in reply to her words. "Watch yerself around him, milady. I canna feel at ease, knowin' him here, and ye without protection."

"I will be careful." Carolyn summoned a smile, drawing the covers closer around herself for warmth. She did not add that she wouldn't be here much longer for him to worry about her. "But . . . will you not stay a while longer? And—talk to me?"

His glance seemed to grow wary. She sweetened her smile. "You could sit down, if you want. I won't try to touch you again, I promise."

With something that could pass for the shadow of a rueful grin the earl sank down on the mattress on the other side of the bed.

"In truth, I've no' held a conversation for a long time, milady. Even when I was still one o' the livin' polite socializin' was never a skill at which I excelled."

"I—" Carolyn stopped short, inclining her head somewhat sheepishly. "How—am I supposed to address you? My lord? Earl . . . ?"

The touch of a smile curved ghostly lips. "I dinna suppose ye'd call me husband, now?"

Carolyn shook her head, feeling an answering

215

smile tug at the corners of her mouth. "No." But how utterly impossible, the difference her heart felt at the thought of him as husband, as opposed to Erik . . .

"In that case, I'd be honored if ye used me Christian name."

She nodded. Then, brows rising, she smiled. "And—what will you call me?"

Tiernan did not hesitate. "Ye are Elyssa, milady. But I shall use yer new name, if 'twill please ye better. Cara."

Spoken in his Irish lilt, it was the most beautiful word she'd ever heard. She swallowed hard, struggling to find her smile again and failing.

"Tiernan—"

—oh, how strange, to be addressing him so, how achingly sweet, how shockingly intimate—

Carolyn shook her head, shivering at the thought that had vanished even as it crossed her mind. She cleared her throat and tried again. She didn't have much time left. And there were two things, at least, that she had to discuss with Thornwyck's ghost before she could find peace in her own heart.

"Tiernan, I want to . . . help you. If I can. If there's anything that will give you rest . . ."

He inclined his head slightly, brows rising as though in puzzlement. "Rest?"

Carolyn nodded decisively. "Yes. Isn't—I mean, don't you—want—to find peace?"

"What an odd notion."

Tiernan rose and paced slowly the length of the room. On his return he paused on her side of the bed, a faint crease between his brows.

"I never thought o' what would happen after ye returned, t' tell the truth," he mused aloud. "I—didna even know why I could remain, after I died. All I knew was that I must tell ye what I'd never spoken in life. But I couldna find ye, only knew ye would return t' this place, somehow, someday. And I would be here, waitin,' till that day."

Carolyn swallowed hard, staring down at her intertwined hands, feeling his intent gaze fully upon her. God. So that's why he'd not been content at St. Mary's. The vault there was a house for the dead. And Tiernan had been waiting for one of the living . . .

Tears burned behind her eyes. She blinked them away, cleared her throat, stared at the covers.

"Well, if there is—anything—that can be done to help you—" She drew an unsteady breath, losing the battle with sorrow. "I won't be here—much longer, but I know Aunt Beth would—"

"Ye willna be leavin'!"

Carolyn glanced up at him, struck by the appalled, incredulous tone of his voice, and nodded tremulously. "My flight is"—she glanced at the clock that showed past midnight—"tomorrow."

An abrupt change came over him. His brow smoothed, his startled look changed to one of understanding. "But ye would prefer no' t' leave?"

Even as he spoke he sank slowly onto the bed

again, so close to her that she could feel the mattress dip beneath his weight. She refused to even try to understand that paradox, only shook her head.

"I don't want to—but I have no choice, really." It was difficult to think, with him so near.

"What do ye want, then, Cara?"

She bit her lip, swallowing tears, and let her gaze sink to the covers once more. *I want you to hold me while I cry,* she wanted to say. *I want you to be real, alive! I want this fairy tale to have a happy ending!*

"What I want is impossible."

"Nothin' is impossible, *mo rún.* Look at me. Am I no' impossible?"

A shaken laugh tumbled from her lips. She nodded her head, glancing up at him with tears in her eyes. "Yes. Yes, you most definitely are," she agreed. Then, drawing a ragged breath, she tried to compose her features. Nicola's favorite motto had been to part with a smile. She'd lived up to it, too, right to the end, and Carolyn had promised herself to keep that legacy of her friend alive. Drawing another, steadier breath, she straightened her spine and met Tiernan's bright green gaze levelly. After all, there was no telling if she would ever see him again. Each short, precious time could well be the last.

"And because you are," she continued, "I want something real of you to take home with me. A picture. And I won't take a photo of your effigy," she added rebelliously.

"'Tis sad I am t' tell ye there is no' a one o' the

218

O'Rourke family portraits left, milady." Tiernan's voice was suddenly cold, his face hardened into grim, sorrowful tones. "The Warringtons left nothin' when they took Thornwyck. If 'twas o' no value t' them, they carted it out into the yard and set it aflame." A chilly silence momentarily filled the room. "I wanted t' kill them when they burned our weddin' portrait."

Carolyn bit her lip, nodding solemnly. Elyssa would have felt the same.

Desperate to lighten the mood in the room before she really lost her composure, still determined to have something of Tiernan's to cherish and keep, she plucked up her courage and went for plan B.

"Well, I—I did take a picture of the sketch of your wedding portrait in the diary, but I wanted to ask you . . ." Her voice trailed off at the change in his features. He did, quite obviously, not know about Elyssa's sketch.

"Do you want to see it?" Carolyn asked quickly, reaching past him for the diary, shivering at the mingled warmth and unearthly chill that now radiated from him. "She made it shortly after the portrait was begun. Here, see?"

She held the pages open for him and watched with a combination of anticipated pleasure and dread what his reaction might be.

The coldness of his features had vanished, leaving in its place a shadow of sorrow, a tautness around the mouth that spoke too eloquently of his loss. But there was wonder in his eyes, too, and something like the first gentle rays of sunlight that marked the end of a long, cold night.

He straightened and rose suddenly, so abruptly that Carolyn stiffened, startled. Yet he seemed to regret that sudden motion immediately, for he smiled at her crookedly, apologetically, even.

"Ye wanted t' ask me somethin', milady. Remember?"

Carolyn shrugged faintly, oddly disappointed that he hadn't even commented on the ink sketch, but not about to get into something that would only rouse more heartache.

"Um, well, yes, I thought—before, that is—to see if you might not mind so terribly much if I kept the diary . . . but I wouldn't think of taking it now," she added resolutely, meeting his gaze, half afraid to find anger.

One of Tiernan's brows arched, vague humor in the gesture. "Ye'd ask me, no' Lady Elizabeth?"

Carolyn shrugged defensively. "Well, the diary belonged to Elyssa, who was your wife. I'd certainly have asked Aunt Beth before taking it home with me, but it seemed only right that I should ask you first. In any case, this really isn't an issue anymore, so . . ."

A crooked smile gentled Tiernan's shadowed features. "The diary is yers, milady. It always was."

There was a meaning far different from what Carolyn chose to hear in his words, but she only nodded, her throat closing up with something she called gratitude but had little, indeed, to do with thankfulness. "I would like that very much."

Ah, but her words, too, held a double meaning.

Tiernan's mouth curved up into that sensuous, irresistible smile. "'Tis so, milady, whether ye wish it or no'."

Carolyn smiled shakily, her gaze fading softly out of focus while her thoughts were cruelly clear.

It did not matter whether she finally believed his words, did not matter what was proven and what was extrapolated. The night after next she would spend half a world away from here . . . and from Tiernan.

"I don't—suppose—sometime tomorrow night —you'd want to"—she gestured toward the wardrobe—"go hide in my suitcase and sneak off to Vancouver with me, would you?"

Her voice was tremulous, watery, full of unshed tears. She looked at Tiernan with what must have amounted to a beaten-puppy look, for he came closer again until he could have raised his hand and touched her cheek.

"Dinna despair, *grá mo chroí*. All will be well."

The sound of his voice, so full of compassion, so full of the love he had felt for the woman Elyssa, was nearly her undoing. She didn't dare look up at him, but then she did, for fear he would vanish again.

A wounded sound escaped her throat as she found that she was too late. Only emptiness remained where he had been.

Grá mo chroí.

"I'm sorry, Nicola." The words became lost in

a choked, ragged sob. Hugging the covers to herself, Carolyn fell back, blindly staring at the canopy of the bed, shaking with the weight of her grief while silent, bitter tears slipped from the corners of her eyes.

Chapter Seventeen

By two a.m. Carolyn couldn't bear it anymore.
The silence, the loneliness of her room . . . it was
too much. Still dressed only in her nightie, she
stomped into her boots, wrapped her green cloak
around herself, and headed out onto the cliffs.

No one was left awake at this ungodly hour,
and the back door opened without a sound, letting her pass in silence out into the night . . . the
night that would soon give way to her last day at
Thornwyck.

Carolyn bit her lip and struggled to banish the
thought.

The sea winds had subsided, whispered only
softly through the rhododendrons. The soft wool
of the cloak kept her warm but could not banish
the chill in her soul.

Only one more day. One more day and one

more night, all quite possibly without seeing Tiernan again.

Carolyn stopped a few yards from the cliff and stared out onto the quiescent sea. The waves were pure black beneath a cloud-cast sky that let no heavenly light touch the earth.

It was a mild night, at least. Even the sound of the breakers against the harsh rocks far below was muted tonight.

Unlike Erik, the sea, at least, seemed to respect her mourning.

Carolyn sank to the ground, folding the cloak around her and beneath her, not bothered by the fact that she'd likely have grass stains on it later. Rubbing her burning eyes tiredly, she cast a glance over her shoulder at Thornwyck, little more than a shadow except for the faint glow of its lanterns.

Perhaps if she stayed here, between land and sea, at this last place where Tiernan and Elyssa had touched, she'd be able to keep the future at bay, somehow, and exist in the moment forever.

Perhaps . . .

She shook her head wanly and stared out over the sea. Yet the rhythmic, muted pounding of the waves finally conspired with her sorrow and exhaustion to lull her to sleep, because she dreamed.

She was still at the cliffs, still folded within her cloak—a cloak that, strangely, now had a silk lining and soft fur trim—but she knew she was dreaming because the sea below was liquid silver, gentle swells stretching out into infinity beneath a haloed, bright full moon.

And she knew she was dreaming because when she glanced back toward Thornwyck again, Tiernan stood there, dressed not in his usual stark black and white, but in pale gray frock coat and breeches, an ivory shirt almost glowing in the light of the moon.

But she wouldn't complain. It was too sweet to see him again, even if only in a dream. Perhaps she could entice him to stay a bit longer than he had in reality, keep him by her side for the remainder of the night, until the cold morning light stole this time out of time from her.

Yet this was a dream unlike any Carolyn could recall, a dream uncommonly vivid in its sublime detail, its impact upon her senses. The fur trim of her cloak, brushing against her throat and forearm when she shifted, was softer than the softest down. The night wind, too, seemed not so chill, the sound of the waves far below a soothing, compelling rhythm. In the distance, softly, the whickering of horses danced on the breeze.

"Milady."

Her heartbeat quickened at just the timbre of that word, at the deep, subtle current of longing and sorrow and need evident within it. Yet she had no voice, neither to deny him nor bid him closer.

But closer he came all the same, to crouch down before her and stare at her out of the tormented, haunted eyes she knew so well. In his hands was a single blood-red rose.

She blinked, tears filling her eyes from the

brightness of the molten, shifting silver sea haloing the form of her beloved.

"Tiernan."

He reached out and took her hand, enfolding her fingers in his, drawing her to her feet beside him as he rose. Her cloak shifted in the breeze. She saw in the slight widening of his eyes the very instant he realized she wore nothing but her nightdress beneath it, and wondered if he was pleased by her shocking lack of decorum or simply disapproved of it.

No. He was pleased by it, she decided a moment later, when he traced her cheek lightly with the blossom of the rose. Her husband always seemed to be pleased by a breach of propriety.

"Ye shouldna be out here at this time o' night, milady," he reproached her mildly. "And dressed so ill fittingly t' the season. 'Tis too cold for one so delicate. Ye must take care, 'else ye'll catch yer death o' cold."

She tugged her hand free to draw the cloak closer around her, suddenly uncertain again of his mood. "As you wish."

Yet when she would have turned to go his hand on her shoulder stayed her, drew her gently against his side. There was something akin to humor in his eyes as she glanced up at him questioningly.

"I would find a way t' warm ye, milady, if no' for the whole household's easy view o' this place."

He was smiling at her, giving her that rarest of gifts that always made her heart beat just a little faster. A frisson of heat shivered through her, rose to stain her cheeks a deep pink as she understood the meaning behind his words.

"My . . . my chamber is well heated, my lord. Perhaps . . . as you said . . . I should return to it."

She caught her breath at her own boldness even as she spoke the words, knowing it was shameful, wanton even, for a wife to behave so. Yet her husband's touch, if not his words, had told her otherwise in nights gone by.

And tonight the fire in his eyes told her the same.

"Aye. And perhaps I shall escort ye there." His hand took hers again, drawing her toward the castle rising like a mountain from the seaward plain. "T' make sure nothin' ill befalls ye on the way, o' course," he added rakishly, his too often dark countenance transformed by a smile.

Her heart was beating high in her chest, like a trapped bird, stirring her body to life with the knowledge of what was to come. She let him lead her up the stairs, into her chamber, all but unaware of traversing the distance, and watched in silence as he lit the two tapers on the bed-side table.

A multitude of shadows sprang to life in the chamber, dancing through air thick with the memory of peat smoke. Though only a soft glow now remained in the hearth, she felt far too hot beneath the weight of her cloak.

As though reading her thoughts, her husband moved toward her, unclasping the fastening and drawing the cloak from her shoulders, letting it fall unheeded to the floor. Slowly, he reached out and drew the heavy mass of her golden, riotously curling hair forward until it spilled like sunshine across her shoulders. Though her hands remained at her sides, she saw the smoldering intensity of his eyes and gloried in it.

The faint tremor of his hand as he touched the thick curtain of her hair spoke eloquently in the silence between them. With a flick of his hand he tossed the rose onto the still mussed covers of the bed she had left some hours earlier, unable to find sleep.

Silently, he stood before her, watching her. Waiting. Drawing rein on his passion, even as she allowed the quickening sensations in her own body to grow into desire, into wanting, hunger.

She drew an unsteady breath and closed her eyes, letting her head fall slowly back as he stroked the line of her throat, as lightly as though she were a bird, captive in his hand. His fingertips trailed down slowly across her collarbone, and though his hand was separated from her skin by the fine linen of her nightdress, it did not matter. She could feel the heat of his touch, the vibrant passion of it, through the linen.

His fingers lightly brushed one breast, and the barest touch of his lips came to her throat. She arched reflexively and sought the cool, thick silk of his hair with her fingers, breath breaking as his hand cupped her breast possessively and his arm came around her back, pulling her softly against him. The heat of his body branded her through the barrier of clothing, quickening the beat of her heart.

"Trobhad, grá mo chroí."

The fluid words were a sigh against her throat, a caress. Of their own accord, her hands slid around his neck, along the delineated muscles of his arms, his shoulders, telling him without words that his beauty struck her to the heart, that she loved him, that she wanted him, while he whispered to her in Gaelic, lilting words on hot breath against the skin of her throat, her jaw, and cheek.

She didn't understand the words, for she had never learned that ancient tongue, but he spoke it often, here, in the sanctuary of her room, when he came to her, loved her. Perhaps he did not wish her to understand. Perhaps it was better that she did not.

His hands were working on the laces of her nightdress, baring more skin to his eyes, his mouth. Lips and teeth captured the tip of one breast, scalding her through the thin linen, loosing a burst of pure fire deep in her belly. Her hands clenched on his shoulders, for all strength was flowing from her legs and her knees felt perilously close to giving way. His arms tightened around her back, lifting her, drawing her flush against his lower body. The smoky air of the room surged into her lungs in a long, shivery breath at the perfect fit of their bodies, hard against soft. He caught her face in gentle, urgent hands, captured her mouth with his own, invading, searching, promising heaven as he rocked himself against her once, slowly, devastatingly.

There was only the ragged sound of their breathing in the cool silence of the room. Slowly, Tiernan released her and stepped back to arm's length, features taut with hunger, eyes blazing emerald in the glimmer of the candle flames. He shrugged out of his coat, letting it drop to the floor beside her cloak. His gaze never left her, only grew hotter at the knowledge that she was watching, was glorying in the sight of his tautly muscled torso as the ivory shirt followed the path of the coat. He kicked off shoes and hose, and still she did not avert her eyes, though her cheeks flamed hotter than the noonday sun in summer.

When his hands went to his breeches her courage finally deserted her, her gaze flying to his face instead. There was a smile there, a tiny curving of full masculine lips as he shed the remainder of his clothes and stepped toward her.

He wasn't laughing at her, wasn't mocking her, and yet her own lips trembled in her struggle to smile. Trembled even more when his hands slowly gathered the fabric of her nightdress and drew it over her head.

"Ye are beautiful, *a ghrá.*"

She flushed hotly at his intent perusal, watching the lowering of thick, sooty lashes, the tightening of those beloved features in stark hunger.

"Beautiful," he repeated against her skin, lowering his mouth to her shoulder, following the path of his gaze across the swell of her breasts, across her ribs and the gentle curve of her belly. He sank to his knees before her, shamelessly touching and tasting, until the sensations became unbearable and she felt her knees buckling. Yet she did not fall; Tiernan caught her up against him easily and carried her the two steps to the bed and laid her down upon it gently, placing the rose on the pillow beside her head, as though she truly was someone cherished, beloved. At times like this she almost dared believe it.

At times like this, more than ever, she yearned to tell him of her feelings for him, to whisper to him words of endless devotion and undying love, even as he whispered his words of passion.

But she knew better. Knew that the faint accent of her words would remind him again of who she was, of the differences between them—differences of blood, of beliefs, of language; differences that could only be forgotten here, in this time of passion and need, with the intoxicating touch of skin upon skin, and blood racing much too swiftly for conscious thought to prevail.

She caught her breath sharply as he lowered himself over her, hard muscle and hot skin, fitting so perfectly against her. His weight pressed her into the mattress, shutting out all the world except for him, his touch, his almost desperate intent to love her, as though only in this could he find absolution for his remoteness during the days. That shattered-emerald gaze remained fixed on her own widening eyes, drinking in every nuance of her reaction as he parted her legs with his, shifted his body against hers more intimately yet. His mouth drank in her broken breaths as his hands continued to stroke her body, driving higher the hunger, the need already there. Urgently, restlessly, she returned his touch, gliding her hands over his powerful shoulders, down his back, nails flexing into his skin as the tremors deep within her grew with each caress, with each slow stroke of his tongue against her own.

Still, he was not close enough to her, never close enough. Her spread hands slid wantonly down to the small of his back, lower still, urging him without words to come to her. A harsh groan tore from his lips as he arched against her, into her, banishing the distance between them. She clung to him as he began to move, welcoming him into her body as she had welcomed him into her heart so long ago, soaring with him, as one, into a storm-tossed heaven that knew neither kin nor creed.

When they fell back to earth he did not pull away and go, as he had on those nights when he'd first come to her, leaving her crying with the loneliness that remained after he had gone. Instead he held her tightly against him until their heartbeats had slowed, until the tremors had ebbed. He touched her with unhurried, lingering kisses, kept her in the harbor of his arms, stroking her gently, soothing her, cherishing her. Even when he rose he did not do so to leave, but to build up the fire and bring a warmed water pitcher and basin to the bed to bathe from her skin the cooling sheen of sweat, the traces of their passion, with such devastating tenderness that embarrassment and shock could not claim her. The gentleness of his touch, the intimacy of it, inexorably stirred the embers of hunger into awakening yet again. She reached her hand up to him, questioning, inviting, blushing with her own wantonness but loving him too much to hide her desire, to cheat him of knowing how very deeply he affected her . . . how very deeply she loved him, needed him, though she did not speak the words.

An odd light shone in his clear green eyes as he took her hand and showed her all that he, too, might never be able to put into words.

The insistent beep of the radio alarm on the bedside table tore Carolyn out of the darkness of sleep. She fumbled blindly for the snooze button, then lay still beneath the tangled covers, staring blearily at her green cloak hanging over the chair in her line of vision. God. She must have sleepwalked up here, because she couldn't even remember returning to her room last night. . . .

Ah, but the dream she remembered. Carolyn felt herself blushing a deep, deep shade of crimson over the explicit, graphic detail of it, the awareness of it in her body, still . . . and, after a moment, found tears well from beneath her closed lashes at the heartrending beauty of it, at the wrenching sadness of knowing that Tiernan and Elyssa had had so very much love to give and so very little time to give it.

Carolyn's lips tightened into a bleak line as she clutched the covers to her chest and blindly stared up at the bed's canopy in the first faint light of morning that penetrated the half-drawn drapes.

Only in dreams could it be like that. In dreams, and in fairy tales.

Chapter Eighteen

"Miss Carolyn, Lady Elizabeth would like to see you when you have a moment. She is down in her study."

Startled by the knock on her door and Ben's voice, Carolyn sat up, blushing. Though it was early yet, she'd been sprawling on the bed for some time, fully dressed, waiting for a reason to move, other than breakfast. She'd gotten up to let the kittens out half an hour ago, yet snatches of last night's dream still replayed spontaneously in her mind, hazy but shockingly real.

She exhaled sharply, staring at the white rose in its crystal vase, standing in solitary splendor on the night table, and suddenly realizing that the butler would be awaiting a reply from her.

"Thank you, Ben. I'll be down in a bit," she

called through the door. Aunt Beth's surprise; yes.

"Very good."

Carolyn barely heard Ben's smart reply. God. The last thing she wanted was a lengthy, possibly cheery farewell. She'd still do her damnedest to leave with a smile, but right now she didn't want to be cheered up. She wanted to have someone to commiserate with for the next 24 hours, to mourn all the things that could never be, all the love that was lost before it could begin.

But Aunt Beth wanted to see her. And Carolyn had some things to tell her, too, things that had better not be delayed, if Tiernan was right about Erik.

Woodenly, Carolyn pushed off the bed, then stared at herself in the mirror on the dresser.

How could it be that she looked no different than she had two weeks ago? How could her soul be turned upside down and not even a shadow of it touch her face?

Her lips tightened mutely in acceptance of merciless reality. Then, without another backward glance, she strode out of the room.

Halfway down the stairs Carolyn could hear Lucy's voice, drifting up from the foyer.

" . . . put a lock on the bloody kitchen door, too, I will!"

The hostess was on her knees in front of Serendipity, fiercely scolding the gray Persian. Serendipity simply sat there, poised on the rug, tail meticulously tucked in around her front paws, looking royally indifferent.

Carolyn smiled in spite of herself, though the smile never reached her eyes. "Might as well give up, Lucy. You'll never get her nose out of joint unless you keep the honey in a safe."

"Well, I just might do that!" Lucy huffed. "Though I've a feeling his lordship wouldn't have a bit of trouble cracking that for this beast, either." Straightening, she flashed Carolyn a welcoming smile. "Good morning to you, luv. Mr. Chandler said to give you his regards too. He left early on business this morning, you know, but he said he'd look forward to having supper with you tonight, if he got back in time. If not, he said not to wait for him."

Heading toward the dining room, Lucy remarked over her shoulder with a brilliant smile, "Such a charming fellow, isn't he?"

Carolyn's smile faded. "Yes." It was a good thing Lucy couldn't see her face, she mused as she crossed the hall to her aunt's study. She still wasn't sure about Tiernan's warning—Erik really did seem like a basically nice guy. But if Tiernan was right, and Erik was a con man, and she'd spent a whole day alone with him . . .

It didn't bear thinking on. And yet it had to be dealt with—now.

Fighting her grief over departing with a plan of action, Carolyn brusquely knocked on the door to Aunt Beth's office.

Lady Elizabeth looked up at her over wire-rimmed reading glasses and smiled brightly, waving her into the room. "Ah, Carolyn. Good morning! But come, sit down, dear. There's a small matter I've wanted to discuss with you—"

"Me, too, Aunt Beth," Carolyn interrupted. "Something important."

"Oh?"

Carolyn took a deep breath, glancing at the sheaf of papers on her aunt's desk as she sat down in the wing chair across from her.

"Tiernan—" Her voice failed her as images of the dream swept over her again. She shook her head and lowered her voice to barely above a whisper as she met her aunt's eyes intently. "Tiernan came to my room again last night. He said . . . he said that Erik is dangerous. That he has forged some writ by Grandpa Ed, detailing Thornwyck as an unpaid stake in a horse-race wager with his own late father."

"That's . . ." Aunt Beth began, then abruptly fell silent. A faint crease between her brows was all that betrayed her consternation. "Well, Mr. Chandler has always spent a lot of time in the library in his past visits, going through the history books and such," she finally admitted softly. "And while that's not at all unusual for a guest to do, I don't suppose it would have been difficult to find something with Father's signature on it."

Carolyn took a long, slow breath. "So you think it's possible Tiernan is right?" Her voice was choked with alarm and anger at her own naiveté, that she could have been so completely taken in by Erik's charm and charisma. "We could be in danger! We should call the police—"

Aunt Beth's look effectively silenced her. "And say what, dear? That a ghost has told us one of our guests is a confidence man?"

Carolyn closed her eyes. She'd known that wasn't an option yet—not until they had proof. "Perhaps Tiernan knows where those papers are. If we can find them—"

"*Then* we could be in real trouble, Carolyn," Lady Elizabeth finished for her. "If Mr. Chandler really is what his lordship suspects him to be, it might be dangerous to let him know we're on to his tricks."

"But if we do nothing—"

Aunt Beth shook her head. "I didn't say that, dear. I will tell Ben to keep his eyes open. But don't tell anyone else, and don't let Mr. Chandler become suspicious."

"All right." Carolyn pursed her lips, frowning. "I don't like leaving you to this, Aunt Beth. . . ."

Lady Elizabeth's features brightened into a genuine smile. "Which brings me to the reason I summoned you here," she began eagerly. Glancing down at the papers on her desk, she paused, looked at Carolyn again, and then shook her head with a sigh. "Oh, dear, this morning has not at all turned out the way I'd imagined it."

Carolyn only smiled sadly. The date on her flight ticket was tomorrow's. "I had a wonderful time here, Aunt Beth."

Lady Elizabeth smiled in return, then looked at her rather crossly. "Well, the mood is certainly ruined, but I might as well get on with this. I've been spending a bit of time in my barrister's office in Killarney this last week, you see."

She held out the bound pages to Carolyn and

huffed impatiently when Carolyn didn't move. "Well, take them. You might as well have a copy too."

Carolyn read only a single word on the top page: *Testament*. Her hands curled into fists in her lap.

"You needn't look so worried, dear." Aunt Beth chuckled mildly, seeing her reaction. "I'm not dying yet, and I don't intend to for a good while to come. I just want to talk over some details with you."

"With me." Carolyn blinked and stared at her aunt, who shrugged her shoulders in return.

"It's very simple, really. You see, the Warringtons have preciously little interest in Thornwyck, outside of financial gain. At the first sign of expense they'd put it on the market. And I hadn't realized till you came how much it means to me to see this place in . . . caring hands."

A sudden understanding dawned in Carolyn. "Aunt Beth—you should think about this—"

"But I have, dearest," Lady Elizabeth interrupted gently. "And I want to tell you now, myself, not have Mr. Henderson or some other balding barrister read out my words to you after I am gone."

She sat back, meeting Carolyn's concerned gaze openly, serenely. "I know you have a life of your own on the other side of the ocean. You have a job, and friends, and a home back there. But I would like you to consider this: Consider staying here, as assistant manager of Thornwyck—with full salary, of course—so you'll know your way around the books, and all when it's time for you to take over the estate."

Carolyn stared at Aunt Beth for a full minute, dumbstruck. Then logic kicked in with a somewhat befuddled vengeance. "But—" She swallowed, shaking her head. "That's impossible—I mean, with immigration and all that, and—I can't just stay here—"

Lady Elizabeth smiled brightly. "Yes, you can, dear. Mr. Henderson—my barrister—has already looked into the legal aspects, contacted the proper authorities, and assured me there will be no problem if you should decide you wish to stay. You can fly back to get your things, of course, or we can have them sent over. If you want to accept your new position, that is."

"I—" Tears had sprung to Carolyn's eyes, blurring the prim and proper figure of her aunt. She suddenly felt like that shy, timid child again, who had spent her Sundays dreaming of knights and castles and fairy godmothers.

Words wouldn't come. Carolyn's teeth sunk into her bottom lip, and the tears welled over, to run, scalding, down her cheeks. Embarrassed, she rubbed at her eyes, then looked up at her aunt with a watery smile, then lunged right over the top of the desk and caught Lady Elizabeth in a hug.

"You've made me the happiest creature on this earth, Aunt Beth."

"I'm glad, dearest."

Blushing from her uncharacteristic lack of restraint, Carolyn slid back into her chair with a somewhat sheepish smile.

But Aunt Beth wasn't looking at her, not precisely. Her gaze was fixed on the space just behind Carolyn's chair, and her lips were curved in a perfectly satisfied smile.

"I thought you'd like that, old chap."

Carolyn twisted around. Behind her stood the ninth Earl of Thornwyck, his hands resting possessively on the back of her chair. And he was smiling.

Chapter Nineteen

For Carolyn, the remainder of the day passed in a whirlwind of dazed euphoria, between going down to Killarney to see Aunt Beth's lawyer, unpacking her things, and then quickly repacking one bag. She still had to leave tomorrow—to officially quit her job, send her things on their way in an overseas container, and say her good-byes back home.

As evening darkness descended softly over the land, Carolyn hung the white rose in the wardrobe to dry, then wandered out onto the cliff again, wrapped into her cashmere cloak. Kerry-blue waves rolled toward shore, dashed as plumes of spray against the rocks of the ragged coastline.

She was no longer afraid of standing here, ten feet away from the edge. Was she really connected to Elyssa? It still seemed impossible. But the serenity that enfolded her like the softest summer wind, the joy and utter certainty that this was where she belonged, spoke more clearly than any theories of the impossible or possible.

This was her home. And she was here to stay.

Her very own happy ending . . .

Carolyn's eyes misted again as she stared out over the ocean. The sky blurred into light and the sea into darkness, while the cool, never-ending sea breeze whipped her hair back from her face. She decided right then to let it grow past her waist. Like Elyssa's.

Carolyn brushed the tears from her eyes, laughing shakily, silently, into the wind. She suddenly felt as if she need only spread her arms and she could fly, borne away upon the timeless wind. As though she need but turn around to see Thornwyck as it had been nearly three hundred years ago, a coach-and-four waiting before the door, perhaps, and tenants working in fields and living in whitewashed cottages with thatched roofs lashed down against the winter gales—

"Jesus Christ, Cary, are you suicidal?"

There was no mistaking Erik's voice. Strong hands yanked her back before she could turn, held her tightly against his chest even when she tried to pull away.

"You scared the hell out of me!" Erik whispered harshly against her hair. "Standing not three steps from the bloody edge of the cliff . . . !"

Carolyn could feel the tremor in his body, hear

the concern in his voice, the anger. She gently twisted from his embrace, but he held on to her hand.

"It's okay, really," Carolyn assured him with a smile. Tiernan's warnings had not left her mind, but they were even more difficult to believe face-to-face with handsome, charming Erik. "There's no danger here now—"

"No danger!" Erik pulled her farther back from the edge, made her walk with him toward the castle. "Don't you know what happened to the blasted earl? There's this little thing called erosion, Carolyn. It can make that rock cliff about as solid as fruit crumble!"

He stopped, finally, turning her to face him, and ran a hand through his sandy hair, agitated. "Just do me a favor, okay? Stay back from that drop."

Carolyn nodded mutely. It wasn't worth the trouble to explain her reasoning. And, in any case, she didn't want to bring up Tiernan's name in front of Erik. Instead, she started back toward Thornwyck.

Erik fell into step beside her, his arm coming to rest lightly around her shoulders. She didn't bother shrugging it off.

"I got some news from Aunt Beth today," Carolyn finally volunteered, to forestall any other topic . . . among other things. "I'll be coming back here in a few weeks."

Erik pulled up short and faced her squarely, catching both of her hands in his. "That's great! Did you get more vacation time?"

She met his elation with a vague smile. "Not exactly."

"But you'll be staying awhile?" he queried eagerly.

Carolyn's thoughts whirled, crystallized. "Yes," she responded brightly, smiling. "Actually, I'm moving here."

Perhaps she shouldn't have told him this—but perhaps knowing there would be a witness would make him think twice of taking advantage of an old woman. "Aunt Beth has asked me to help with the . . . family business."

Something like suspicion crossed Erik's features, and then was replaced by a hopeful smile. "Was that the only reason you decided to stay?"

Carolyn sighed, stepping back until he let go of her hands. She would have been happier if he'd been angry at her revelation, angry that she might be here to foil his plans.

"Erik, please, we've been through that. What we have won't go beyond friendship, and if you can't accept that, then let it end right here."

His countenance darkened momentarily, but finally he nodded.

"I'm—sorry. I guess it's—" He grinned disarmingly, shrugged, and fell into step beside her again, taking out a cigarette from the pack in his shirt pocket and lighting it before continuing. "You affect my rational thinking, Cary. I'll try harder not to forget myself again."

Carolyn nodded, but as soon as they were inside the castle she excused herself and headed down the hall alone. It was a good half hour before dinner would be ready, and there was a Gaelic-English dictionary in the library that would make the time pass far more pleasantly than Erik's company.

"Carolyn, dear, are you or aren't you going to come to supper?"

"What—?" Glancing up from the book in her lap, frown still in place on her brow, Carolyn blinked to find Aunt Beth standing in the doorway to the library. "Oh. I guess I got distracted with this. . . ." She gestured at the book in her lap, smiling sheepishly.

Lady Elizabeth nodded. "I'll say you were distracted. I called you to supper a quarter of an hour ago, on my way past, and you said you'd be over in a minute. You didn't fall asleep, did you?"

"I wish," Carolyn replied jokingly to her aunt's mild teasing. "Just look at this, though." She heaved herself out of the armchair and crossed to the door, holding up the open dictionary to Lady Elizabeth's surprised face, then snatching it back before her puzzled aunt could read a single line.

"It says here that *cogais* can mean 'a prodigious large, red, carbuncled nose,' or 'a huge frog,' or 'a large pinch of snuff.' And that's not even all." She frowned at Aunt Beth accusingly, voice plaintive. "How in the world could anyone ever hope to learn this language, even with an almost photographic memory? Not to mention the pronunciation! It has nothing whatsoever to do with the way a word is spelled!"

She heaved a sigh, shut the dictionary, and plopped it down on the nearest desk before heading for the door.

"Why are you trying to learn it?"

Carolyn sighed again, then shrugged. "He speaks it sometimes. And Elyssa never learned it."

"Ah," Lady Elizabeth replied after a moment, as though that reasoning made perfect sense. "Well, for one thing, dear, you had the wrong dictionary."

"The wrong—?"

Aunt Beth nodded, barely hiding a smile by turning and heading down the hall toward the dining room. "His lordship would hardly be speaking Scottish Gaelic, you know. While it's quite similar to Irish, there are differences. The accents, for example." She sent Carolyn a bright smile. "We do have the proper dictionary, of course. And I'm sure Maura would be happy to help you with your studies, if you asked her. Lots of people in this area speak Irish, you know."

"That's right, they do, don't they?" Carolyn echoed happily. The prospect of being able to discuss the language with a living person instead of cursing at the page of a dictionary abruptly brightened her whole outlook on life.

"Certainly. It is by no means a simple language to learn, as you pointed out, but—"

"It escapes me why anyone would want to,"

came the abrupt comment from Erik, who was striding down the stairs.

"Ah, good evening, Mr. Chandler," Lady Elizabeth returned as politely as ever as he joined them on the way to the dining room. Carolyn forced a smile for Erik, marveling at how consummate an actress her aunt was. She only wished she'd inherited some of that talent.

"It's a fascinating language, Erik," Carolyn retorted somewhat disapprovingly, foregoing a greeting.

"It's a dead language, Cary," he corrected her with no little scorn. "I shouldn't waste my time trying to learn it. Everyone here speaks English, so why bother?"

"I take it you don't speak it, then?" Carolyn pursued the subject despite Aunt Beth's warning look and the fact that they'd entered the dining room.

"Why in the world should I want to?" Erik stared at her, contempt at the very thought in his eyes, and Carolyn wondered suddenly how she could ever have thought of him as charming. But she only shrugged and gave him a disappointed smile.

"Rats. And I was hoping you could give me lessons when I come back. Oh, well, I guess I'll have to ask Maura after all."

The look on Erik's face as he took a seat across from her was almost comical, except for the sharp glint of anger in his eyes. Aunt Beth wisely refrained from saying anything, and that pretty much set the tone for dinner conversation.

*   *   *

Carolyn tossed and turned in bed that night, waiting, hoping that Tiernan would appear again.

Memories of last night's dream returned in the darkness, bringing a flush of heat to her face and a restless hunger to her body.

She'd never imagined it could be like . . . *that.* Had never imagined how lonely, how devastatingly empty her solitary bed could be after but a single night of knowing what love was, even if only in a dream.

But Tiernan didn't come, much as she longed to see him, needed to speak to him. Long after midnight she finally consigned herself to sleep, knowing that the kittens would wake her if Tiernan appeared.

He did not.

Erik was there with the rest of the staff to see her off the next morning. He gave her a brotherly hug and waved with the others as Cummings drove her and Aunt Beth to the airport.

The month she was gone seemed like forever, and yet the days flew past. There was so much to do, she barely had time to sleep, but too much time to think—about Tiernan's warning, about Tiernan, the dream of loving him . . . and its apparent yet utterly impossible consequences.

She was pregnant. She, who had avoided getting close to any man, who hadn't so much as dated since high school, was pregnant from a dream of making love with a ghost.

* * *

Lady Elizabeth was there to greet her at the arrivals terminal, and Carolyn flew into her aunt's arms, nearly bowling her over in her happiness at being back. Cummings snatched up her bags, as before, and together the three of them headed out to the parked Rolls.

"How—have things been, Aunt Beth?" Carolyn made herself wait with the question until they were in the privacy of the car, well underway to Thornwyck. How, or when, she would tell her aunt about the baby was a problem yet to be resolved in her mind.

"Well, we've had a terrible cold spell the last few days, even had a bit of hail the other night. There was a young Austrian couple who stayed for a week's honeymoon, but they left last Friday. Oh, and Lyle sprained his ankle a few days ago, chasing after Tippens—"

"Aunt Beth!" Wide-eyed, Carolyn stared at the woman beside her.

Lady Elizabeth blinked in surprise. "Oh, you mean . . . ? Of course you do." She nodded somewhat distractedly. "Well, Mr. Chandler is still here, and will be for another month or so, though he's out on business right now. But he's done nothing strange, and we have been keeping an eye on him."

Carolyn sighed in relief, sinking back into the leather upholstery. "Thank God."

"But I'm afraid the frost killed the roses, though it did wonders for the ivy on the courtyard wall. You should see it now . . ."

Smiling, Carolyn closed her eyes and listened to her aunt recount everything of even the least importance that had happened in the last four weeks. If nothing else, Lady Elizabeth's easy chatter helped to subdue her excitement at returning to Thornwyck and to speed the passage of time. It seemed like only minutes had passed when Cummings pulled up in front of the main door of the mansion.

"Glad to have you back, Miss Carolyn."

Carolyn was so happy to be back herself that she gave the stunned Ben Masters an exuberant hug. The rest of the smirking staff got the same treatment, amid much laughter and good-natured jests.

"I'm afraid you'll have this room to yourself now, dear," Aunt Elizabeth commented as she escorted her upstairs a moment later. "Your kittens have grown like weeds, and as of last week they've taken up with Serendipity."

"Oh, no." Carolyn clapped her hand to her mouth, only half in jest. "God, not as apprentices, I hope?"

"Not as yet, I'm glad to report." Aunt Beth chuckled, opening the door to Carolyn's old room and letting Masters carry in her luggage. "Now you relax for a little while; have a nap, whatever you like. I'll see you at supper in an hour or so, if you feel up to it. Else I'll have Lucy bring you up a tray—"

"I'll see you downstairs for dinner," Carolyn

interrupted with a smile. Aunt Beth obviously remembered her first arrival at Thornwyck. But, aside from the haunting awareness of another life growing within her, she felt wonderful, no different than before. And, since she'd slept on the flight in an effort to make time pass more quickly, she had an eight-hour head start on jet lag.

"It's good to see you home, dear."

Carolyn, having taken Elyssa's diary out of the bottom drawer of the desk and the dried white rose out of the wardrobe, turned to look at her aunt. "It's good to be home," she said quietly, never having meant any words she'd spoken more than these.

But Lady Elizabeth was looking at the rose in her hand. Carolyn placed the diary on the night table, and the rose atop it, then met her aunt's gaze in silent understanding.

"I'll see you at supper," Lady Elizabeth finally replied simply, turning to leave Carolyn to the quiet sanctuary of the bridal chamber. After a moment Carolyn sat down on the bed, then lay back with a long sigh.

There was no trace of Thornwyck's ghost. He'd not shown up to welcome her, but, as always, she could feel his presence in the castle.

Carolyn smiled shakily. She turned her head to stare at the dried white rose, then laid her hands gently over her flat belly and silently wondered what Tiernan would say when he found out.

* * *

Carolyn was early in the dining room. Lucy served her the usual orange juice, then hesitated.

"Hear that, Miss Carolyn?" The black-haired woman shot a quick, worried glance out the rain-sheeted windows. "'Tis the scream of his lady wife, it is. When he done and taken her over the cliff—"

"Lucy!"

Guiltily, the hostess stepped back from Carolyn and the window to glance at Lady Elizabeth.

"That's quite enough," Aunt Beth scolded mildly, seating herself across from Carolyn. "Please, could you get me a glass of wine before supper?"

"Of course, Lady Elizabeth."

Carolyn stared at Aunt Beth, then glanced after a quickly retreating Lucy. Rain pattered against the windows in waves of changing intensity. "Can't we tell her the truth?"

Aunt Beth smiled vaguely. "Well, we could try. But Lucy so loves that frightening ghost we have here, I do believe it would be a lost cause."

"Perhaps we could put something in the paper, revising history," Carolyn suggested. "That the ninth Earl of Thornwyck didn't murder his wife, and—"

"And prove it how?"

Carolyn made a face. Aunt Beth smiled crookedly, looking instantly contrite for her choice of words, but Carolyn only shrugged. They didn't mention Erik or Tiernan for the remainder of the evening, though Carolyn silently rejoiced in the awareness of her beloved ghost's presence.

She got to bed late, exhausted despite her in-flight naps. With a deep sigh, Carolyn switched off the light on the bedside table and buried herself under the covers.

And thought of Tiernan.

Lying in that bed brought back the memories she had kept so carefully at bay. Carolyn stared up at the canopy in a room thick with the color of night and remembered a night of glorious love that had taken place nearly three hundred years ago.

And now a child was growing within her.

Carolyn knew the testimony of time would have swept away the last of her denials and rationalizations, even if she had not gone to see her doctor. No amount of stress had ever delayed her monthly time, and she'd never been lucky enough to get off without at least a day of pure agony. That was why she'd asked that illogical question in her doctor's office. And she'd received her answer.

It was unthinkable, of course. Impossible. But no more so than nearly getting killed by dancing on the cliff with Tiernan. She had been Elyssa then, in his time. And she had been Elyssa in the dream . . .

. . . the dream that had no more been a dream than her encounter with him during the storm.

Muffling a cry against the pillow, Carolyn squeezed her eyes shut, breathing raggedly. While she'd been away, it had all been so unreal, everything that had happened, so far away and outlandish. But now—now everything around her, everything she saw, served as witness to the paradoxical truth.

With a long, harsh sigh, she turned onto her back, trying to resort to logic in the face of the impossible. The cliffs—it had to have something to do with the cliffs, because both times . . .

But she'd been out on the cliffs many times without slipping into the past!

It had to be more than the cliffs. A time of day, of the month, of the year? Matching conditions to those of the past that came so suddenly alive?

Carolyn shook her head impatiently. She was grasping at straws, trying to explain the inexplicable.

Suddenly she stilled, then scrambled to turn on the light and retrieve Elyssa's diary from the bedside table.

> *October 10*
> *I am quite certain now that I carry my Beloved's babe. I told him this Morn, and it seemed he was Pleased. I do not think he hates me so very much anymore—he calls me* grá mo Chroí, *his darling. Pray to God that our trials are over.*

Carolyn had known the exact words of the entry, of course, had seen them against her closed eyes for weeks. But reading them again, black on yellowed vellum, still shocked the breath from her lungs. She stared at the radio clock, then turned off the light and slowly lay back.

Midnight had slipped by. It was now the morning of October 10—the date chiseled in marble on the tomb of the ninth Earl of Thornwyck.

Carolyn pulled the covers over her head and solemnly vowed that nothing in the world would get her out onto the seaward grounds that day.

Chapter Twenty

The morning of October 10 dawned cold and clear, with last night's rain turned to ice on plants, roads, and puddles. By noon the temperature had dropped further, and the fires in the halls of Thornwyck were stoked high.

Except for a brief walk through the rose garden, Carolyn stayed inside all day, going through the books and records of the bed-and-breakfast business with Aunt Beth. She had no intention of being drawn, by whatever powers at play in this ancient place, to the seaward cliffs.

Finally, it was evening. Nothing unusual had happened all day . . . which was precisely the way Carolyn liked it.

Erik still hadn't returned from his latest business trip. Carolyn didn't particularly look forward to their reunion but knew that it was inevitable. In the meantime there was Tiernan to think about . . . and the child.

After dinner that night, in her room, came the anxiously awaited, and simultaneously dreaded, visit from the earl's ghost.

As it usually happened, Carolyn felt his presence beside her, suddenly, and much more intensely than when he wasn't visible. She looked up from her diary, then ceased writing and leaned back in her chair.

A faint smile curved the corners of his mouth. He was dressed, as usual, in white and black. He was breathtakingly handsome, as usual, green eyes bright as cut emeralds and coal-black hair loosely curling to the top of his shoulders, feathering across his brow.

"Welcome home, Cara."

She smiled uncertainly. This wasn't going to be easy. She snapped her diary shut and placed it into the top drawer of the desk, then rose from the chair. Realizing she was only wearing an oversized T-shirt, without a bra, she folded her arms across her chest.

"Na bí cho socharach."

Carolyn frowned, then searched her mind for the clearly pronounced words. So he knew she was studying Irish, did he? She wondered what else he knew, then shied away from the thought. That topic would be broached soon enough.

" 'Do not' what?" she finally asked, giving up on the last term. She hadn't reached the Ss in the dictionary yet.

Smiling at her studious frown, Tiernan clarified, "Shy. Dinna be so shy."

Carolyn made a face but didn't uncross her arms. He chuckled and leaned against one of the bedposts. "'Tis glad I am t' see ye again, *a ghrá*. This house isna the same without ye here."

She stared at him for a moment, reveling in his presence, in his dark, masculine beauty, in the love shining from his eyes. Then a sigh lifted her shoulders.

"I have some news for you, Tiernan."

"Good news, milady?"

Carolyn searched his eyes, his features, for any hint of teasing or mischief. There was none, and that made her revelation all the more difficult. She crossed to the bed and sat down on it, hard.

"You—don't remember. Do you?"

Tiernan followed her around the bed and braced his hands against the canopy frame, smiling gently.

"What is it I have forgotten now, *mo rún?*"

Carolyn closed her eyes for an instant and shivered. She should have known. Should have known that he'd remember this no more than he had remembered dancing with her on the cliff.

Opening her eyes, she looked up and met his gaze. To her surprise, her voice held steady. "That last night. The night before I left . . . after you warned me about Erik . . ."

"Aye, I recall it well enough," Tiernan interrupted angrily, his brows furrowed. "He hasna been here for the last—"

"This doesn't concern *him*." Carolyn took a

deep breath, then let it out slowly. "That night—that night, you—we—"

She shook her head, exasperated at her sudden, belated bout of shyness. "We slept together that night. I thought it was a dream, because I was Elyssa, but—"

Tiernan's shocked stare made her voice trail off. "Slept—together?"

She nodded, flushing crimson. "Made love."

The frown returned, furrowing arched black brows. "I canna believe—"

"Well, you'd bloody well better believe it!" Carolyn burst out, suddenly angry, though her voice remained a gruff whisper. "Because you're the only one I've slept with since I was eighteen, and I sure as hell didn't conceive by myself!"

Tiernan straightened abruptly, stiffly, his expression almost comical. "Conceive."

"As in pregnant, with child—whatever you call it in your time! Your child, damn you!"

Carolyn surged to her feet and stormed across the room to the window. She pushed aside the drapes and braced her hands on the cold wood of the windowsill, staring out into the dark, mist-shrouded night through a haze of tears.

"I was out on the cliffs—just like the first time—just like so many times since. And just like the time you came and danced with me . . ." Her voice trailed off and she cleared her throat of the taste of tears. "Just like that time, you were . . . real. We could touch. . . ."

There wasn't a sound from Tiernan. Carolyn buried her face in her hands, wearily rubbing at her eyes, and finally turned around again. He had not moved, was still staring at the bed.

"Can you explain this to me?" she demanded tiredly.

He slowly looked up at her, her face, then her flat belly, then shook his head, still silent. She would have given just about anything at that moment to know what he was thinking. But she only leaned back against the windowsill, hard wood cushioned by the velvet drapes.

"Just forget it." She couldn't—but he could. There wasn't anything he could do about it, anyway. Carolyn closed her eyes for a moment, gathering strength, then fixed the earl with a level stare.

"That forgery you mentioned last time, when you warned me about Erik—I want to know where he keeps that hidden. Is it here? At Thornwyck?"

Tiernan stiffened. Eyes narrowing, he advanced on her, one step, two.

"Dinna tempt the devil, Cara. That man is unpredictable as the winter storms. If he should discover ye in his chamber—"

"So it is there!" Carolyn cried triumphantly. "Where, Tiernan? Where does he hide it?"

When the earl only shook his head minutely, features shut forbiddingly, Carolyn stormed up to him, stopping mere inches away.

"You've got to tell me, Tiernan. If I can find that paper, we'll have something on him. We'll have proof, so that if he tries any funny business—"

"Uist! Hold yer peace, and speak no more o' this. I dinna want ye near him, Cara." Despite the flowing accent, his voice was harsh, leaving no room for argument.

Carolyn spun away, expelling a sharp breath. "You're not being reasonable!" She flung herself onto the bed, staring up at its canopy. Remembered suddenly, vividly, being in this bed with him—

She punched the nearest pillow, cursing.

"Milady, such is hardly fit language for—"

"Oh, stuff it!"

After a number of seconds Tiernan's utter silence drew her attention. She looked up at him with a sigh, then shrugged, slumping back again.

"I'm sorry. Look, women these days can curse just as well as men. I've cut it out since my university dorm days, but I guess you never forget."

She shot him a quick glance and found he still hadn't moved. "Where's the paper, Tiernan?"

He ignored her question and slowly paced the length of the room.

"It would be a lot safer for me to search his room while he's not here," Carolyn mused aloud. She received no reply. Tiernan kept pacing.

"And it'll take me longer to find it if I don't know where it is."

Still nothing. She shut her eyes for a moment and drew a deep breath, then started to push up off the bed—only to find Tiernan suddenly towering over her, bare inches away. She shrank back, not out of fear but because she didn't want to touch—*through*—him again. The first time had been quite unnerving enough.

"Ye came into me time again."

Carolyn propped herself onto her elbows and managed to shrug. He was still close to her, so close she could see each inky eyelash that shadowed smoldering green eyes.

"'Tis a good thing ye didna dance longer wi' me that night, then."

Carolyn pressed her lips together. She had wanted to discuss this *before*. Not now. Not when he was stalling, trying to distract her from what she planned to do tonight. What she would do tonight.

She inched back and rolled off the other side of the mattress.

"Wait."

Something about his voice stopped her halfway between the bed and the door, yet she did not turn back.

"Ye said ye were out on the cliffs . . . like that time we danced."

Carolyn nodded, not wanting to play his game but too curious about the past to resist. "But I've been out on the cliffs dozens of times. And nothing ever happened, except for those two . . ." She broke off and turned to face him, shaking her head. "Look, just tell me where this damned paper—"

"Aye, *ye* were on the cliffs often," Tiernan cut her off, features taut and hard. "But 'twas only those two times that I was there wi' ye, Cara."

Carolyn stared at him, open-mouthed. For an

instant she thought her knees might give out. She flung out on arm toward the wall to steady herself.

No time of day, or month, or year, or other obscure combination of circumstances, her mind formally answered that burning question. Just the cliffs . . . and the ghost. Just that simple.

She did sit down then, sliding along the wall to fold down on the ground. She could feel Tiernan coming closer and finally looked up to find him crouched before her.

"We could test this theory, Cara."

Carolyn stared at him, shivering, feeling the timbre of his voice like a physical caress. It was tempting—oh, God, was it tempting. . . .

But the chance of getting the implicating document out of Erik's room was one that she couldn't afford to miss.

Shoving to her feet with a curse, Carolyn turned toward the door. He'd succeeded in distracting her, all right. But she *was* going to get that forgery—and then she'd consider this gate to the past.

"You won't keep me from this, Tiernan. No matter what you say, I'm going to get that piece of paper and expose Erik. And I'm going to do it *now*."

"Cara."

Her hand on the door knob hesitated for only a heartbeat.

"'Tis in a large Bible, *a ghrá*. In a suitcase on top o' the wardrobe."

266

With a sigh, Carolyn turned around. "Thank you."

Tiernan stood directly behind her. His gaze was intent, his features taut with lines of tension, worry.

"I canna always be where I wish it, Cara. And I canna do injury t' the livin'. That is for the Dark Ones, and I'll no' be one o' them. Like ye, Chandler can hear me, see me, if the darkness is far enough away, and if I be wantin' t' be seen. Yet he'll no' flee from me in blind terror."

Carolyn nodded slowly. "I understand." She took a deep breath and straightened before him. "And I'm still going. I know where Aunt Beth keeps the master key—I'll be back here with that forgery in no time flat."

She smiled encouragingly, but Tiernan's gaze didn't soften.

"Milady . . ."

"Yes?"

His expression was remote, fraught with pain. Carolyn moved closer, concern rising. "Tiernan?"

"That night, Cara . . . when ye—when ye came into me time . . ." He sighed, closing his eyes briefly. "Ye felt what Elyssa felt?"

Carolyn's breath rushed softly from her lungs. She could find no words, only nodded, then realized he could not see. "I—yes."

Tiernan's mouth tightened; whether in anger or shame, she could not say. A muscle in his jaw spasmed.

"Ye were right, the first time we spoke, milady.

I didna give much affection t' me wife in the short while we had together, and I never—never gave her words o' love in a tongue she could understand."

"She knew, Tiernan."

His eyes snapped open, the hard green gaze scouring her. Carolyn mustered a smile. Oh, how wrong he had been, how blind in his stubborn pride. Elyssa, in her love for him, had seen so very clearly. No woman alive could have misunderstood the power behind each of his kisses, each gentle touch. Even the not so gentle ones.

"She fell in love with you the first time she saw you, I think." A small sound escaped her throat, not quite laughter. "Just like I did."

"Cara—"

Carolyn shook her head, backtracking out of where this might lead. "She knew you loved her, in the end. You must know, from her diary—"

"I never read her diary, *grá mo chroí*."

A puzzled frown creased Carolyn's brows. "But . . ."

His shoulders heaved with an unsteady sigh. He glanced at the ancient leather-bound book, at the dried white rose lying atop it. "Oh, many's the time I could have read over yer shoulder, had I but wanted t'," he reluctantly agreed with her unspoken argument. "But I didna. Perhaps . . . Perhaps I was bein' too much the coward t' face what she had written. T' know what she thought o' me."

"Oh, Tiernan . . ."

Carolyn reached out to him, stopping her hand

a hair's breadth from his skin. So that's why he'd not known about the ink drawing of their wedding portrait . . . The earl's eyes slid closed, as if in pain or pleasure, yet he remained perfectly still.

"I can feel the warmth o' yer hand, *mo rún*." There was wonder in his voice, and sadness and pain as his breath caught. "I would give me unnatural existence t' touch ye just once more, hold ye t' me—"

On a broken sound of pain, Carolyn spun away and fled downstairs to get the master key from the safe in Aunt Beth's study.

His child.

Mary, Jesu and Joseph. The woman he could not so much as touch with his insubstantial hands carried his babe.

Tiernan stared after her as she rushed down the stairs, feeling as though he was dying all over again—shock, confusion, disbelief. And then the joy rose in him.

His child.

Had he a body, he would have wept. He could only watch Carolyn stride down the hall to Chandler's chamber, master key clutched in one hand, movements lithe as a cat's.

His child.

The overwhelming joy vanished, suddenly, swept away by a rising, cold flood of dread.

'Twas the past coming to pass all over again: his wife and babe endangered by the man who was Marshall, and he helpless to aid her. The only

*difference lay in that before he had not been able
to save her because he had not known of the danger. Whereas now he knew—but could not raise a
hand against the bastard.*

*Raging in his helplessness, Tiernan watched his
beloved open the door to Chandler's chamber and
disappear into the darkness inside as though swallowed by the depths of hell.*

It was the first time she had ever done anything illegal, aside from occasionally pushing the
speed limit. Carolyn's heart was near to pounding out of her chest and her whole body trembled
with adrenaline as she silently closed the door to
Erik's room behind her.

In the dim beam of the flashlight the chamber
looked like any of the others, ancient and
elegant, though permeated with the smell of
cigarette smoke. Carolyn spotted the suitcase
on the large oak wardrobe and got it down
with the help of a chair. The suitcase was
unlocked, and inside it was a massive, antique-
looking Bible.

A time-yellowed, fragile sheet of paper lay
folded in half between two pages in Revelations.
Carolyn snatched up her prize and quickly
replaced Bible, suitcase, and chair as they had
been before. Switching off the flashlight, she
tiptoed out the door.

She had it! God, she'd actually done it!

With shaking hands she silently closed the door
and locked it again. She had the proof they'd
needed—!

"Such a shame. I'd really hoped it wouldn't come to this."

Carolyn spun around with a choked cry at the first sound of Erik's quiet voice.

He was standing in the darkness of the hall-way, leaning casually against the opposite wall, the usual briefcase under his arm. There was no telling how long he'd been there. His face was inscrutable.

Carolyn backed up one step down the hallway, then another. Her mind was spinning in circles, screaming at her to flee, louder and louder with each heartbeat.

"I wouldn't run if I were you."

Carolyn froze. For the first time she saw the muzzle of a gun pointed at her out of the shadows of Erik's form. Her hands clenched around the flashlight; the folded paper nearly crumbled in her grip. The air seemed to stick in her throat, making it impossible to draw breath.

Erik smiled, that same innocent, boyish smile he'd so often charmed her with, though this time it didn't touch his eyes. He stepped forward to unlock the door, his cold stare never straying from her.

"Won't you come in for a while, Cary? There's a great deal we need to discuss, you and I."

Carolyn felt like a deer walking toward a loaded rifle on the first day of hunting season. Erik closed the door behind her, switching on the light and glancing around the room.

"You do show promise, I must admit," he commented conversationally, nodding approvingly.

"Very neat, very tidy. I wouldn't even have noticed you'd been here."

After a moment Erik relaxed into one of the chairs, gesturing to another. The gun had vanished again, but Carolyn felt no safer. She remained standing just inside the door, loathe to come near him.

"Don't be shy, sweet. Make yourself comfortable. And do tell me how you found out about that old thing."

Carolyn pressed her lips together and sat on the edge of the chair, not bothering to deny her knowledge of "that old thing." She had to play along with him until she could get away and call the police. Just for a little while . . .

But her mind wasn't coming up with a single credible answer to Erik's question.

"I'm waiting, Cary."

Carolyn met his gaze mutinously. "The ghost told me." Then she held her breath, waiting for him to explode into a fit of rage, to fly at her. But Erik only raised his brows, then chuckled, shaking his head.

"That old bastard sticking his nose into things again, is he? What else did he tell you, sweet?"

The transformation from humor to fury in that last sentence was so swift, so complete, Carolyn nearly shrank back in her chair. "Nothing."

Erik rose, laughing softly, a sound than sent shivers down her spine.

"Nothing! You know what, Cary? I believe you." He stopped in front of her, smiling beatifically. "Because if he knew anything at all, he'd never have allowed you to go looking for that useless bit of scrap paper!"

Erik's voice never rose, never became loud enough to carry beyond the walls of his room. Carolyn said nothing, only sat stiffly in the chair.

"Ahh. You'll have to marry me now, sweet." He smiled at her sudden, wide-eyed stare. "And I just know you'll be the perfect wife to me."

Fighting panic, Carolyn drew a slow, unsteady breath. "Erik, please understand that I don't intend to marry anyone, and—"

"No, Cary, sweet, I don't think *you* understand." He settled back into his chair, smiling still. "You wouldn't want to precipitate any—shall we say *unfortunate* accidents. Would you?"

Chapter Twenty-one

Carolyn swallowed hard. "What do you mean? What—accidents?"

Disgust and fury rose like bile in her throat at Erik's charmingly boyish smile that suddenly showed all the cruelty of a youth torturing a helpless animal for the sport of it.

"Well, that all depends on you, sweet."

He rose again, lighting a cigarette, and slowly paced the room. Carolyn clenched her teeth, stiffening her spine. "Whatever you're planning, you must know I won't go along with it."

"Ah, but you're mistaken there," Erik corrected her mildly, as though speaking of which wine goes best with which dish. "I am quite certain that you *will* go along with this. You see, you've made it very obvious how fond you are of your dear Aunt Beth."

Carolyn froze. Rage turned slowly, inescapably to stark terror. Her throat was so dry, she could hardly rasp out the words. "What have you done to her?"

Erik drew on his cigarette, brows raised innocently. "Nothing, of course." He snatched the forgery out of her hands as he walked by and sat down again on the chair across from her, smiling. "Not yet."

Carolyn shoved herself to her feet, backing up two steps toward the door. "We have that wonderful modern contrivance called a telephone, you know. One call to the police and—"

"And what? You'd have me arrested for asking you to marry me?" He waved the writ in the air, smiling coldly, then crumpled it. "I discarded this plan quite a while ago, in favor of a much more pleasant one. And don't think there's a damned thing you could ever prove against me. I've become rather good at this over the years, if I do say so myself."

He took the lighter from his shirt pocket and watched for a moment as the aged paper took flame, then tossed the burning ball into the ashtray on the desk beside him. "Such a wonderful thing, fire. It leaves no evidence at all if it's hot enough."

Carolyn suppressed a shudder at the images his words raised in her mind, at the thought of what crimes this man had already committed with impunity.

"But what if something were to happen to Lady Elizabeth?" she pointed out logically, tearing her gaze from what was quickly becoming a heap of ashes. "And the police knew that you were planning to do her harm—"

"Cary, Cary." Shaking his head, Erik rose and crossed the room toward her. She backed away.

"Your aunt is old, sweet, over seventy. She has a heart condition, you know. Takes pills for it every morning. All the cops would find is an old woman dead of natural causes, and the ramblings of some foreigner. They won't believe you, no matter what you say, because all they'll see is this little gold-digger niece who shows up for the first time just as the old lady is getting on in years. I, on the other hand, am an exemplary guest who has been coming here for years, who's on wonderful terms with everyone on the estate, as even the people in town can attest to. The worst that'll happen to me is a day of questioning down at the station, ending in sincere apologies for my inconvenience. Then I'll be back. And I'll find you, believe me. And you won't know the meaning of the word sorry until that day."

Carolyn slapped away the hand that was rising toward her cheek. "Don't touch me!" Her hiss was as low as his words, but none the less venomous for it. She backed up another step as Erik advanced, hating with all her soul that condescending smile on his lips, that cruel, triumphant glint in his eyes. Either he was mad, insane with his own imagined power, or . . .

She refused to consider the alternative. Clutching the memory of Tiernan inside her, Carolyn prodded, "Why are you doing this? You want the estate, right? So why not just buy it? It's not worth that much, and you're rich enough."

Erik's smile changed, in a way that made Carolyn's blood run cold.

"Don't ever insult my intelligence like that again, sweet. Your aunt wouldn't sell this place to save her life and you know it." He caught her chin in his hand and held it bruisingly. "Yeah, I want the estate. We go back a long way, you know, this place and I. But that's none of your business. I know the old crone made you the sole heir, knew it long before she ever told you. But I didn't lie to you when I said I'd fallen in love with you, and I don't enjoy having my affections thrown back in my face. I want you, Cary, make no mistake. And I always get what I want."

With that, he let his hand drop. Carolyn clenched her fists to keep from rubbing at her chin, refusing to give him the satisfaction of seeing that he'd hurt her. He walked past her toward the door and paused in front of it, fixing her with a cold stare.

"You may have your choice, sweet—agree to marry me, live happily here, and watch your dear old aunt live out the remainder of her years before the estate falls to you—and me. Or you may be contrary and difficult—and dig an early grave for the both of—"

Erik leapt aside an instant too late. The suitcase tumbling from the top of the wardrobe glanced off his shoulder and sent him staggering. Cursing viciously, he kicked at the leather luggage. "And the first thing I'm going to do when I'm in charge here is call in some damned priest and get rid of this bloody ghost!"

He glared at her, but she showed none of the emotions he seemed to be waiting for. Carolyn showed no emotion at all. A blank facade settled over Erik's features, a mask of calm self-assurance.

"I won't rush you into giving me your answer, Cary. Go back to your room and think it over. I'll look in on you in fifteen minutes." He opened the door gently, despite the rage still burning in his eyes.

Carolyn pushed past him, but his hand clamped over her arm, halting her in the doorway, though he did not turn her toward him again.

"Remember now, sweet. Don't do anything foolish. Because if I—ever—see anything even remotely suspicious, your dear aunt will be dead long before the cops could even get here. And that's a fact, Cary, not a threat."

His hand released her. Carolyn made herself walk, not run, though the muscles of her stomach and back were tight enough to cramp. She strode down the corridor with angry, not terrified, strides; only after she rounded the corner did she break into a run.

For the first time since coming to Thornwyck Carolyn locked the door behind her. She rested her forehead against the polished wood, nails digging into her palms, and whispered with barely a breath, "Oh, God, Tiernan. What do we do now?"

The ghost of Thornwyck remained silent and absent. For ten minutes Carolyn paced her room, frantically racking her brain for an answer. Erik was testing her, testing to see how gullible, how scared she was. But she couldn't go to Aunt Beth now—not yet. He might be watching her door, might be in the hallway, listening to each word she said.

Perhaps if she waited until he was asleep, she could sneak downstairs and call the police. . . .

But if what he'd said was true, she couldn't even do that—

"Carolyn."

The quiet word froze her in place. Fifteen minutes . . .

"Open the door, sweet."

Her hands began to shake. She crossed the room, stopping a foot away from the doorway.

"Open the door."

Her mind was racing. He wouldn't dare break in, would he? Aunt Beth and the staff would hear that. And as soon as Erik was out on business again she could tell her aunt the truth. They could go to the police—

But he had a gun. There was no telling what he'd do.

The doorknob turned. "Carolyn." The voice grew softer, so faint she had to strain to hear it. "Your beloved aunt will be dead before morning if you don't let me in."

He could be bluffing. He could be lying

through his perfectly straight teeth. But she couldn't be sure.

Carolyn opened the door and stepped back.

"Very good, sweet." He smiled at her as he stepped through he door. "You're a fast learner. I like that."

Erik closed the door softly, sauntered into the room, and sat down on the bed. Carolyn kept her distance, stiff and wary.

"Have you come to a decision, Cary? I'm sure you've had plenty of time to think about how much your aunt's life is worth—and your own."

Carolyn's teeth were clenched so tight her jaw ached. There was only one option, really: Play along with him. For as long as it took to get help, somehow . . . But she needed time.

She nodded. "All right; you win. But—you have to give me time. To—to prepare for the wedding. Next spring, let's say. It would seem suspicious if—"

Erik shot off the bed, jerking her against him, with his hands like manacles around her upper arms. Her gaze flew up to his face, found features utterly bland despite the violence.

"I've told you once, sweet, don't insult my intelligence. Now, I'm going to give you another chance. Try again."

Carolyn clenched her stomach muscles to keep from shaking, from giving him the satisfaction of knowing he terrified her. She pressed parched lips together and forced a thin smile.

"I—think the end of the month would be

fine for the wedding, Erik. That should give us enough time to plan it."

The bruising hands fell away from her arms. "Your wish is my command, love. The thirty-first will be perfect—a Saturday. I'll begin making the arrangements and leave you to make the announcement to your aunt."

Carolyn stood stock still while he kissed the crown of her head and then strode toward the door. Just before opening it he turned back to her, smiling still.

"And another thing: I know you don't lock your door. Don't start any new habits now, sweet. And don't think to try any fancy nonsense, like hidden recorders or cameras, because you won't get away with it. The sooner your aunt is dead, the sooner you'll inherit, don't forget. And I won't mind you speeding up my plans in the least."

With that, he was gone. Carolyn stared at the closed door unblinkingly, forcing her thoughts into coherence, refusing to give in to the blind panic reaching out to embrace her.

She didn't sleep that night. Just after dawn of another cold, clear day, Carolyn sought out Lucy and borrowed her green Renault for a "secret" trip into Killarney. Knowing Lady Elizabeth's birthday was approaching, Lucy agreed with a conspiratorial smile. Mr. Chandler, the hostess replied to Carolyn's casual inquiry, hadn't come down for breakfast yet.

Carolyn stopped at the first public telephone in town to call the local police station and, under the guise of working on a magazine article, tested Erik's bluff.

To her horror, it held. If no crime had been committed, if no proof existed of any crime, a suspect could not be apprehended. Questioned, perhaps—but not held. It was just as Erik had said.

Carolyn got back to Thornwyck long after dark. She'd bought a woolen shawl for Aunt Beth, to have an alibi, and then spent the whole day driving aimlessly across the countryside, struggling desperately with the web of threats Erik had woven around her . . . and finding no way of escape that wouldn't endanger her aunt.

Exhausted, Carolyn hurried down the quiet hallway, intent on getting to her room as quickly as possible without seeing anyone or anything. It was the large, neon orange piece of paper tacked on to one of the dining room doors that slowed her step and finally brought her to a complete, stunned halt.

WARNING: Due to current weather conditions promoting erosion, the seaward grounds are extremely hazardous and unsafe. Guests should refrain from venturing past the old curtain wall, as several sections of the cliff have already collapsed.

It was signed, "The Management."
Collapsed? The cliff?
Clutching the bag with the scarf, Carolyn ran into the dark kitchen and retrieved the flashlight

before heading for the back door, hands shaking. She didn't even pause at the sight of another copy of the warning note, posted on the inside of the garden door. Heedless, she flew out into the icy night, past the remains of the curtain wall, only to stop short, incredulously, heart leaping into her throat at the sight before her.

It was gone.

The cliff began a good fifteen yards closer to Thornwyck than it had that morning. Gone was the grassy spot where she'd danced with Tiernan all those days ago, gone the place where she'd sat that night, staring out over the sea, and woke in her dream to find him by her side.

Carolyn stumbled forward three short steps and shone the ineffective beam of the flashlight into the darkness ahead of her, as if expecting it to disprove this new reality.

It didn't. A huge section of the cliff, forty feet or more thick, had split off and now lay in sharp-edged boulders and splinters of rock far below the reach of her flashlight, down where the eternal surf pounded against the base of the cliff.

Gone . . .

Wrapping her arms around herself, Carolyn harshly pulled herself together.

What had happened was utterly logical, of course. Wet weather, then cold weather; moisture expanding to ice in tiny fissures of the rock with the force of a slow-motion explosion . . . in short, erosion. One of the most elementary forces of nature, the kind of stuff taught in primary school.

It had been happening, as Aunt Beth had pointed out, for as long as this island had existed. But tonight it had stolen from Carolyn the only place where she had ever slipped into the past, to be with Tiernan in the flesh, to hold him, touch him. . . .

With a soft cry Carolyn dropped to her knees on the short, springy grass, her breath a cloud of white before her. Just last night he'd offered her the chance to come here with him, to, perhaps, return to the past, be with him again—and she had refused. And now . . .

Now it was too late.

Carolyn sucked in a ragged breath and drew herself to her feet, struggling for dominance over her thoughts. There was no proof whatsoever of their crazy theory, no proof at all to suggest that this time slip wouldn't happen again, somewhere else. Perhaps there had been much different conditions at work, other than the location and the presence of Tiernan's ghost. Perhaps . . .

She straightened her spine and, with determined strides, headed back toward Thornwyck.

Perhaps she could drive herself stark, raving mad, here on the cliffs, trying to second-guess what should be impossible in the first place. And while that would help her, insofar that she'd no longer have to deal with Erik, it certainly wouldn't do Aunt Beth any good to have a basket case on her hands.

Regaining some measure of control over her

emotions, Carolyn resolutely returned the flash-light and headed up the stairs toward her room. She was on the middle landing when Erik's voice broke the silence of the hall.

"I missed your company over dinner, Cary. As did your aunt."

Sudden fear blossoming like ice in her gut, Carolyn clenched her hands into fists and slowly turned around. Erik was standing on the bottom step, leaning against the banister and smiling up at her. Unhurriedly, he climbed the stairs to join her.

"You didn't tell Lady Warrington about our wedding yet."

Carolyn swallowed hard and shook her head, not wanting to meet his cold gaze yet afraid to let him out of her sight. Her hands clenched around the plastic bag with the violet shawl. "I had some shopping to do. And I—needed some time alone."

Erik nodded, lightly stroking her cheek. "You don't bruise easily," he commented softly, cap-turing her chin as he had the night before, only gently now, carefully. "Good. But you still shouldn't go out on the cliffs—especially at night, and alone. It's very dangerous there, you know."

Before Carolyn could pull away he drew her against him with an arm around her shoulders and started up the stairs with her. Carolyn stiff-ened until she thought her body might splinter into a thousand pieces with the strain.

"And did the cops tell you what you wanted to know?"

Erik's words froze Carolyn in midstep. The arm around her shoulders tightened and drew her onward, down the corridor toward her room. "I—"

"Don't try to deny it, Cary." Erik cut her off, his voice soft, gentle, coaxing. "I understand you had to do what you did, and I even admire you for it. But don't fool yourself, sweet, and don't underestimate me. I don't want to hurt you. But if you'd done anything but ask questions, you would have returned to find everyone wearing black tonight."

They reached her room, and Erik led her inside, ignoring her token resistance. Once through the door he let her go. Carolyn stepped away, under the pretense of turning on the lights.

"You had better learn a more convincing way of expressing your fondness for your future husband," Erik commented drily. "Anyone watching us might not fully believe that you're madly in love with me."

Carolyn forced her body to relax and shrugged, struggling to keep her expression indifferent as she placed the gift-wrapped shawl in the top drawer of her dresser. "You wouldn't want people to think I'm easy, would you?"

"Christ, no." He smiled broadly and leaned against one of the bedposts. Carolyn remembered Tiernan standing in that same spot and felt her stomach twist with revulsion.

Another thought struck her. She swallowed hard, grasping frantically at the pieces of a plan, then leaned against the opposite bedpost to face Erik. Praying that some of Aunt Beth's theatrical bent might be in her blood after all, and help her to rise to the occasion, Carolyn crossed her arms and put on her most casual front.

"Speaking of which, I feel there's something you should know—before I make the announcement to Aunt Beth. It would only be fair to tell you, before . . . Well, in case it might change your mind about wanting to marry me."

She could see the tension suffusing Erik's body, see the sudden cutting edge of anger in his eyes, but forced her body to remain relaxed even when Erik stepped away from the post, closer to her.

"And what might that be?"

Carolyn pursed her lips and shrugged. "I'm pregnant."

"What?"

She tilted her head at him and bit her tongue to keep her expression blank. She'd never heard his voice so quiet before, not even when he'd threatened her life or Aunt Beth's. "I said, I—"

He jerked her forward hard, up against him. "I heard what you said! Whose is it? Damn you, answer me!" he rasped, features twisted with fury.

Carolyn pulled back. To her surprise, he released her. She took another step back and came up against the edge of the bed, feeling the sweet taste of a smile touching her lips, as Tiernan's mouth had, that night, so very tenderly. . . .

"What did you expect? That I lived like a nun back home?" she challenged mildly, despite the fear and triumph blossoming in her blood. "Well, I didn't. But my boyfriend and I split up just before I came here. He was very rich, you know, and his parents—"

The explosion was instantaneous, cutting off her ramblings. Erik's openhanded blow threw her onto the bed, leaving the metallic taste of blood in her mouth.

"Goddamn you, bitch!" He towered over her, his face that calm, utterly unaffected mask again, his voice never rising above a whisper. "You'd better fix that little *problem*, sweet—"

"We're not back home, Erik!" she reminded him, taking almost savage joy in the pain of her split lip. She'd succeeded in making him lose that icy control, if only for an instant. "We're in Ireland. It's not as if I can just walk into any—"

"You're a smart girl—you'll think of something," Erik cut her off coldly. "I know you will, sweet. Because I sure as hell won't have you breeding someone's bastard when we marry!"

Whirling, he stalked out of the room.

The triumphant smile died before it could ever rise to Carolyn's eyes. Her hand rose to her mouth to stifle a cry and came away bloody.

When we marry . . .

Oh, God, she should never have opened her mouth, should never have . . .

But now it was too late.

Clutching her abdomen, she curled up on the covers, shaking with silent sobs.

289

Chapter Twenty-two

She had fallen asleep with the lights on.

Carolyn blinked against the brightness, then let out a startled sound as she caught sight of the dark shape on the bed beside her, his hand almost touching her face.

"Chuir e saoile ort!" A string of muttered imprecations followed the rasped words, but the earl was already straightening, rising off the bed. "He struck ye hard! I would kill him for that if I could, milady."

Carolyn stared up at the ghost, one hand rising to her face in sudden awareness of how she must look, eyes red and puffy from crying, her face bruised from Erik's blow.

"Tiernan—"

"I told ye no' t' go t' his room! God be me witness, I told ye 'twas too dangerous! But ye wouldna listen." He paced to the windows and, with a flourish of motion, drew the velvet curtains shut. It seemed to Carolyn that he was so angry, he hardly noticed what he had done.

But then, he could, after all, touch . . . things. But not people. Could not, no matter how much she yearned for it, touch her. Perhaps never again, not even in the past . . .

Her tongue probed the small, already scabbed cut on the inside of her lower lip. "You saw . . . what he did?" she finally asked in a voice barely above a whisper.

Tiernan spun to face her. "Aye. Saw and heard. I told ye . . ."

At her desperate look he actually bit back the remainder of his words. Giving all her attention to moving, Carolyn pushed off the bed, kicking off her running shoes and halfheartedly straightening her sky-blue sweater. She crossed to the dresser and stared at her reflection in the mirror to find that her face wasn't bruised after all. Wetting one of the washcloths with unsteady hands, she pressed it against her hot, dry eyes.

"I won't—" The hands holding the cloth fell away from her eyes, pressing against her mouth even as her voice broke. The words she had thought to speak calmly, resolutely, came out in a wail muted by the damp cloth. "God, I won't do it! I'm not going to kill this child! I—I can't."

Shaking her head, she whirled to stare at Tiernan's coldly set features, desperately seeking reassurance from him. "But I won't be able to lie to him for long, Tiernan. Won't be able to hide—"

Her breath broke, and she choked back a sob.

"Hush, now. Dinna worry on that account, *grá mo chroí*. He'll no' be near ye long enough t' know that ye've lied t' him."

The rich, soft whisper of his Irish brogue brought Carolyn's head up out of her hands. She swiped at tears with the cold, damp washcloth and shook her head. "But—"

"*Uist.* I'll find a way, Cara. I'll no' leave ye t' him, I promise ye that."

He stood close to her now. She could see the glimmer of tears in his eyes, brilliant green catching the light, glittering with emotion.

"But for now do naught t' rouse his anger," he advised her, his words and tone gentle. "Be agreeable; be polite. Make him believe, if ye can, that ye've accepted his rule, that ye've forgiven him for his deceit and trickery, that ye've fallen in love wi' him. That way ye'll be as safe as ye can be."

Carolyn pressed her lips together, the taste of blood salty on her tongue. "I'll try. But what if he's heard us talking . . . ?"

"He canna hear what we say when I am here, *mo rún*, unless it be wi' his own ears. His new-fangled toys dinna work well in me presence, just like the old clock. But ye must mind each word ye speak, milady, t' anyone."

Carolyn nodded faintly, a frown line deepening between her brows. Newfangled toys; did Chandler have the whole estate bugged? Did he have taps on the police phone lines? Perhaps even in Mr. Henderson's office, to find out about Aunt

Beth's change in her will? And where else?

There was no way for her to know.

"All right." She nodded again, with more conviction this time, and even found a watery smile. "I'll do my best."

"Good." Tiernan stepped back, and she caught herself just as she would have followed him. She put the washcloth away, instead, watching him from the corner of her eye. "You saw what happened to the cliff?"

His features changed abruptly, growing cold and remote. "Aye."

"We could go and test our theory tonight, couldn't we?" Carolyn suggested, actually managing a conversational tone. "I—I don't feel much like sleeping and . . ." Her voice trailed off at Tiernan's somber look.

"'Tis too late, *a ghrá.*"

"What—what do you mean?" The words tumbled from Carolyn's lips, senseless words, redundant words, because in her heart she already knew the answer.

Gone . . .

Tiernan hesitated, pacing the length of the chamber once, then again. He stopped not half a step before her, emerald eyes cold and hard, hiding his pain. "When ye went out t' the cliff this eve . . . I went wi' ye, Cara. As I'd done before."

And nothing had happened.

The silent words rang through Carolyn's mind, echoing over and over. She sat down hard on the bed, pressing her hands to her lips to stifle a cry. Tiernan followed her, crouching down

294

beside the four-poster so that his eyes were level with hers.

"Mayhap our . . . theory wasna as sound as we believed," he suggested gently, the very tone of his words only adding to her anguish. "Mayhap the cliff was but incidental, and ye'll cross into me time again some other place. . . ."

"Do you really believe that?" Carolyn demanded softly, meeting his wounded gaze, too wrapped up in her own grief to keep silent words that could only bring more pain, for him and herself. She'd never be able to touch him again, hold him, escape from the terrible reality of Erik's tyranny. . . .

Tears blurred her vision, blurred the face that abruptly moved out of her line of sight.

"It doesna matter what I believe, *mo rún*," Tiernan insisted, his voice low yet firm. "We had no way o' knowin' if our idea was even near t' the truth, Cara. It could have been a matter o' coincidence, nothin' more."

Carolyn swallowed hard, blinking away tears. Tiernan was pacing the room again, hands in his pockets. She pulled herself together and nodded. "You're right, of course."

She didn't believe a word she said and he knew it. She could see it in his eyes when he stopped in front of her again, gazing down at her.

"We canna change the past, *a ghrá*, and little good has ever come from frettin' over it. What's done is done, dinna forget that." He folded down beside the bed again and reached out as though to touch her. His hand drifted down the side of her face with barely a breath separating it from her skin.

"Rest, Cara. Tomorrow will come soon enough, and ye'll only harm yerself and the babe wi' too much worryin'."

Carolyn nodded again and wrapped her arms around herself as the ghost of Thornwyck slowly faded from her sight.

She slept in late. Consequently, by the time she got down to the dining hall, Aunt Beth had already left for town.

"But she won't be long today, Miss Carolyn," Lucy informed her while pouring the usual raspberry tea. "Lady Elizabeth's just gone to pay a quick visit to Mr. Henderson, is all."

"Oh." Carolyn drew a slow, deep breath, at once appalled and relieved by this temporary reprieve in breaking the news of a surprise wedding to Aunt Beth. "Could you tell her that I'd like to see her when she comes home?"

"Certainly, luv. If she doesn't stop at Darby's, she should be back afore noon."

"Thanks, Lucy."

The hostess flashed her a quick smile that sobered after a glance out the seaward windows. "But you be sure not to go near the cliffs, now, you hear? Saints, we thought the walls were coming down around our ears when that thing gave way yesterday! Like an earthquake, it was."

"No one got hurt?"

Lucy shook her head. "No, thanks be. And the weather's supposed to be getting warmer, too, or so they say. This is not at all like our usual fall, Miss Carolyn, oh, not at all. But the weather is going mad all over the world nowadays, isn't it? I don't know what this'll come to—"

The sound of porcelain shattering on the marble tiles of the other side of the swinging doors cut off Lucy's words and sent the hostess rushing toward the kitchen with a cry of dismay.

Carolyn cringed faintly at the sound of Lucy's tirade—whether she was scolding one of the cats or one of the staff, Carolyn couldn't make out. Adding a spoonful of honey to her tea, she took a cautious sip of the steaming liquid, then sat back with a sigh.

All the emotions that had run so perilously wild last night, the sorrow and pain and seemingly endless despair of the future, were more manageable again, now, with the rational light of day surrounding her. And Tiernan was right, of course. No sense crying over spilled milk.

At least Erik wasn't with her this morning, though he'd probably be furious that she had missed their usual breakfast at eight.

With another sigh, Carolyn let one hand trail inconspicuously down to her belly. Before, she hadn't known how to tell Aunt Beth about the baby. Now she didn't dare tell her, since Erik expected her to be taking care of "that little problem." But what if she told Aunt Beth, and everyone else, that it was Erik's child? He couldn't kill them all, could he?

But many things could happen to an unborn child. Then he'd grieve right along side of her, of course, but it would be Tiernan's child who paid the price.

No. Tomorrow, she'd go into town and do research enough to be able to make Erik believe she had done as he demanded. And she would trust Tiernan to find a way to keep them safe.

"Carolyn, dear? Oh, there you are. Lucy said you'd wanted to see me. Mr. Henderson came back from his vacation today and I had an interesting chat with him about that possibility of Mr. Chandler successfully forging—"

"He was wrong, Aunt Beth." Carolyn put down the wedding etiquette book she'd taken to reading in case Erik came into the library and steeled herself to lie to her aunt.

Lady Elizabeth sat down in one of the chairs across the round table, looking puzzled. "He was wrong?"

Carolyn nodded but stared down at the tabletop, following the curves and lines of the wood grain, terrified of betraying the lie, the despair that was a living thing inside her. "Tiernan . . . was wrong," she finally expanded on her laconic statement. "Erik has no plans of using any kind of forged document to get control of Thornwyck."

That much, at least, was pure truth. He was using *her*, not a piece of paper, to get the estate. Forcing herself to look up, Carolyn curved her lips into the parody of a smile. "He's—he's in love with me, you see, and wants to marry me. And I've—said yes."

"You did not!" Lady Elizabeth shot to her feet, nearly toppling her chair. For the first time since she'd known her aunt Carolyn saw her blanch. "But what about—Carolyn, dear, I thought—"

Carolyn waved off Aunt Beth's question, putting as much conviction as she could muster into her words. "I think Tiernan's just jealous of Erik. That's why he made up this whole thing—he still thinks I'm Elyssa, and so he doesn't want me to be with anyone else. Besides, everyone here has known Erik for years, and they all say he's a very nice man."

Lady Elizabeth frowned down at her severely. "Are you very sure about this, Carolyn?"

Carolyn shut away everything innocent and naive and pure inside of her and painted a wistful smile onto her face. "I know it sounds sudden, Aunt Beth, but I had time to think about things while I was back home, and I really missed Erik. He—had asked me to marry him before, when I didn't know that I'd be staying, and I turned him down. When he asked again the other night . . ." She smiled and shrugged her shoulders. "I said yes."

The knowledge that Erik had asked her before she'd known about the change in the will seemed to calm Aunt Beth somewhat. Frowning still, but looking more confused now than appalled, she sat down again across from Carolyn. "Well, I suppose . . ."

Carolyn summoned her brightest smile. "I'm so glad to have your blessing in this! You know I never thought I'd ever get married. But . . . I guess I just hadn't met the right man."

The look Aunt Beth shot her was far from approving. "And you're so sure now that you have, dear?"

Carolyn nodded. She didn't dare say the words, because she knew her voice would have broken on the lie. It was hard enough bearing up under Lady Elizabeth's scrutiny. When her aunt rose at last Carolyn heaved a silent sigh of relief.

"Well, all right, then. If this will make you happy, I'll not stand in the way of the marriage. Have you set a date yet?"

Carolyn nodded and held her breath as she answered. "The last of the month. We—we didn't want to wait any longer," she added quickly at her aunt's shocked expression.

"Well." Lady Elizabeth shook her head, still frowning. "Well. I suppose I'd better see about having preparations made, then. It won't be a terribly big wedding, with such short notice, will it, dear? Or are you inviting—"

Carolyn shook her head. "It'll be very private, Aunt Beth. Just the bare minimum. I don't think any of my friends could make it over here on such short notice, and Erik didn't mention any family coming, either."

"Oh. Well." A distracted, pensive look had come over Aunt Beth.

"Will you speak to your minister and ask him to perform the service?" Carolyn continued quickly, determined not to give her aunt much time to think about this sudden change of heart. "You know how I am with church-going and all that."

"Oh." Lady Elizabeth frowned down at her, then nodded decisively. "Well, of course I will, dearest. Reverend Thomas—he's a very nice man, very nice. You'll like him. Why don't I go right now and give him a call? Perhaps you can meet with him later on this week and go over the details of the ceremony."

"That'd be great." Carolyn bit her tongue, smiled, and watched her aunt walk toward the door, then hesitate.

"Oh—before I forget—be sure to stay well back from the edge when you go out to the cliffs, won't you, dear. You've probably seen the warning signs I had Ben put up, but I just thought I'd remind you. . . ."

"I'll be careful, Aunt Beth."

"Do, please." Lady Elizabeth nodded, then turned and with purposeful steps left the library. Strains of music began drifting down the hall from the Blue Room, where Maura had started her harp hour again.

Carolyn stared at the book open on the table in front of her, her vision blurring.

" . . . and cares of tomorrow must wait till this day is done."

Maura's words sent Carolyn fleeing from the library and out onto the grounds. Her aimless, agitated wandering took her through the rose garden, past the fountain, and past the trees and shrubs, quickly losing their leaves in the colors of fall.

Already the cold snap seemed to be fading. Though Carolyn could still see her breath, the ground was no longer frozen.

Tiger and Lily were having a ball in the falling leaves, chasing them and each other. Carolyn scooped up the little tom, ruffling his neck fur and nuzzling his face. Unlike Lily, who was a rag doll with a running motor in anyone's hand, Tiger only fidgeted in her hold, impatient to get free so he could continue his delightful play.

"That old bat must be blind as well as stupid."

The harsh scoff sent Carolyn whirling around to find Erik behind her, scowling as he possessively placed an arm around her shoulders.

"You don't lie worth a damn, you know that? Christ, a five-year-old could've seen through that act." He pulled her close, but she turned her face away, unable to stop the tension stiffening her spine, no matter that Erik and Tiernan had both, for different reasons, told her to be agreeable.

Tightening his hold, Erik jerked her against him more forcefully, angrily, mindless of the kitten in her arms. Tiger let out a bloodcurdling yowl, struggling to free himself from the suddenly too-close quarters. Erik yelped, caught the flailing cat, and threw him viciously to the ground. Tiger scrambled away toward the trees, and a second orange streak followed at full speed.

"Damn rats! If they weren't so useful in making a good first impression, I'd . . ." He broke off, rubbing his jaw. A thin line of blood bisected the neatly trimmed blond beard.

"Aunt Beth believed me," Carolyn replied to Erik's last accusation, careful to keep any hostility out of her voice while wanting nothing better than to kill him for the way he'd mistreated the kitten.

Erik grunted noncommittally. "Damned lucky for the both of you."

Carolyn only shrugged and resumed walking. Erik stayed close beside her, lighting up a cigarette as he matched her step. For several minutes he remained silent while the tension in Carolyn rose higher and higher until she thought she would scream. He was too dangerous when he was silent.

They had climbed the gentle rise north of the estate, and the Thornwyck chapel lay before them in the early afternoon light. Before Carolyn could turn away to head back toward the castle Erik caught hold of her arm and pushed open the old wooden door.

"This would be a perfect place to get married, don't you agree?" Smiling, he gestured around the dim interior with the hand holding his second cigarette. "We could even invite *his lordship* to the wedding." He took a slow drag and blew smoke into the musty air, watching her as he spoke. "It's not such a long way up, from the crypt."

"Not a long way at all," Carolyn agreed after a moment of gaining control over her disgust and shock. "Will you keep a seat empty for him in the front row?" She added with a smile, "if we get pews into this place before the wedding?"

Erik's laughter echoed off the empty, white-washed walls and chilled her soul. Without a word he pulled her from the chapel and strode back down to Thornwyck.

It was Lyle, the gardener, who found Tiger dead outside the base of Rory's Tower the next morning. He couldn't show Carolyn the body, no matter how much she argued and pleaded, said he'd buried it already. He only told her that the kitten looked like it had fallen from the tower, and thus broken its back. Carolyn believed Lyle. But there was no way Tiger had *fallen* from the tower.

Dashing tears from her eyes, she balled her hands into fists and swore that Erik would pay for this.

Chapter Twenty-three

Carolyn had never imagined that two weeks of such terror could pass so quickly. Everyone congratulated her on the upcoming wedding, and it was unfathomable to her that so many people could be fooled so easily with her lies. Erik spent more time with her than ever, being the perfect gentleman to all appearances, seeming to believe her charade except for the occasional warnings not to double-cross him. He never asked about the baby again, and that alone was proof of his confidence in his own power.

Her only talisman against despair was the awareness of Tiernan's presence, though he'd not appeared to her again since the night after the cliff's collapse. Aunt Beth's birthday came and went, with a big celebration that seemed to include most of the people of the outlying area, but all Carolyn knew was that Erik never left her alone. With him beside her, she was introduced to all of Aunt Beth's gentleman friends. She ate next to him, walked the grounds with him, danced with him, and finally managed to flee from the crowded great hall and the live folk band, claiming very real exhaustion. She could only be thankful that the brief bouts with morning sickness had already passed, unnoticed by her husband-to-be.

After a quick bath Carolyn dressed for bed but lingered by the window. The seaward grounds and mist-shrouded courtyard looked just as they had that night, when her visit to Thornwyck had felt like a wonderful dream, and her waking hours had not been filled with anguish and despair.

She pushed off the windowsill, eyes bleak and lips tightened into a bitter line. With wooden motions she climbed into bed and lay staring up at the canopy in darkness, one hand against her still flat belly.

There was no silent presence in the room, no sudden ceasing of the clock's steady, quiet ticking. No shadow standing at the foot of the bed, looking down at her with bright green eyes . . .

"Oh, Tiernan, where are you? Why won't you even let me see you. . . . ?"

There was no reply. Carolyn shut her eyes tightly. Perhaps he could not appear now. Perhaps he could not even hear her. Perhaps, despite his words, he knew there was nothing a ghost could do to help her. . . .

She opened her eyes and stared up at the

canopy again. "If you'd just come to me for a little while, it would help," she argued softly against her own logic. "I—love you, Tiernan O'Rourke. And I miss you so. . . ."

The door to her room opened with but a whisper of sound, then closed again. Carolyn pushed upright and stared into the darkness by the door, remembering her first night at Thornwyck. Suddenly the lights came on, shattering her hopes.

"In love with a dead man, are you, Cary?" Erik shook his head, voice mocking and angry. "How pathetic."

He crossed to the bed, laughing coldly. "You'd never make your living as an actress, you know," he added without heat or anger, a simple tidbit of information coldly tossed her way. "What about you, ghost?" he challenged the silence of the room, turning full circle on his heel, looking about as though expecting an apparition. "Can you hear me, Earl? You've been so quiet these last weeks. How do you feel about our wedding?"

Carolyn gasped as Erik's hand shot out and closed cruelly around her arm, pulling her to her feet. Yet even in his anger, Erik's voice was but a hiss, too low to attract attention.

"You might think about this, you bastard. If you keep playing dirty tricks on me, she's going to be paying double for every one! You hear me?"

"Erik, stop it!" Carolyn tugged against his grip and pried at his hand. "Listen to yourself, for God's sake. You're talking to a ghost!"

He stared at her, then shoved her away, muttering under his breath. "He'll listen, just you wait. If he knows what's good for you, he'll keep his bloody pranks to himself!"

He fixed her with an intent look and smiled slowly. Carolyn, though in a dark green flannel nightie, felt naked under that coldly burning stare. She scrambled under the covers again, but he jerked them away from her.

"Erik—"

He dropped the duvet onto the floor and stepped closer. Carolyn shrank back.

"It won't do you any good to scream, you know—not that anyone would hear, with that party going on downstairs. But it would upset your aunt terribly."

Carolyn's back was shoved up hard against the headboard. She shook her head frantically. "Don't—"

Erik smiled, that utterly charming smile that had masked his depravity so well before. "Relax, sweet. I can wait until our wedding night. After all, it's only a few days away."

Without another word he turned and strode out of the room.

Shaking, Carolyn lunged off the bed and, despite his warnings, locked the door. Then she hauled the covers back onto the bed and scrambled beneath them, wrapping herself tightly into them, choking on her own tears.

She couldn't play along with this anymore, couldn't pretend even civil acquiescence any longer, even had he still believed her act. Because she still didn't know enough to turn him in, and in less than a week she'd be wearing that obscenely expensive wedding dress he'd picked out for her, and the lacy, erotic lingerie, and this pretense would become reality—

"*Leig d'anail.* Rest, *mo rún.* Rest easy."

"Tiernan!"

Her whisper was no louder than a broken breath. The earl's ghost was sitting on the far edge of the bed suddenly, gazing down at her with troubled green eyes. It was all she could do not to throw herself into his arms, and that only because she knew that, no matter how solid he looked, she would pass right through him and end up on the floor.

"He canna hear ye now, milady. He has gone t' his chamber."

Carolyn caught her breath on a sob, her hands clenched into fists as she pushed up to sit facing him. "Then talk to me! Please, stay with me. I need to hear your voice—"

"Hush, *a ghrá,*" he soothed her softly, leaning closer, all but touching her. "I am with ye, Cara. Never doubt that. And dinna be afraid. I'll no' let him harm ye, even if it takes me eternal soul t' keep ye safe."

Carolyn hugged the covers more tightly around her, shaking. "How can you stop him? You can't even touch him!" The words were bitter, fraught with the cold touch of logic.

"I will do all I can, *mo rún;* trust me. I will find a way t' keep ye safe. He has taken ye and our unborn babe once, and I swear t' God he'll no' do so again!"

Carolyn felt her heart constrict at the unshake-able conviction and intent evident in his features, but shook her head sadly. "Oh, Tiernan. It would take a miracle to stop him."

He tilted his head, eyes filled with a love so real she thought she should be able to touch it. "Aye. But dinna despair, Cara. And dinna lose hope. God willin', ye may get yer miracle."

She looked at him, tears in her eyes, wanting so much to believe his words, to believe in even the faintest chance that everything would still work out, it near tore her apart.

Over the next four days what time Carolyn didn't spend in the gym she spent shut into the Blue Room, getting callouses on her fingertips from the taut metal strings of the harp. If Aunt Beth thought her behavior odd, she refrained from broaching the subject.

That night, like all the nights since Lady Elizabeth's birthday bash, Carolyn lay awake in bed, waiting for a ghost that seemed, once again, to have abandoned her.

Shortly after midnight the wall clock ceased its hollow ticking.

"Tiernan?" Heart in her throat, Carolyn reached over to turn on the lamp on the bed stand, afraid of whom she would see. But the soft light revealed a figure shrouded in darkness by the door, a man dressed in black with a white rose on the lapel of his frock coat.

"Oh, God, it *is* you." Her held breath escaped in a rush. "I was so afraid it would be him. . . ."

"Hush, Cara," Tiernan interrupted gently, moving to stand by one of the bedposts. "He'll no' bother ye afore the weddin'."

He hadn't; that was true. Hadn't done a thing to terrify her since Aunt Beth's birthday. And that, in itself, kept her off balance. It was not like Erik to show any kindness. Perhaps he simply felt too secure in his power to bother with his tricks; or maybe he was up to something else. . . .

Carolyn shook her head to escape the thoughts and stared up at the earl's ghost, despair flooding through her yet again. "Tiernan, the wedding is tomorrow!"

"I know," he soothed her, his voice low and lilting. "And I want ye t' go through wi' the ceremony, Cara. Be beautiful, *a ghrá*—for me, for I'll be watchin'."

Carolyn bit her lip and squeezed her eyes shut to contain her anguish. Still, hot tears leaked out from under her lashes, spilling down her cheeks. "I—I don't know if I can—" Her voice broke on a ragged breath.

"Ye can, Cara. Ye are stronger than ye think, stronger by far than that coward."

She blinked at him through her tears. "But—"

"*Uist,* now." His hand rose toward her face and halted just short of touching her, of wiping away the tears. "No more o' this, *mo rún.* Think o' the babe. 'Twill no' be good for him t' have his mother so distraught."

Carolyn almost laughed at his words. God, if something didn't stop Chandler from carrying through his plans, the babe would be dead before it could ever be born! But she didn't speak the words, only nodded, smiling wanly for Tiernan. Any thought of the child brought out the lioness in her, and the earl knew it, just as he knew she would fight to the last before letting this baby be taken.

"That's better. Now, try t' sleep, Cara. Ye need yer rest, and ye've had far too little o' it these past weeks. I'd no' have ye swoonin' when I need yer presence most, *grá mo chroí.*"

Her breath caught in her throat as hope rose like an spring within her. "You have a plan?"

The words were less than a whisper, less than a breath of wind.

But Tiernan didn't answer. He met her widened gaze a heartbeat longer, then abruptly faded away.

Shaking, Carolyn turned out the light. Then she curled up under the down comforter, cradling the covers against her chest, and watched the minutes change to hours on her radio clock, counting down the last remaining moments of her freedom.

Chapter Twenty-four

The day of Carolyn's wedding dawned cold and clear, with a chill northern wind sweeping fallen leaves and fragments of low cloud and night mist away from the land. Lucy and Aunt Beth fussed over her all morning, until finally she stood before the full-length mirror brought into her room, hair braided in a coronet around her head, frothy lace and yards of white satin sprinkled with crystal and pearls surrounding her like a spider's web.

"Goodness, don't you look quite the sight, Miss Carolyn," Lucy breathed from just behind her, clasping her hands in front of her chest. "Like a princess, I swear!"

Carolyn caught her aunt's gaze in the mirror, then turned from the image of herself she could no longer bear.

"Thank you both for all your help," she offered

in a choked voice, assaulted by emotions as far from what a bride should be feeling as was humanly possible. "I—"

"You've nothing to thank us for," Aunt Beth insisted, shaking her head and straightening a fold of fabric in the bridal gown. "It has been a long time since we've had a wedding at Thornwyck, hasn't it, Lucy? And never with such a beautiful bride."

Carolyn managed a smile. She felt dizzy from lack of sleep and too much adrenaline in her system. She'd not slept last night, after Tiernan had left, nor the night before. And she'd not seen the ghost again since his encouragement to be strong, to be beautiful. One of those, at least, it seemed she had accomplished. The other . . .

"Miss Carolyn? Lady Elizabeth?" A knock followed, but Aunt Beth was already answering the door before Carolyn could take a single step toward it.

"Reverend Thomas is down in the great hall, Lady Elizabeth, with Mr. Chandler," Ben Masters reported. "They are ready and anxiously await the bride." He cleared his throat and inclined his head toward Carolyn. "And may I add that the bride does look absolutely stunning?"

Carolyn straightened her spine, returning the butler's sincere smile. "Thank you, Ben."

"Go ahead and tell them to proceed to the chapel, won't you?" Aunt Beth ushered the butler out the door, then shooed Lucy out, as well, before stopping in front of Carolyn.

"Now, dear, this is your last exit, you know.

Are you still certain you want to be doing this?"

Carolyn froze her lips into a smile and nodded. "Yes, Aunt Beth. I'm going through with the wedding." She took Lady Elizabeth's arm and turned toward the door. "Now, please, let's be going. I don't want to be late."

The entire ceremony passed without a single glitch. Wooden chairs had been brought into the chapel, candles lined the walls, even the stained-glass windows on the seaward side had been polished to let in the afternoon sun.

Carolyn's voice shook no more than any nervous bride's when she gave herself into the power of the monster who was Erik Chandler.

Tiernan remained invisible. Only the certainty of his presence warmed Carolyn's soul, and the pale hope that, perhaps, he did have a plan to bring this horror to an end.

The diamond solitaire Erik placed on her finger was like the coldest of chains around her heart. Her hands shook so badly, she nearly dropped his ring, but he caught it and guided her hands, smiling all the while. Only she knew that it was not a smile of love and contentment, but of coldly calculated victory. His hands on her face, when Reverend Thomas announced that the groom might kiss the bride, were no more giving than steel.

The congratulations and well wishes from everyone assembled were like the fragments of a nightmare to Carolyn. It wasn't she who shook hands, gave and received kisses and embraces,

315

who followed Erik like an adoring wife back to the great hall, leaving the chapel and the tomb in its vault to the whisper of the sea wind. It was some creature more automaton than human, doing just what was expected of it, while thoughts and soul were frozen in bleak despair.

Lady Elizabeth was seeing off the minister when Erik drew her along to the front door, calling out before the man of God could leave.

"Reverend Thomas—another minute of your time, please, before you go."

"Oh—why, certainly, Mr. Chandler."

Carolyn stared up at Erik, at his smiling, open, charming face, and wondered how such evil could live in such a handsome body.

"We've been having some trouble with an apparition . . . a ghost, if you will," Erik explained to the minister, acknowledging the sudden tightening of Carolyn's hand around his with no more than a fond smile at her. "We'd be much obliged if you would bless this house, and try to—well, try to lay to rest the spirit that's been wandering these grounds. Especially seeing how it's All Hallow's Eve today . . . ?"

The balding man blinked up at Erik in consternation, then glanced at Lady Elizabeth. Aunt Beth had obviously not mentioned Tiernan as a problem before. "Well, I—"

"Come, why don't I show you where he's usually seen? Carolyn, sweet, go ahead and take your aunt back to the hall, won't you? We'll only be a minute, I'm sure."

Blanching, Carolyn watched Erik lead the

minister off toward the stairs. Her hands were clenched into fists where they held the skirt of her dress off the floor.

There was no doubt in her mind that Erik would take the minister into her room. What she didn't know was how much injury a man of the cloth could do to the earl's ghost.

God, what if he really did exorcise him?

The thought left her dizzy, breathless, off balance.

"Don't you worry, dear," Aunt Elizabeth reassured her, taking her arm and drawing her back toward the great hall. "There've been many things tried to expel his lordship from Thornwyck over the centuries. And, so far, no one has managed to evict him from his rightful home."

Carolyn held tightly to her aunt's arm and could only pray that she was right. Facing a life with Erik Chandler without the presence of Tiernan would be more than she could bear.

Carolyn excused herself from the after-dinner celebration soon after Erik's horrifying announcement. For the last time alone in the sanctuary of her room, she slammed the solid oak door shut, then tore the veil out of her hair and cast it onto the floor. Tears rose to blur her vision. Shaking, she leaned against the dresser, her face in her hands, using all her self-control to keep from crying out in rage and despair.

. . . *the good Reverend Thomas seems to have been quite successful . . .*

Damn him! Damn that deceitful, spiteful, evil man!

But wasn't that what she'd wanted, too? To see Tiernan find peace?

Carolyn straightened with a breath too close to a sob, and turned to brace herself with both hands on the dresser top. She stiffened with a startled sound as the earl's image filled the mirror beside the reflection of her own face.

"Tiernan—!" The relief that washed over her was enough to make her knees weak.

"Nay, dinna turn," he rejoined softly, staring into the looking glass and meeting her gaze in it. "'Tis All Souls' Night this eve, Cara. *Oíche Shamhna*. Dinna ye know 'tis the night t' conjure up an image o' yer true love, yer future betrothed? Many a lass would spend hours wi' tricks, starin' into flame or water, hopin' t' catch a glimpse o' a face."

Carolyn's eyes filled with tears again, yet she refused to break the bond of their shared glance. The ring on her finger felt cold, alien, a shackle whose weight crushed her soul.

"I'm glad you're still here." The words were close to a sob.

Tiernan made a rude sound, straightening up. His image disappeared from the mirror, and Carolyn turned around, unwilling to let him out of her sight for even an instant.

"Bloody false priests couldna touch me in life and willna do so now, ye can be sure o' that."

Seeing her fear and relief, his expression softened. "I'd no' leave ye, *grá mo chroí*. I promised ye that, remember?"

She nodded jerkily, feeling the breath catch in her throat. No, he'd not leave her; he'd remain here, would be watching as Erik defiled her, body and soul—

"Dinna lose hope, Cara."

His soft words drew her gaze up from where it had sunk to the smooth, polished wood of the floor beneath the window. She found him standing not an arm's length away, watching her intently.

"And dinna forget whom ye saw in the lookin' glass this night, *mo rún*," he added, more softly still.

Carolyn's breath broke on a wounded sound. "This is no fairy tale, Tiernan!" She held up her hand to him, the hand bearing that hated ring, a hand shaking with its burden. "I'm married to him! There's not going to be any knight in shining armor charging to my rescue. There are no happily ever afters—"

She whirled away from him with a sob, pressing her face into her hands, her eyes squeezed shut, struggling to draw breath against the burning tightness of her throat. The gradual withdrawal of Tiernan's presence intruded on her pain, spun her around again.

He had stepped back, was fading, like a shadow disappearing into night as the sun sinks behind storm clouds.

"Cry if ye must, *a ghrá*. But remember that I'll

319

no' let him harm ye. I'll no' forsake ye, no' for the devil's own company."

Carolyn stared at the empty room and bit her lip until she tasted blood to keep from crying. "Tiernan . . ."

"Éist le fuaim na gaoith," came the disembodied whisper into the sudden silence of the room. "Listen t' the sound o' the wind. It tells the same tales, still, as it did when the O'Rourkes lived within these walls." The voice was soft, musing.

"Tiernan, don't go yet—"

"Come out t' the cliffs wi' me, Cara, afore Chandler comes here. Never ye mind the dress," the invisible ghost added impatiently when she began struggling to get out of the wedding gown. "Come wi' me. Hurry, *a ghrá.*"

Throwing logic to the winds, trusting in the words of Thornwyck's ghost, Carolyn snatched up the layered skirt, glad the train had already been detached before dinner, and rushed out of her room.

The sharp raps of her heels on the wooden stairs and then on the marble tiles of the hall echoed crazily around her, matching the frantic pounding of her heart. No one saw her flee down the hall, out into the darkness of the night, where the cold sea wind tore at the flowing fabric of her wedding dress—no one but the man from whom she fled, the man who would possess her, body and soul, with ruthless cruelty.

She was halfway across the garden when she heard Erik's voice, carried on the cold October wind, and spun back, heart leaping into her throat.

He was in the courtyard, a lone figure in a black tuxedo, striding with quick, slightly unsteady steps toward her. On the mountainside behind him, far in the distance, two bonfires flickered in the velvety darkness like the red, blinking eyes of some otherworldly monster.

Carolyn whirled and made for the cliffs at a run.

God, he was drunk. She'd noticed him imbibing during dinner, celebrating his own personal victory. What would he do to her later tonight, with that cold, callous control frayed by too much liquor?

The wind howled up the face of the cliff, tearing at her dress. Dark clouds hovered like black, convulsed towers over the water, testimony to the violent air currents.

Carolyn's hands knotted into fists, heart pounding wildly inside her chest as she paced the springy ground of the cliffs, glancing around frantically for Thornwyck's ghost. "Tiernan, where are you? Why did you bring me here? The old cliff is gone!"

There was no answer but the howling wind, and no place to hide on the open, flat seaward grounds. No lies would take the edge off Erik's fury when he reached her.

Carolyn cast a last, longing gaze out over the whitecapped sea, wishing she was in truth the witch Tiernan had once called Elyssa, wishing she could turn herself into one of the sea birds and soar away into the cloud-torn heavens.

"You little bitch."

The voice, no less venomous for its slight slur, cut like a lash through the sound of the wind, tearing her away from the sea sprawling below to meet the face of scalding fury.

"Is this how the eager bride awaits her husband?" Erik snarled at her, catching her by the shoulders and hauling her close in a bruising grip. "By running away into the night? Did you think you'd escape your *wifely duties* out here, sweet?"

Carolyn shook her head, meeting his ice-cold blue eyes with as much courage as she could muster. She could feel his breath against her face, quick and hot and liquored, could feel his chest rising and falling against the hands she raised to keep him at bay. "Erik, I—"

"You what?" He cut her off harshly, nearly panting with the force of his rage. "*Needed some time alone*, like you did that day you went to town to call the cops?" He shook her roughly, pulling her away from the precipice, shoving her forward, toward Thornwyck, dragging her by the arm when she moved too slowly for his taste. "Well, sweet, you'd better learn right now that you'll need exactly as much time alone as I tell you, and not a damned minute more. You try another of these bloody escapades and you won't have the chance to draw up a will, my darling bride!"

"Neither will you, *a anlaith*."

"Tiernan!" Carolyn spun in midstep as the form

of the earl appeared behind her in the darkness of night. Breath surged into her lungs and rushed out again in a silent litany of his name. The appearance of an angel wouldn't have looked half as welcome to her as the ghost of Thornwyck.

But Tiernan was staring past her, at Erik. "Step aside, *mo rún*," he commanded softly.

Before Carolyn could move Erik's hands shoved her out of the way. Biting out obscenities, he stormed past her, but ground to a halt not two steps away from the earl.

"Well, I'll be damned. Our little ghost finally got up the guts to show himself. You missed the wedding, Irishman. And you're too late; she's a married woman now—mine! Just as Thornwyck will be mine as soon as old Aunt Beth is out of the way."

Carolyn's breath came on a voiceless cry at Erik's gloating words. So he'd had no intention of letting Aunt Beth live out her natural life! The bastard! But there was nothing to stop her from betraying the truth of his schemes now. She had nothing left to lose. All she had to do was run back to the house and tell everyone. . . .

"That's where ye're wrong, ye spineless bastard," Tiernan growled softly, words flowing together in his Irish lilt. "She'll never be yers. And if ye'll no' leave her be, I'll make ye rue the day ye ever laid a hand on her!"

"*You* will!" Erik burst out laughing. "You're a ghost, in case you haven't noticed, *your lordship*. And next time I'll make damn sure to get a Catholic priest to bless the house, and send you

323

on to oblivion where you belong!"

Tiernan took several small steps back, closer to the edge of the new cliff. He replied to Erik's sneer in flowing Irish, speaking too fast for Carolyn to understand. But she could see her new husband's tanned complexion darkening with each word the earl spoke, until Erik surged forward, enraged.

"Cut out that gibberish, damn you!" Wild laughter broke from Erik's lips. "Can't even speak a civilized language, can you?"

Tiernan backed away once more, one step closer to the end of land. Erik laughed again at the seeming retreat.

"Go crawl back into your tomb, Earl. I think we'll have it sent back to St. Mary's before my wife and I go on our honeymoon!"

"*A cladhaire*. Coward!" The words were soft, taunting, lilting. "*Anlaith*. Tyrant!" Tiernan smiled coldly, standing tall and proud not three feet away from the drop. "*Ainmhí*. Brute! Are ye learnin' this dead tongue yet, Chandler? The wee children speak it, and easily so. I'm thinkin' that they be smarter than ye are."

"You—"

"*Is truagh liom thú*. I pity ye, Chandler. Ye're a fool as well as a coward. Ye'll never have Thornwyck, just like Marshall never held it, no' even wi' all his treachery!"

Erik's hands were clenching and unclenching. "I don't know any damned Marshall, you pathetic apparition. And if you don't pull a real quick vanishing act, I'll be the owner of Thornwyck a hell of a lot faster than you think! Then you can share your tomb with Carolyn!"

"*An chuimhin leat, a cladhaire?* Dinna ye recall the last time ye tried this? Dinna ye recall fleein' from me t' this very place, in mortal terror o' yer life? Ye were a coward then, Chandler, as ye are a coward now. Afraid o' me ghost!"

"You lying bastard!"

Tiernan laughed, the sound whipped away by the wind. Spewing curses, Erik launched himself forward, and Carolyn's eyed widened in sudden understanding a fraction of a second before Tiernan's plan bore fruit. Not even a cry escaped her throat as Erik lashed out at the Earl of Thornwyck, at his beautiful face, in a vicious punch that should have thrown Tiernan backward, head over heels into the emptiness gaping behind him.

Yet Erik had exactly as much success in touching the ghost of the ninth earl as she'd had, that night in her chamber. With a cry of rage and shock, Erik passed right through Tiernan's solid-looking form and soared headfirst over the precipice. His scream echoed eerily for a few seconds, then only the roar of the wind and the pounding of the waves far below met her ears.

Carolyn stared at the edge of the cliff, at the ghost coming slowly toward her. "Tiernan . . . ?"

He met her widened gaze, triumph and sadness glittering in those bright, shattered-emerald eyes. "I promised ye, *mo rún,* that I'd see ye safe from him. I love ye, Cara. *Táim i ngrá leat.*"

Carolyn nodded, shaking with the surge of adrenaline in her blood, but then a broken sound escaped her throat. "Tiernan, you're fading away! Don't go yet—"

"I'm sorry, *grá mo chroí*. I have t'. But ye'll be safe now. And ye'll forever have me love, Cara. Forever."

It was a goodbye, Carolyn realized with a soul-gripping flood of horror. "Tiernan! No . . . oh, dear God, please, no. . . ."

But he was disappearing before her eyes, fading into the darkness of the night, until not even the bright glitter of his eyes remained, or the pale shadow of the white rose on the lapel of his coat.

"Táim i ngrá leat. . . . "

"Tiernan—!"

Gone.

For an endless span of heartbeats Carolyn stared into the space where Tiernan had stood.

I canna do injury t' the livin'.

The words he'd spoken to her that night flitted crazily through her head. Yet he had harmed Erik . . . killed him, most likely.

I'll no' forsake ye, no' for the devil's own company.

Blinded by tears, Carolyn gathered up the voluminous skirt of her wedding gown and inched forward to peer down the face of the cliff, praying for the sake of Tiernan's soul that Erik was still alive.

Chapter Twenty-five

The man who had terrorized her for the past month lay crumpled on a ledge some 80 feet below her, nothing more than a tangle of limbs in the gathering darkness, one arm sprawled out into empty space.

"That's for Tiger, you bastard," Carolyn whispered coldly, inanely, hardly knowing her own voice. For a moment she stared down at Erik, feeling nothing, now—calm, only. Shockingly, obscenely calm, when she might well be looking at a corpse.

But she could still sense Tiernan's presence. Which meant, perhaps, that Erik wasn't dead yet. That, as long as Erik lived, Tiernan would not pay the price for saving her.

An ambulance. She should go and call an

ambulance. So some doctor could save this vile creature's life . . .

With wooden motions, Carolyn backed away from the cliff and turned toward Thornwyck. By the time she reached the remains of the old curtain wall she was running, hands knotted in the skirts of her wedding dress. She yanked open the back door and ran full-tilt toward Aunt Beth's study.

"Ah, dear, I was wondering where—"

"I think you'd better call an ambulance, Aunt Beth," Carolyn cut her off, coming to a rough stop inside the room. "My . . . husband seems to have fallen down the cliff."

With an utterly unladylike expletive Lady Elizabeth shot to her feet, snatched up the cordless phone on her desk, and began punching numbers.

The ambulance arrived far too quickly, trained experts working with calm, competent efficiency to save the life of the man lying on that ledge partway down the cliff.

Carolyn stood by, in jeans and a sweater now, surrounded by Aunt Beth and Lucy and Ben and Cummings and a number of the mansion's guests. She answered the questions put to her by the ambulance driver, and otherwise watched, wide-eyed and in silence, as Erik, strapped securely to a stretcher, was brought up over the edge of the cliff and hustled into the ambulance. She sat just as silently beside Aunt Beth while Cummings sent the Rolls screaming down the narrow coast road in hot pursuit of the emergency vehicle.

By the time they had reached the hospital and entered the emergency ward, Carolyn had convinced herself that Erik was dead. The haunting awareness she'd had of Tiernan's presence had disappeared without a trace, while before it had followed her across half of Ireland.

Gone . . .

"They'll take good care of him, dearest, don't you worry." Aunt Beth was there beside her, guiding her to one of the chairs in the waiting area, her pale, slender hands tight around Carolyn's. "We may be living in the sticks, but we do have some very fine doctors here—"

"I hope he dies."

The flat, harsh words were all that came from Carolyn's lips. She saw her aunt's shocked look and knew that she had spoken half a lie, for if Erik did die, Tiernan might never return. Yet there was no certainty that, even if Erik lived, Tiernan would be restored to her. The horrible certainty that she would never see him again had settled like an icy fist around her heart, squeezing the life out of her. With a sudden, gut-deep realization, Carolyn understood how people could die of grief.

"But, Carolyn, dear—"

She shook her head and sank down on the nearest chair, oblivious to the bright lights, the sporadic announcements over the PA system, and closed her eyes. "It was all a lie, Aunt Beth."

How odd, that she should be able to speak of Erik's schemes so utterly unemotionally, so

329

casually, as if she was speaking of yesterday's mild fall weather. But the relief she'd been sure would come with the words, with cleansing herself of the lies, was absent. Still, she continued speaking, keeping Tiernan's beloved face fixed in her mind's eye.

"All I've told you since I came back was a lie. Erik would have killed you if I hadn't done what he said. He knew you'd changed your will, knew it even before you told me—"

"Carolyn, you're not making any sense—"

A cold laugh trickled from her. "I know. I never thought there were—" She cut off her own words, shaking her head. "No, that's not true. Everyone knows there're real monsters out there, the kind that abuse small children, that revel in dealing out pain, that love to kill. I just never thought I'd run across one."

Aunt Beth's hands around her own had grown progressively tighter, until Carolyn gently loosened her grip. "He wants Thornwyck badly enough to kill for it. Maybe he had your lawyer's office bugged, but he knew before I did that you'd changed your will, that I'd inherit Thornwyck if anything happened to you. That's why he gave up on the forged writ of debt. I found it, in his room. He caught me, told me he'd kill you if I didn't marry him."

"Why—Carolyn, you could have—"

"No." She shook her head, her voice suddenly gruff. "I tried calling the police, from a pay phone in Killarney. He knew about the call. And they— they only confirmed what he'd told me—that without proof threats alone couldn't get a man arrested."

Aunt Elizabeth nodded, frowning. "He must have somehow tapped the telephone lines. Good God!"

Carolyn nodded jerkily. "That's what I figured too. But there was no way to find out how far his damn web of control went without risking your life." She shuddered.

"Well, love, we can certainly have the police step in now, and—"

"No." Rising, wrapping her arms around her body, Carolyn stared down at Aunt Beth. "We can't. Because we don't have any proof yet, aside from my word." She shook her head frantically. "I won't risk him getting off with a warning, Aunt Beth. He'd come back and kill you, and me, and my baby!"

All color bled from Lady Elizabeth's already pale features. She looked up at Carolyn and whispered, "Your . . . baby?"

Carolyn's arms tightened about herself, lowering until her hands lay against her still flat belly. "You want to hear a good one, Aunt Beth? One that'll really put to the test your belief in ghosts?" She laughed shakily and paced back and forth for a number of steps. Aunt Beth rose and stopped her with ice-cold hands around her own.

"I dreamed, one night," Carolyn began, her voice no more than a whisper, "before I went back to Vancouver. I dreamed of being Elyssa, of—making love with Tiernan."

"No!" Lady Elizabeth's expression was downright comical. But Carolyn wasn't laughing.

"Yes. There was something about the cliffs—some gate into the past, or something, maybe on the part that's now gone. Don't ask me how, Aunt Beth—but it looks like the ninth Earl of Thornwyck is going to have an heir, after all."

Lady Elizabeth sank down heavily on the nearest chair, slumping against the backrest, shaking her head slowly from side to side, staring at the white wall on the other side of the waiting room.

"Tiernan was with me out on the cliff tonight," Carolyn continued, softly, painfully. "He stood at the edge and goaded Erik into striking him, knowing Erik would fall. He would have killed you anyway, you know, the bastard. I didn't want to believe it before, thought that he would be true to his word and leave you in peace if I married him. But his patience had run out. He wanted Thornwyck now."

Carolyn placed a hand on her abdomen again, fierce protectiveness surging through her, battling some of the grief. "And he would have killed my child as soon as he found out that I'd lied to him about having the abortion he ordered."

"God Almighty!" The words were soft but clear. Lady Elizabeth added a number of other, more forceful exclamations, before straightening, and then rising to her feet.

"I think you had better rest awhile, dear. I'll keep an eye out for the doctor, if he should come with any news."

"But—"

"No. No buts. Don't you worry, I won't breathe a word of this to anyone except Ben. But if the bastard survives his fall, he'll be in for pure hell at Thornwyck, I can assure you!"

Carolyn drew a shaky breath and shook her head. "What if he had others working for him? How can we—"

Aunt Beth gently but forcefully pushed Carolyn down into a chair. "Hush. I don't know who his hirelings were, or even if he had any, but if he did, I'll wager they're long gone for fear of being exposed. In any case, there's not much we can do about it now. I'll have Cummings start making inconspicuous inquiries around town tomorrow. Somebody's bound to know something. And I'll see Mr. Henderson and tell him to have someone come in and check his office."

Sitting down beside her, Aunt Beth laid an arm around Carolyn's shoulders and drew her close. "Until then, you stop making yourself crazy. Tomorrow will come soon enough, and all this worrying won't do the baby any good."

Carolyn pulled away slightly to stare at the fierce and yet gentle features of her aunt, struck to the heart by the similarity of Aunt Beth's advice to the words Tiernan had spoken. The last of her defenses against her grief crumbled, and she cried quietly on her aunt's shoulder, grieving for the loss of a love that had truly been hers only in a dream.

Chapter Twenty-six

The evening dragged on interminably. Carolyn's tears had dried hours ago, and the agonized voice in which she'd told Aunt Beth everything, purging her soul of all the lies Erik had forced her to tell, had grown hoarse and finally fallen silent.

She watched the minute hand of the wall clock make its rounds, sweep by hour after hour, while doctors and nurses and clients and their relatives came and went, announcements blared over the speaker system, and the fluorescent lights in the ceiling fixture flickered petulantly. Heartsick, Carolyn searched for any trace of Tiernan's presence, until her eyes grew too heavy to keep open and sleep finally claimed her.

" . . . wake up, dearest."

Carolyn blinked awake, straightening stiffly in the molded-plastic chair, squinting against the

335

bright lights. "Aunt Beth?"

"The doctor just came out, dear. I had a talk with him, but I didn't want to wake you, in case we'd be staying longer."

"How—how is—?" She trailed off, not even able to bring herself to say Erik's name.

"Not good, but a damn sight better than he might have been, considering the fall he took."

Drawing Carolyn to her feet, Aunt Beth leaned closer, her voice lowered. "They lost him twice in the ambulance, but managed to jump-start his black heart again. He's unconscious now, and might even stay that way for a good long while, according to the doctor, thanks to a concussion. But, amazingly enough, he didn't break anything except a leg. The doctor said we were lucky he was so drunk. He's gotten off with a dislocated shoulder and various bruises and scrapes, but he'll live . . . and will probably wake up again too. But they can't be sure about that."

Carolyn said nothing. She should feel relieved to know that he lived, that, perhaps, Tiernan would return. After all, Erik had taken that fall all by himself, with only his own rage to push him.

Yet Tiernan hadn't returned. And the despair that he had paid the ultimate price for her safety grew inside her with each passing minute, into a huge, gaping void that would swallow up her soul.

"Come on, dear. Let's go home. The hospital will call if there's any change."

Carolyn blinked, focused on the tiny form of

Aunt Beth, still holding her arm, and nodded vaguely, walking beside her out of the hospital emergency ward. The drive home passed in silence, and Aunt Beth made no move to stop Carolyn as she headed straight for her room.

She cried, there, again, cradling Elyssa's diary and the dried white rose against her chest, cried the tears Elyssa never had the chance to spill for the death of her beloved. She cried for a long time, huddled in her solitary bed with only Lily for company, until no more tears would come. The last numbers she saw on her digital clock before she finally slipped into the merciful oblivion of sleep were 5:26 a.m.

By the time Carolyn came downstairs in the morning, eyes red and swollen, not bothering even to try to hide her distress, Aunt Beth had already left for town.

"She's gone to see Mr. Henderson, luv," Lucy offered quietly. "Are you sure you won't have something other than char? Mr. Chandler will be all right, just you wait and see. But you have to look after yourself, you do. Let me bring you some nice, fresh waffles."

With a shuddering breath Carolyn hid her face in her hands. No one except Masters and Cummings knew about Erik, and for the sake of trapping him, it had to remain a secret for a while longer yet. But Carolyn didn't know how much longer she would be able to play this role.

"Oh, Lord, Miss Carolyn, I didn't meant to upset you some more—"

"It's all right, Lucy." Straightening, Carolyn

waved off Lucy's concern. "And I think I'd like those waffles, after all." With a very deliberate, somewhat watery smile, she added, "I've got to think of the baby, don't I?"

"Oh! Miss Carolyn, but you—oh, my goodness!" Lucy sputtered for another minute, going from confusion to enlightenment, and finally heaped on utterly sincere congratulations. "That's so wonderful, luv! I'm so glad for you!"

By noon everyone at Thornwyck had come to cheer, comfort, and congratulate Carolyn several times. She bit her tongue each time wishes for Erik's speedy recovery were expressed, and was silently appalled that no one seemed to realize Tiernan was gone.

She finally withdrew into the Blue Room, shutting the door firmly behind herself, and passed the hours with the harp.

"Ah, here you are, dear. I thought I heard someone playing."

Startled, Carolyn glanced at the door to find Aunt Beth closing it as softly as she'd opened it. Carolyn let her hands drop from the metal strings to her knees and watched Lady Elizabeth cross the room, now bright with autumn sun.

"I've had Mr. Henderson do some inquiring," Aunt Beth began somberly, taking a seat on one of the armchairs with blue velvet upholstering. "He's managed to find out some rather fascinating facts about our Mr. Chandler."

Carolyn swallowed twice to make sure her voice worked. "Oh?"

The sound was rusty and drew her aunt's

gaze. There were questions in Lady Elizabeth's gray eyes, but she only continued sharing her news. "His parents were both American—but his grandmother was English . . . and a Warrington by birth."

Aunt Beth paused, while Carolyn stared at her mutely.

"I remember her, from a long time ago, you know. I forgot what exactly her relation to me was—an aunt, I think. She eloped with a visiting American. It was quite the scandal, though I didn't much understand it, as young as I was. But her father disowned her for it. She managed to outlive all of her generation, probably out of spite, and should rightfully have inherited a good part of the Warrington wealth . . . including Castle Warrington and Silverstone Manor in England, and Thornwyck here in Ireland."

Carolyn made a low sound of disbelief. "It's— it's just like the last time! Just like in Elyssa's time. This bloody obsession with owning the estate got them killed, and nearly you, too," she ground out angrily. "Erik had more money than he could ever spend in one lifetime! Why couldn't he just buy any other damn castle? Why did he have to . . ." Her voice trailed off, broken.

"He was probably told all his life that these estates should rightfully belong to him. If his grandmother was as bitter about being cut out of the will as your mother was about it . . ." Aunt Beth shrugged. "He's a ruthless man. Sick, too, I think," she added, gesturing to her head. "And he set about getting back what he thought was his."

"*I* didn't turn out like that!" Carolyn protested, still angry. "Despite my mother."

Lady Elizabeth rose from her chair and slowly crossed to the mullioned windows. "Dear, I can't explain to you why one man becomes a mass murderer and the next one doesn't, all other things being equal."

Carolyn snapped her mouth shut and said nothing.

"I've had Ben search the whole estate with a fine-tooth comb, and you wouldn't believe the things he's found. I can't believe Mr. Chandler could have set up all those bugs without anyone finding out."

Aunt Beth tapped one finger against her lips, then broke into a smug smile. "Ben will be setting up the recording equipment in Mr. Chandler's room tomorrow, using the microphones that were in your room. He's always been a fair hand with electrical things. I don't think Mr. Chandler would find anything, even were he well enough to look around. And he certainly won't find his pistol or any of his bugs in working order."

Carolyn took in that new information with mixed feelings, remembering Erik's threats about trying something like this. But this time *he* wouldn't be in control.

Then she looked up at her aunt. "You think he'll be home soon?" Her stomach churned at the mere thought of facing Erik again. Facing him without Tiernan . . .

"Better to be prepared, dear. There's no telling how long this unconsciousness can last. For myself, I'm rather hoping he'll wake up soon, because he'll be hurting like the very devil, after that fall, and I don't intend to give him so much as a single bloody aspirin!"

Aunt Beth's warlike mien was irrationally comforting to Carolyn. Yet even if they did succeed in having Erik convicted, it still wouldn't bring back the ghost of her beloved.

"Tiernan—Tiernan is gone," Carolyn finally whispered into the silent, sunny room, staring at dust motes dancing in the air.

Aunt Beth sighed, leaning against the paneled wall of the study where a sunbeam gilded the wood. "I know, Carolyn," she replied after a long moment of silence, in a voice weary and sad. "I—can feel it. The place is empty, now, without him."

Carolyn closed her eyes as the pain in her throat and heart grew unbearable. She hadn't wanted to believe it, had hoped, prayed, that her aunt would have some alternative explanation for the disappearance of Tiernan's presence.

"He said he couldn't harm the living, Aunt Beth. And that—that he would keep me safe from Erik. . . ." She drew a ragged breath, staring at her aunt through a shimmering veil of tears. "Even if it meant damning his soul."

Lady Elizabeth sighed again. "Now, dear, don't be so hasty in thinking the worst. Perhaps he has finally found rest, knowing you are safe."

She straightened away from the wall and gestured around the room. "Besides, last night was Samhain."

The same kind of smile Carolyn had seen on her aunt's face so long ago, when Lady Elizabeth had first told her about the ninth Earl of Thornwyck, once again lit weary, time-lined features. "You know about Samhain, don't you, dearest?"

Carolyn couldn't quite muster a smile in return, only shook her head. She knew enough about Halloween, but she desperately wanted the distraction of Aunt Beth's voice and any tale she might have to tell.

"Ah. Well, Samhain is the Celtic New Year's Eve, you see, when the Sun God and Samhain, Lord of the Dead, were honored. In ancient times they would light up huge bonfires on the hilltops to frighten away evil spirits. And the night before Samhain was Mischief Night, where the ghosts and faeries would be about, curdling fresh milk, snatching gates off the posts and hiding them, riding people's horses to exhaustion. . . . Making— all sorts of mischief," Aunt Beth summed up with a smile. "But on Samhain Night . . . It was the time when the Otherworld became visible to mortals, when prying into the future was particularly fruitful. And it was the night when the gates of heaven and hell opened wide, and the souls of the dead came to visit their homes and warm themselves by the hearth fires." She shrugged, brows high. "Mind you, some of the folks probably didn't much want to see their long-dead relatives. I think that's were those scary pumpkin lanterns eventually came from, don't you?"

Carolyn smiled wanly at her aunt's attempt at humor. "And you think Tiernan . . . you think he's at rest, now, because he could find his way into heaven?"

"I think it is possible, dear."

Possible. Carolyn bit her lip, remembering too well Tiernan's words. She'd never believed in heaven or hell, had never given much thought to what happened after death. But in her mind's eye, with the cruel clarity of her cursed memory, played a scene from a movie she'd seen once, where grotesque black shadows dragged a soul down to damnation, oblivious to screams and pleas. Now, on the next replay of the scene in her memory, the man was Tiernan—and he wasn't screaming. He was only staring at her, with undying love shining from his eyes, as the shadows hurtled him into darkness.

All the candles had burned down again. Carolyn set the flashlight onto the stone tomb, and, one by one, lit the new tapers she had brought, until flickering light bathed the marble effigy.

Carolyn shut off the flashlight and watched the dance of smoky shadows and golden light on the still, beloved features. The tears that had overcome her the first few times she'd performed this simple task remained absent. Her mourning had gone beyond that.

It had been over two weeks since the wedding. Over two weeks of living day to day, retrieving her overseas container from Dublin and tiring more quickly than usual. Over two weeks of no news from the hospital other than that Erik was still fading into and out of consciousness, though no brain damage was detectable.

Over two weeks without the slightest trace of Tiernan, two weeks without the comfort of his smile, his soothing voice, the awareness of his presence . . .

He truly was gone. Even though Erik lived, Tiernan had paid the price for injuring one of the living. Had, very likely, damned his eternal soul . . . to keep her safe.

Except she wasn't safe. Erik Chandler was still alive.

And Tiernan's babe was growing within her with each day. In another few months not even the loosest clothing would be able to conceal her condition. And if she and Aunt Beth didn't manage to have Erik arrested—and convicted . . .

It did not bear thinking on.

After a last, awkward, silent prayer to a God she hadn't paid much heed to for most of her life, Carolyn left the vault. Darkness filled with the rustling of huge rhododendrons met her, embraced her. Without bothering to turn on the flashlight, she made her way from the chapel back to Thornwyck.

Aunt Beth waited for her at the door, as she did each night. Eyes somber with understanding, with shared grief, she escorted Carolyn into her study, guiding her into one of the stuffed leather chairs before meeting her gaze.

"The hospital just called, Carolyn. I'm afraid you're not a widow yet. As a matter of fact, Mr. Chandler has finally regained full consciousness, and he demands to be taken home."

Chapter Twenty-seven

"I—sent Cummings to get him," Aunt Beth continued softly, carefully, watching her.

Carolyn felt the ground tilt beneath her. She'd had enough time to prepare for this—it shouldn't come as such a shock. But it did.

"Everything is ready, dear," Lady Elizabeth continued reassuringly, sinking into the chair behind her desk. "We'll keep Mr. Chandler in his room upstairs, where you can watch over him. And every single word he speaks to you, every threat he makes, will be recorded. He's in no condition to harm anyone right now, and with any luck you can goad some implicating small talk out of him."

Drawing a ragged breath, Carolyn stiffened her spine and nodded. "All right." She could do this. Had to do this. Erik had to be stopped.

Adrenaline flooding her system, she strode upstairs into her room and placed the despised wedding band on her hand again.

The Rolls pulled up in front of the main door beneath the light of the courtyard lanterns. A heavy mist hung in the cold night air, glowing in the light. From the porch Carolyn watched Cummings get out, then pause and look at her expectantly.

After one last glance at Aunt Beth, Carolyn straightened and stiffly approached the car. "Let's bring him in, then," she told the chauffeur warily.

"Of course." Cummings opened the back door.

When Erik made no move to get out Carolyn stepped around the chauffeur and peered into the back of the car. Her husband lay slumped against the headrest of the front seat, motionless.

"Mr. Chandler, we've arrived."

He didn't stir. Cummings cleared his throat and tried again. "Mr. Chandler—"

"Enough already. Hold yer tongue, man." The inert form stirred with a groan; then he turned and stuck his head out the door, frowning severely.

Glittering eyes fixed on Carolyn and brightened. "Cara."

She saw the faint smile touch the full lips of a clean-shaven face; an instant later her world spun itself away. For the first time in her life Carolyn fainted.

"Cara!" Before Tiernan could haul himself out of the Rolls, Cummings caught up Carolyn and headed inside with her. Lady Elizabeth was there, too, suddenly, watching him with bright eyes and a soft, uncertain smile on her face.

"Ah, Lady Elizabeth." Tiernan started easing himself out of the backseat, awkward with the cast, fighting the dizziness that swirled through his head with every breath. "What a pleasure 'tis t' finally meet ye face t' face. Though, I'm afraid I willna be greetin' ye properly," he added with a crooked, strained grin. "I'm thinkin' I'll be joinin' me wife."

The words had hardly left his lips when he collapsed facedown onto the seat.

"It was the shock, nothing more, your lordship."

"Then why will ye no' let me see her? Yer man is strong enough t' help me t' her room, is he no'?" Tiernan glowered up at the fragile old woman standing beside his bed, the woman he'd watched grow from infancy to dignified old age, who presently ruled over him with as iron a hand as his father ever had. "I'd walk meself, if no' for this piece o' plaster around me leg," he added mutinously. "And I tell ye again, Lady Elizabeth, I didna faint—I was merely overcome by dizziness."

"As soon as Carolyn wakes, I will bring her here," Lady Elizabeth offered mollifyingly. "I won't have her open her eyes to see your lordship and drop straight into a faint again."

Tiernan sank back into the pillows with a grunt of pain and acquiescence. "Aye, well enough." He shut his eyes for a moment, exulting, almost, in the pain of his bruised body, for the pain of injury was a mark of life. Life!

"Lady Elizabeth?" A soft knock sounded on the door before it opened. "Lady Elizabeth, Miss Carolyn is waking up. I think you'd better come."

"Is she ill?" Tiernan was halfway off the bed before the white-haired old woman shot him a quelling glance.

"Only a bit confused, Mr. Chandler," Lucy replied with a quick smile before backing out of the door again and closing it softly.

"You will stay in that bed, your lordship, else you will find yourself back in the hospital. When you are strong enough to rise I will let Ben bring you the crutches, and you may then do so. Do I make myself clear?"

"Aye." Tiernan met Lady Elizabeth's no-nonsense glare and lay back with a crooked grin that went a long way toward softening her expression. "Ye should have met me Da. I do believe he would have taken t' ye at first sight."

With a harrumph, Lady Elizabeth turned and strode out of the room. Tiernan watched her go and schooled himself in patience. He had waited nearly 300 years to be with his wife again; he could wait a few more minutes.

"Tiernan . . . !"

"Easy, dearest. Just lie still; you'll be all right in a moment."

Carolyn blinked, then rubbed at her eyes. She was on the large four-poster bed in her room, still fully dressed. "Aunt Beth? God, I had the most awful dream. . . ."

"I know, dear."

"You know?" Frowning, Carolyn sat up—slowly. Dizziness faded quickly, leaving only confusion. "How could you—?"

"It wasn't a dream, dear."

"Oh, God." Closing her eyes, Carolyn lay back down. "How much of it wasn't a dream?"

"Well, that all depends. You staying at Thornwyck wasn't a dream. Nor was Mr. Chandler's scheme to take over the castle, nor was his lordship helping Mr. Chandler see the face of the cliff up close. Nor was his coming home."

Carolyn stared at her aunt, tears suddenly welling from her eyes. "I—" She curled up on her side, burying her face in her hands. "I thought I heard Tiernan's voice. When Erik looked at me from inside the Rolls—" Her voice broke, giving way to ragged breaths.

"Ah. Well, you see, that is the interesting part."

At the enigmatic quality of her aunt's voice Carolyn looked up. There was a smile in that voice, and delicate smugness, like that of a mother about to present her daughter with a long-yearned-for present.

But Erik was back.

"I—I should go talk to him," she finally ground out, pushing up off the bed, forcing herself to be strong for the baby's sake. "The sooner we can get this over with, the better."

"Yes, perhaps you're right. Are you sure you feel up to it?"

She shot her aunt a shaken but determined look. "Yes."

"Very well." Turning, Lady Elizabeth led the way down the hall to Erik's room. Carolyn drew herself up straight as she entered, determined to let Erik see only cool composure.

"Ye look well, *a ghrá*," came the soft, lilting voice from the man on the bed. "Ye didna take harm from seein' yer husband again, then?"

Carolyn stared, open-mouthed, dumbstruck. It wasn't Erik's voice that greeted her—not Erik's slight drawl, or the cruelty never long missing from him in those last weeks.

"Ye looked like that the first time ye saw me," the voice continued, musing, rich with mirth. "I dinna know whether t' be flattered or offended. Surely ye'd no' be put off by a few bruises?"

Carolyn closed her eyes, listening, and knew that it should be Tiernan she should see when she opened them again.

It was still Erik—lying on the bed, bare torso covered with fading scrapes and cuts and bruises, the down duvet drawn to his waist, the unmistakable bulge of the toe end of a cast poking out on the side.

Though, on closer inspection, it wasn't Erik. It was someone who looked a lot like Erik. The beard was gone, making him look younger . . . kinder. And his hair was just a shade darker, and his eyes—they were no longer that icy blue, but a rich shade of dark turquoise, like the stormy, silt-laden sea on a clear day. . . .

"Well, I'll leave you two alone. I'm sure you have much to talk about."

Carolyn snapped her gaze from Erik-who-wasn't-Erik to the door, in time to see Aunt Beth slip out through it.

"Trobhad, grá mo chroí. Come here, love."

The softly spoken words went through her like a knife. She knew them. They were the same words Tiernan had spoken to her, that night, when she had been Elyssa. . . .

"No!" Rational thought reasserted itself, stood in victory over wishes and hopes and dreams. "I won't let you play with me like this, Erik. You've got what you wanted. I won't have you mock me now."

"Ah." Tiernan nodded slowly, pensively, watching his wife through half-lowered lashes. She stood stock-still, stiffer than a board, hands knotted into fists by her sides, her bright blue eyes and golden hair shimmering in the lamplight. A smile curved the corners of his mouth. He was the luckiest man alive.

"I dinna suppose there would be aught I could say," he mused, crossing his arms in front of his chest, "that would make ye believe me words. Though I could tell ye how I scared ye that night in yer room, when ye tried t' touch me and yer hand passed right through me. I could tell ye about that stormy night we danced on the cliffs, when ye came into me time. I could tell ye about another night, when ye were in the past— when ye were Elyssa, sweeter than a maiden yet burnin' like the brightest o' flames. I could tell ye that ye have yer miracle, *mo rún*, and that ye'll no' need that spot on the cliffs and the presence o' a ghost t' touch me again. Or I could tell ye how glad I am t' see ye are both well, ye and the babe."

Carolyn had backed up across the room, until her shoulders came up against the solid oak door. She was shaking her head, staring at him as though . . . as though he were a ghost.

He couldn't help but smile at the thought. "Come here, me heart," he repeated softly. "Me love."

"No—"

"Aye," he countered somberly, yet smiling. "I didna think t' ever see ye again, either, Cara. For ye'd no' go t' hell, and I surely thought that was where I'd be headin'."

"This is impossible."

Tiernan raised his brows but did not release her from his gaze. "Aye. Ye did say that I was."

He saw the recognition of his words in her expressive face. Slowly, step by step, she came toward the bed, still shaking her head. But her kerry-blue eyes were wide in wonder now, no longer narrowed in hate and suspicion.

"Chandler brought about his own death, *a ghrá*. Perhaps 'tis because o' his *aingidheach*—his wickedness—that God didna judge me so harshly. That He gave me the greatest gift either side o' heaven, *grá mo chroí*: Lettin' me return t' ye."

"But—but how—"

She had sunk to her knees beside the bed, one

trembling hand reaching out to his face, her eyes shimmering with unshed tears, as they had that night in the chapel vault. Tiernan grasped her hand and brought it to his lips, marveling in the glory of the senses—the scent of rose mingling with the faint perfume of her woman's body, the warmth, the texture of her skin against his lips.

"'Twas *Oíche Shamhna,* that night, Cara. The night when heaven and hell open their gates and the spirit world touches that o' the livin'. I dinna know how, *mo rún.* Chandler died, in that contraption wi' all the bright lights. And next I knew, I was flesh and blood again. 'Twas hurtin' like the very devil, I'll tell ye, but 'twas a body, and a chance t' live again. I didna even know *whose* body 'til I overheard them talkin', about me and t' me, there and beside me sick bed. Callin' me 'Mr. Chandler.' Even then, I didna want t' believe it."

"Tiernan." The sound was pure love, touching him like a caress. He watched her teeth close over her lower lip, the gesture painfully childlike. "Can you—can you accept this body, this face, then?" she finally asked hesitantly.

He drew a long, silent breath, then shrugged lightly, embracing the pain of the movement as he longed to embrace the woman beside him. "There's an old sayin', milady, no' t' look a gift horse in the mouth," he replied, mustering a grin. "I'd wager the same be true for miracles. Besides, I'm thinkin' 'twas a fair trade: me unnatural existence for the chance t' touch ye again. Hold ye." He touched her face gently, tracing the path of tears that had, somehow, spilled. "But I know what the bastard did t' ye, all this time. 'Tis I who should be asking that question, milady. Can *ye* accept this face? This form?"

"You don't look exactly like him," she allowed, studying him intently, no revulsion in her features.

Tiernan nodded, relief flooding through him in a warm, buoyant tide, not so much at her words but at the tone of her voice. He grasped her hand, the one that still bore Chandler's wedding band, and removed the diamond ring, tossing it to the floor as he had thrown the one returned to him by the hospital nurse to the ground outside the building.

Carolyn's hands tightened around his in silent gratitude that nearly broke his heart. "I'll no' have ye wear that bastard's mark," he told her gruffly. "Tomorrow we'll go into town and find ye a right proper weddin' band."

She smiled down at him, blinking through tears he was willing to wager she didn't even know were falling. "And I'll dye me hair, Cara," he offered with a smile that soon turned somber. "I dinna want ye wakin' up in the night and thinkin' ye should be afraid o' the man next t' ye."

"Oh, Tiernan . . . !"

She moved into his embrace, then, gifting him with the touch of her silken hair against his chest, the liquid heat of her tears spilling onto his skin, the living warmth of her body.

"Hush, now, *grá mo chroí*." He kissed the tears

356

from her face, smiling, though he felt like weeping himself. "No more cryin', ye hear? We've a weddin' night t' celebrate."

Her eyes shot open even as her body stiffened against him.

"I've recovered well enough, Cara," he retorted with a lopsided grin, bringing his lips to hers. Her lashes drifted closed, but after a moment she pulled away, shaking her head.

"No. Not in this room, we don't."

Carolyn ignored Tiernan's inquisitively raised brows and straightened from the bed, caught between logic and desire. "I'm going to get Ben so he can help you into my room. *Then* we can consider the matter of a missed wedding night."

Before Tiernan could say another word Carolyn rushed from the room.

Aunt Beth came to help, too, of course, and among the three of them they maneuvered Tiernan into her bed, proving his earlier words about recovery a lie. He was grumbling to himself in Irish when Ben excused himself to retire for the night.

"Recovered well enough, are you?" Carolyn couldn't help but tease him, after all the times he'd gotten the better of Elyssa. "You should think yourself fortunate I didn't take you up on your offer."

Aunt Beth shot a glance of mingled curiosity and surprise from Carolyn to Tiernan, delicately cleared her throat, and took a step toward the door.

"I think you'd best both get some rest," she

ordered sternly, but Carolyn saw the glimmer of laughter in her eyes.

"Before ye go, Lady Elizabeth—"

"Yes, your lordship."

Tiernan was pushing away the covers that had been piled on top of him and sitting up in the bed, a frown between his brows. "Kindly speak t' yer Mr. Henderson tomorrow and have him send a letter t' Mr. Chandler's solicitor—ye'll find the address in his wallet—orderin' him t' liquidate all assets, close all bank accounts, and transfer the funds into yer name."

Carolyn stared from Tiernan to her aunt, only to find Lady Elizabeth momentarily speechless.

"But—"

Tiernan shook his head, forestalling her protest. "I willna have a halfpenny o' his blood money. If ye wish, sink the money into the estate. Or donate it t' yer favorite charity. I dinna care, nor do I want t' hear what ye've done wi' it."

Aunt Beth fixed the ninth earl with a long, measuring look, then nodded. "Very well."

"Also, if ye could, have him apply for a change in name for meself and me wife."

Lady Elizabeth smiled at that. "I certainly will, your lordship. Now, good night," she added after a moment, turning to leave the room.

"And Lady Elizabeth—"

Aunt Beth paused at the door, looking over her shoulder. "Yes?"

"I'd be much obliged if ye didna call me 'yer lordship' any longer," Tiernan requested with a sheepish grin. "I feel we know one another better

358

than that . . . and it reminds me too much o' . . . well, that other time."

"Gladly, Mr. O'Rourke."

Tiernan groaned, but the door had already closed behind a smirking Lady Elizabeth. Carolyn shook her head, then turned to contemplate the ninth earl. He had sunk back onto the bed, looking pale compared to the ivory bedding. He was obviously in a good deal of pain, and she was starting to feel bad for teasing him.

"Is—is there anything I can do for you?" she asked solicitously, only to feel heat rising into her face at his very male, very sexy, downright lascivious grin.

"Should I say the words, *a ghrá*, or will yer cheeks burst into flame if I do?" he inquired equally solicitously.

Carolyn shook her head vigorously in response to both the spoken and unspoken question, then turned out the light and proceeded to slip into her flannel nightie.

"Ye have a beautiful back, Cara," came the lilting compliment from behind her, bringing more heat to her face. "I watched ye once, that mornin' ye were so set on yer exercisin' that ye missed breakfast," Tiernan continued, musing. "Ye were wearin' that shockin' garb, the one that fits ye like a second skin, so tight I could see the crowns o' yer breasts when the breeze from the windows blew in and cooled yer sweat. And that one machine . . ." He groaned. "Ah, 'tis indecent, Cara, what ye do wi' yer body on that contraption."

Carolyn nearly choked. She knew instantly what "contraption" he meant—adductor/abductor, working inner and outer thigh and buttocks. Her face burned, but laughter bubbled too. There were a lot of things the ninth Earl of Thornwyck would find shocking in the twentieth century.

"Come t' bed, Cara," Tiernan entreated yet again from behind her. "Let me hold ye, *mo rún*."

Carolyn's face felt flushed. She was being silly, undoubtedly—both to feel bashful and to feel that feverish hunger in her body. But he was right—he could hold her, tonight, and she could lay her hand against his skin and touch him. It was more than they'd had in the past weeks, the past centuries.

After the briefest of hesitations she slipped beneath the covers, thinking inanely that the bed had been much too big for one person to sleep in. Two, it fit perfectly.

"Ye dinna know how I've longed t' touch ye, hold ye." Tiernan breathed into her hair, drawing her close, enfolding her gently in his arms. She could feel him shaking even as she burrowed against him, trembling herself. In the darkness of the room no memory of Erik remained. There were only the arms around her, the hard, warm body against her, and the lilting brogue of Tiernan's beloved voice.

Like the dream.

"Me love," he whispered softly, then again, and again, as though to make up for all the times he'd not spoken the words in the past. "Ah, *grá mo chroí*, I've missed ye," he sighed against her skin, touching his lips to the column of her neck, the hollow at her throat. "Ye canna know how I've longed for ye all these centuries. How I've prayed . . ."

"There's still this matter of a honeymoon," Carolyn pointed out, trying to sound casual while her blood heated to his touch. "The trip, I mean. Erik had arranged for a Caribbean cruise. He—he left the dates open. Of course, we should wait until that cast is off—"

"Mmhh. I should like t' see the world," Tiernan replied dreamily, urging her to shift until she lay atop him, trailing his hands down her back and up again, beneath the soft flannel of the nightie. "I've heard o' *airplanes* and *television*, and *cinemas*. But I've no' left this estate for near t' three hundred years. I'll be lookin' forward t' havin' ye show me the world, *mo rún*."

"Tiernan, I don't think this is such a good—"

"Hush, Cara. Dinna tax me strength arguin' wi' me. Just let me hold ye."

Carolyn was about to point out that he was doing more than just holding her, and that her weight on top of him couldn't possibly feel good with all those bruises, but his mouth found hers, stealing her will to argue. It wasn't long afterward that the realization that his earlier words on recovery hadn't been a complete lie, after all, dawned on Carolyn. He moved slowly, inconspicuously almost, but with great determination, like the tide against the shore. The flannel of her nightgown, which had been between them, was suddenly gone, leaving nothing but the delicious sensation of heated skin on skin, obliterating reason and logical thought. She twisted against him with wanting, but he held her, stilling all but the slightest movements, slowly guiding her body over his until her breath broke and she shuddered as he came into her.

"Cara." He kissed her eyes, her mouth, taking her soft sounds of pleasure and hunger into himself, keeping her body molded to his, nearly motionless. "Hold on t' me, *a ghrá*, forever. Dinna ever let me go."

She whimpered, tilting her hips, trying to get even closer, wanting more, and his arms wrapped more tightly around her yet. Her body was like the plucked string of a harp, vibrating at fever pitch, resonant, reacting to the lightest touch, the slightest of movements. It was as though each beat of his heart, each rush of blood through his veins was a sublime caress, strumming through her flesh, driving her ever higher, out of control, borne on burning storm winds. She felt Tiernan's arms tighten, felt his breath hot against her throat, his teeth closing on her skin with a passion just short of pain while her hands dug into his shoulders to pull him even closer. Then his mouth took hers again, deeply, hungrily, even as his body suddenly spasmed and the abruptly shattered quiescence swept her into an exploding kaleidoscope of sensations.

And it was her name, not Elyssa's, that shivered from Tiernan's lips as she clung to him, shuddering.

His breathing was harsh and ragged, loud against her ear as she came back to herself, pure sensation giving way to soul-deep joy, contentment, and a love she had thought never to hold. And still Tiernan had not released her, had only eased his hold slightly, turning with her onto his side. She touched his face in the darkness, seeing the face of the man who had given her a babe, and moved closer into his embrace.

"Welcome back, Tiernan. Welcome home."

Epilogue

She woke toward morning, body languidly content, and a single intent shining brightly in her mind. Smiling secretly, Carolyn shifted out of Tiernan's embrace and left behind the warmth and comfort of their bed.

She slipped into the chill flannel nightie, then sat down at the desk, mindful to make no sound. In the top drawer, among several fountain pens and sheets of paper, were matches and a stubby candle in case of power failure. Carolyn lit the wick, chose one of the pens and, from the desk's bottom drawer, where she'd placed it when she'd no longer been able to bear looking at it, reverently took out Elyssa's diary.

Slowly, she leafed through the familiar, brittle pages yellowed by time. She'd read them often, those words that traced out the joys and the tragedy of that other's life. And she knew, instinctively and inexplicably, that if she were to return to St. Mary's, the haunting chill would be there still—yet the anguish, the hatred, would be gone.

Carolyn turned to the last written page and read it once again.

October 10
I am quite certain now that I carry my Beloved's babe. I told him this Morn, and it seemed he was Pleased. I do not think he hates me so very much anymore—he calls me grá mo Chroí, *my darling. Pray to God that our trials are over.*

Smiling, eyes misting with tears, Carolyn took up the pen and began one last entry in the ancient diary, an entry dated over two and half centuries after Elyssa's.

November 18, 1994
I am the most blessed woman in the world, for this day my beloved has been restored to me. Not time nor death could steal away the love that is ours.

A tear blurred the fresh ink. Carolyn sat back, blinking and sniffling, but smiling through the tears. She jumped, startled, when warm fingers suddenly closed around her right hand.

Tiernan was standing behind her, the solid wall of his chest fitting against her back, warming her even through the fabric of the nightgown, his features solemn in the shadows of the candle flame. Without a word he brushed a kiss against her temple, then guided her hand holding the pen back to the page, to place below her tiny handwriting a sentence scribed in the bold flourish of another age, a closing to the diary.

Let it be known that Tiernan Padráig O'Rourke, Ninth Earl of Thornwyck, has given up his reckless ways and Surrendered in love to his lady wife, to keep and Protect her, to cherish and love her, until the end of all Days. For by the miracle of Love, nothing stands unconquered.

Author's Note

Tiernan is no ordinary specter, by any standards. While researching appearances of ghosts for this story, I soon realized that the "average" ghost (if one can call any ghost average) would not make a very interesting hero—at least not in a full-length book. Documented specters seldom speak, and even more rarely do they interact with the living in the way I've given Tiernan leave to do, through the power of literary license.

The quoted meaning of *cogais* is taken from *A Pronouncing and Etymological Dictionary of the Gaelic Language* by Malcolm MacLennan (Great Britain: published jointly by Acair and Aberdeen University Press, 1991). I am also indebted to Dr. Grove-White for her help with the Irish phrases; any mistakes are entirely my own.

"Créide's Lament for Cael" is from *Acallam na*

Senórach, "The Conversation of the Elders," a compilation of tales about Finn Mac Cumhaill and his warriors, the Fianna. Other lyrics I've included are taken from traditional folk songs, many of which originate from poetry.

And as far as haunted castles go . . .

They're remarkably numerous in the British Isles, for one thing. I spent a night in such a place once, and though I never saw what was said to be the ghost of a man of ill repute, I can attest to the fact that everyone in our room that night grew surprisingly alert at even the faintest creak of a floorboard. The ghost that had seemed so patently ludicrous in the light of day had taken on a very different aspect once darkness fell.

SPECIAL SNEAK PREVIEW!

ENCHANTED CROSSINGS
MADELINE BAKER
ANNE AVERY
KATHLEEN MORGAN

*Don't miss these three captivating stories of
love in another time, another place.*

A special sneak preview of Madeline Baker's "Heart Of
The Hunter" follows. In this magical love story a Lakota
warrior must defy the boundaries of life itself to claim the
spirited beauty he has sought through time.

ON SALE AT NEWSSTANDS AND
BOOKSTORES EVERYWHERE!

Prologue

Indian Territory, 1877

The two men glared at the Indian who stood between their freedom and a king's ransom in gold.

The Indian was tall, his skin the color of dark bronze, his eyes as black as the bowels of hell. His voice was like slow thunder as he ordered them to get out of the cave and leave the gold behind.

Charlie McBride was willing. Life was more precious than gold. Any fool knew that.

Any fool except Denver Wilkie.

As soon as they cleared the cave, Denver drew his .44 and fired at the Indian. Denver was a crack shot and the bullet struck the Red Stick in the chest, just left of center. Blood oozed from the wound, spreading like crimson tears over the warrior's buckskin shirt.

The Indian fired back. His first bullet struck Denver in the throat, unleashing a fountain of blood.

The second smashed into Charlie McBride's shoulder. He staggered backward, tripped over a rock, and landed on his rump, hard. More frightened than he'd ever been in his life, Charlie stared up at the Indian, certain he was about to be given a one-way ticket to hell.

For a moment, the two men stared at each other, and Charlie felt as if the warrior was probing deep into his soul, prying into the innermost secrets and desires of his heart.

And then the warrior lowered his rifle. "Take only what you need," he said at last. "If you take one nugget more, my spirit will haunt you for as long as you live."

His mouth as dry as the dust of Arizona, Charlie McBride could only nod.

"My body—" The Indian was swaying on his feet now. "Do not leave it . . . out here. . . ."

Charlie nodded again. "I'll bury you," he said. "You have my word on it."

"Inside the cave," the warrior said, his voice growing faint. "Swear it."

"I promise," Charlie said, but the Indian was past hearing.

Slowly, the life faded from the warrior's eyes, the strength left his legs, and he fell slowly, gracefully, to the ground.

Although he was growing a little light-headed

Chapter One

Montana, 1994

She felt it again, a warm breath whispering against the side of her neck, and then a chill, as if a cold winter wind had found its way into the cavern.

For a moment, Kelly didn't move, only stood there with her lantern held high, she was unable to shake the feeling that she was being watched, that unseen eyes were contemplating her with equal parts of curiosity and malice.

But that was ridiculous. There was nothing to be afraid of, she told herself. Nothing at all. If her grandfather was right, no one but members of the family had been in this cave for more than 100 years.

Taking a deep calming breath, she placed the

lantern on the ground and returned to her study of the body that occupied a narrow shelf along the side of the cave wall. The body, wrapped in a faded Hudson's bay blanket, was located exactly where her grandfather had said it would be.

In her mind's eye, Kelly could see the ancient remains on display in the local historical museum, along with a small white placard that named her as the contributor.

Kelly shook her head. She had never truly believed her grandfather McBride's ramblings about the riches supposedly hidden in a cave in the mountain behind the ranch. She had thought all his talk about a wealth of Indian gold guarded by the ghost of a savage Lakota warrior to be nothing more than the confused yearnings of an old man's mind—a jumbled mix of old legends and fables handed down from one generation of McBrides to the next.

A long sigh escaped Kelly's lips as she stared down at the blanket-wrapped corpse.

She believed her grandfather now.

Answering some call she didn't understand, Kelly drew a corner of the blanket back, then blinked in surprise. She had expected to find no more than an emaciated corpse, a skeleton clothed in tattered shreds of deer hide; instead, she saw the well-muscled body of a man dressed in a buckskin clout and fringed leggings. His moccasins were unadorned. He was tall, long legged and narrow hipped. His hair was black and straight and fell well past his broad shoulders. His jaw was strong and square, his cheekbones prominent, his forehead wide. His nose was long and blade straight.

Kelly stared thoughtfully at the dark stain on his shirt front, then frowned in bewilderment. Why hadn't the body decayed? She had the strangest feeling that the Indian wasn't dead at all, that, like Sleeping Beauty, he was merely sleeping away the centuries, waiting to be awakened by love's first kiss.

With a shake of her head, she put away such fanciful thoughts, and then, impulsively, she touched his cheeks with her forefinger. His skin was supple and . . . warm.

Warm when it should have been hard and cold. When it shouldn't have been skin at all. After all these years, the body should have returned to the dust from which it had been made.

A shiver of unease skated down Kelly's spine, and she glanced around the cave, every instinct warning her to run. Abruptly, she jerked her hand away from his cheek. Then she saw it, a small buckskin bag resting against his chest.

Curious, she opened the small sack and emptied the contents into her hand. For a moment, she could only stare at the large medallion resting in her palm.

Fashioned in the shape of an eagle with its wings spread wide, the amulet was about three inches in diameter. And it appeared to be made of solid gold. Even in the flickering light of the lantern, the fetish seemed to glow with a life all its own. It felt warm as it nestled into the palm of her hand.

Kelly stared at the eagle for a long moment, and then, almost of their own volition, her fingers folded over it, and her gaze was drawn to the numerous bags of gold dust and nuggets stacked one on top of the other against the far wall. There was enough money there to pay off the mortgage on the ranch, enough to settle her grandfather's hospital bills. Enough to keep her in comfort for the rest of her life.

Her hands were trembling as she pulled the blanket over the face of the dead man. She couldn't put his remains on display. She knew somehow that he wouldn't want that. Tomorrow, she'd bring a shovel and bury the Indian in the farthest corner of the cave, where he could rest undisturbed.

Kelly sighed. The body had rested there, undisturbed, for over 100 years. She wasn't going to bury it so *it* could rest in peace; she was going to bury it for her own peace of mind.

As she stepped away from the narrow shelf, she felt the warm breath against her neck again.

Put it back.

Kelly whirled around, her gaze searching the cavern's dim interior for the source of the deep male voice. But there was no one there.

Suddenly anxious to be gone from that place of death, she slipped the medallion into the pocket of her jeans. After folding her grandfather's map, she stuck it inside her shirt.

For now, she would leave the treasure as she had found it.

For now, she wanted only to go home.

Her bootheels made soft crunching sounds as she hurried toward the entrance of the cavern. The cave was long and narrow, with a high, rounded ceiling and a sandy floor.

Blowing out the lantern, Kelly left it on the ground inside the mouth of the cave. The opening was only a few feet high and barely wide enough for her to fit through. It had taken her over two hours of intense searching to find the cave at all, and then it had been by sheer luck.

Kelly squinted against the sunlight as she stepped out of the cave. For some reason, she had expected it to be dark outside.

Her grandfather's old gelding, Dusty, whickered softly as she stepped out of the cavern. She patted the buckskin's neck, suddenly glad for the presence of another living creature, and then she swung effortlessly into the saddle and reined the horse toward the Triple M.

Riding away from the cave, Kelly slipped her hand into the pocket of her Levi's, her fingertips moving over the golden eagle.

From behind her, she heard a low rumble, like thunder echoing off the mountains, and then she felt it again, that chill that was colder than the north wind.

Seized with a sudden uncontrollable fear, she drummed her heels into the gelding's sides and raced for home.

Chapter Two

As she ate dinner later that night, Kelly studied the golden eagle, intrigued by the intricate carving. It was the most beautiful thing she'd ever seen, tempting her touch again and again. She marveled at the rich feel of the gold beneath her fingertips, at the delicate lines that formed the bird's deep-set eyes and sharp beak. The wings were exquisite, the talons honed to fine sharp points.

Rising from the battered kitchen table, she quickly washed up her few dishes, took a long leisurely soak in a bubble bath, then settled into bed with pillows propped behind her back so she could read.

But she couldn't concentrate on the book. She kept thinking of the body in the cave. How long had it been there? A hundred years at least, she thought, because the Triple M had been in her family about that long. Why hadn't the body decayed? She stared at the eagle standing against the table lamp beside her bed. Why had the body of the Indian felt warm to her touch?

Kelly shook her head. Surely that had been a product of her overactive imagination. But she had not imagined that long, lean body. He must have been quite an impressive man in his day, tall and broad shouldered. She knew somehow that his eyes had been as black as sin, that his teeth had been straight and white, and that when he smiled. . . .

She laughed softly, uneasily. What was the matter with her, fantasizing about a man who'd probably been dead for over 100 years! First thing tomorrow she would bury the body. It made her uncomfortable just knowing it was there.

She was about to switch off her bedside light when she saw a dark shadow at the window. All the air seemed to leave her body, and her heart suddenly seemed too big for her chest as she watched the shadow pause, then move on.

For a moment, she was frozen with fear. Then she bounded out of bed, ran into the living room, and grabbed the shotgun from the rack over the fireplace, grateful that her grandfather had taught her how to shoot.

Heart pounding, she stood behind the front door, listening, waiting. For the first time, she realized just how alone she was. Her closest neighbor was five miles to the south. She couldn't pick up the phone and dial 911 for help.

Far in the distance, she heard the lonely wail of a coyote, and then there was only silence, a silence as deep and dark as the grave.

She stood there for a quarter of an hour, her whole body tense. And then, gradually, the sounds of the night returned. She heard the frogs croaking in the pond behind the house, the song of a cricket, the soft sighing of the wind, and she knew somehow that whatever had been lurking in the shadows had gone.

It took her a long time to fall asleep that night, but when sleep finally came, she dreamed of a tall, dark-skinned warrior with hair as black as midnight and eyes as deep and dark as fathomless pools of liquid ebony. . . .

In the morning, her fears of the night before seemed foolish. Kelly had never been one to be spooked by shadows in the night. She'd lived alone in Los Angeles ever since her father had died five years ago. Lived alone and like it, but when Grandpa McBride's health started failing, she had tried to convince him to come to LA and live with her. But her grandfather had refused to leave the Triple M. Like Kelly, he had cherished his independence. She knew he would have died alone if the hospital in Cedar Flats hadn't called to inform her he was there. She'd taken a two-week leave of absence from her job with Wolfe, Cullman, and Chartier and flown to Montana to be with him.

Kelly felt a familiar tug at her heart as she thought of her grandfather. In days past, when she was a little girl, her family had spent their summers at the ranch, and Grandpa had charmed her with tales of the Old West, repeating the colorful tales his great-grandfather, Charlie McBride, had once told him, tales of Indian fights and buffalo hunts and mountain men.

Her grandfather had been on his deathbed when he'd told her about the gold his great-grandfather, Charlie, had buried in a cave in the mountain behind the Triple M.

"Gold?" Kelly had said with a grin. "If there was any gold up there, don't you think someone would have found it by now?"

"It's there, girl. My great-grandpappy told me so."

"Why didn't he spend it?"

"He was afraid of it, afraid of the ghost who haunts the mountain."

"Ghost!" Kelly had exclaimed.

"I've seen him, Kelly girl," her grandfather had said, his gnarled hand squeezing hers with surprising strength.

"Really?" Kelly had asked, leaning forward. "When? Where?"

"When I was younger and braver. I followed my great-grandpappy's map and found the cave. The gold's in there, girl, a fortune, just like he said."

"And you never touched it?"

"Oh, I took a little dust now and then, when I

386

needed it. But something told me not to try to take more than I needed. Now it's yours, Kelly. Use it wisely."

Those were the last words her Grandpa Frank had said in this world. He was asleep when she went to visit him the next morning. He'd opened his eyes, smiled at her, and then, with a sigh, he was gone.

And now the ranch, and the gold, belonged to her.

After a quick breakfast, Kelly went out to the barn and saddled Dusty. She had a grave to dig, and it was a long ride to the cave.

Kelly approached the cavern with a growing sense of unease. Chiding herself for her foolishness, she slipped on a pair of heavy work gloves, removed the shovel she'd tied behind the saddle, and ducked into the cave.

Pausing near the entrance to light the lantern she'd left the day before, she felt her heart begin to pound as shadows came to life on the walls. The cavern was roomy inside, high enough for her to stand erect once she was inside.

Nothing to be afraid of, she told herself. The dead can't hurt you.

Her booted feet made hardly a sound on the soft, sandy earth as she went deeper into the cave. She wouldn't have to dig a very deep hole, she decided, just deep enough to cover the body.

Her heart was pounding like a runaway train as she drew near the ledge, and then her breath caught in her throat.

The ledge was empty.

The body was gone.

Not believing her eyes, Kelly ran her hands over the surface of the earthen shelf, searching for some sign that a body had actually been there, that she wasn't losing her mind. Nothing.

And then she saw it, the faded Hudson's bay blanket, crumpled in a heap beneath the ledge.

For a moment, Kelly felt relief. She hadn't imagined it after all. The body had been there, and now it was gone.

Bewildered, she stared at the blanket. Gone, she thought. Gone where?

Lantern in hand, she searched the floor of the cave for some sign that an animal had dragged the remains away, but there was no sign of animal tracks, no footprints other than her own.

She laughed at that. Of course there were no footprints. Ghosts didn't leave footprints.

With a cry, she turned on her heel and ran toward the entrance of the cave, scrambling out of the narrow opening as if Satan himself were snapping at her heels.

She dreamed of the Indian again that night. She was walking in the moonlight when suddenly he was there beside her, his black eyes glowing like dark fires. He gazed at her for a long moment, the awareness growing between them, and then, quite unexpectedly, he brushed his knuckles against her cheek. The touch exploded through her like lightning, and while she was trying to recover, she heard a voice echo in the corridor of her mind. A voice that was husky with warning. His voice. *Put it back.* And then he was gone.

She woke to find the sheets tangled around her legs, her brow damp with perspiration.

Unconsciously, she reached for the golden eagle she'd placed beneath her pillow, and as her hand closed around its smoothness, she heard the warning again. Only this time it wasn't a dream, and she didn't hear the words echoing in her mind.

She heard the words, spoken clearly, from the shadowed corner of her room.

"Put it back."

On the verge of terror, Kelly scrambled across the bed and switched on the light, her eyes wide as they searched the room.

There was no one there.

Chapter Three

Harry Renford stared at the young woman seated before him with obvious disbelief.

"Pay off the loan?" he said, repeating her words as if he hadn't heard her quite right. "You want to pay off the loan?"

Harry sat back in his chair, his hands folded on the desktop as he studied her face. Kelly McBride was a pretty girl, with long, curly brown hair and large blue eyes. He'd known her grandparents, Frank and Annee, for years. Annee had died almost ten years ago, but Frank had stayed on at the ranch, alone. He'd gotten pretty feeble in his old age, but he'd refused to leave the Triple M, and the ranch, located some 30 miles southeast of town, had fallen into a state of disrepair.

Old man McBride had died three weeks ago, leaving behind a mountain of hospital bills and a sizable mortgage. It had been in Harry's mind to buy the Triple M when it went on the market and discover for himself if the rumors of a hidden gold mine were true. It had seemed a safe investment. If there was no gold, and he doubted there was, Harry planned to turn the Triple M into a guest ranch. But then Frank's granddaughter had shown up to claim the old place. He'd made her what he considered to be a generous offer for the ranch—an offer she had politely, but firmly, refused, thereby upsetting his carefully thought-out scheme.

Harry shifted in his chair. He wasn't a man who liked to see his plans upset, especially by a young city girl who probably didn't know the difference between a dandy brush and a hoof-pick.

"Well, that's fine, Miss McBride," he drawled. "Just fine. But where, if you don't mind my asking, did you get the money?"

"I don't believe the source of my funds is a requisite for paying off the loan, Mr. Renford."

"No, no, of course not. Well, it will take me a day or two to get the necessary papers drawn up. Why don't you come back on, say, Friday afternoon?"

"Fine. Until then, Mr. Renford."

Outside, Kelly drew a deep breath and let it out in a long sigh of relief. She was glad to be out of Harry Renford's sight. She didn't like the man, though she didn't know why. It wasn't his looks, she mused. He was quite a handsome man, with a shock of wavy blond hair that was just

392

turning gray at the temples, a charming smile, when he cared to use it, and light gray eyes. It was his eyes, she decided now—they were cold and unblinking, like the eyes of a snake.

Well, as soon as she paid off the mortgage on the ranch, she wouldn't have to deal with him again. Tomorrow she would drive into Coleville and see about selling some of the smaller nuggets. She didn't dare do it here. Cedar Flats was a small town where everybody knew everybody else's business. She didn't want to have to answer any questions about where the gold had come from.

Frowning, she started down to the sidewalk to where she'd left her car. In a few days, she'd have to decide what to do about the ranch. When she'd first arrived, it had been in her mind to sell it, but once she'd seen the place again and remembered the good times she'd had there, she'd known she couldn't sell the old ranch. It had, after all, been in her family for over a century. Still, it was horribly run-down. The house and the barn were in need of painting inside and out; the corral fences needed new rails. There was no stock to speak of, except for Dusty and a couple of aging chickens.

Nevertheless, she was here, and she was here to stay, even though it meant relocating, quitting her secretarial job with Wolfe, Cullman, and Chartier, and finding other employment.

Kelly laughed softly. She didn't need to work anymore. Having access to those nuggets was like having a trust fund. She was set for life.

She was unlocking door of her car when a man appeared beside her.

"Miss McBride?"

Kelly hesitated a moment before answering. "Yes?"

"I'd like to talk to you."

He was Indian, she thought, noting his dark skin and high cheekbones, though there was nothing particularly sinister about that. There were lots of Indians in Cedar Flats. Most of them lived out on the reservation.

"Talk?" Kelly said. "About what?"

"The Triple M."

Kelly glanced around, reassured by the presence of other people nearby. "What about it?"

"I'd like to buy it."

Kelly glanced at his faded green shirt, the sleeves of which were rolled up to his elbows, exposing bronze forearms thick with muscle. Frayed blue jeans hugged his legs; his feet were encased in a pair of run-down black boots. She doubted if he could afford to buy a cup of coffee.

"I'm sorry," she said politely. "The ranch isn't for sale."

She opened the door and slid behind the wheel, but before she could close the door, the man took a step forward, placing himself between her and the car door.

"Could we go somewhere and discuss it?" he asked.

Kelly shook her head, thinking that his voice was as deep and rich as dark chocolate fudge.

"Please."

The word seemed torn from his throat and she had the sudden unshakable feeling that this was a man who hadn't done much apologizing in his life.

She looked at him then, really looked at him for the first time, and felt a shiver of apprehension skitter down her spine. He looked remarkably as she had imagined the dead man she'd found in the cave would have looked when he was alive.

Kelly's heart begin to pound as she noted the similarities. Like the body in the cave, this man was tall and dark. His thick black hair fell past his shoulders. His legs were long; his shoulders were unbelievably broad beneath the almost thread-bare shirt. He seemed made of solid muscle. His eyes were as black as obsidian, just as she'd imagined those of the dead man would have been. His nose was straight as a knife edge, and his mouth . . . oh, my, she had never seen such a sensual mouth on a man in her whole life.

He stared down at her, one black brow arching slightly, as if he knew exactly what she was thinking.

"Are you sure we can't discuss it?" he asked in a voice as seductive as candlelight and champagne. "Maybe grab a cup of coffee in the motel coffee shop?"

"I'm sure," she said, wondering if he was truly suggesting what she was thinking. "Now, if you'll excuse me—"

Kelly stared pointedly at his muscular forearm, which was resting along the top edge of the car door.

His dark eyes flashed with anger as he stepped away from the car.

In an instant, Kelly shut the door and locked it. Shoving the key into the ignition, she gave it a twist, put the gear shift in drive, and pulled away from the curb.

But she couldn't resist a look in her rearview mirror. For some reason, she had expected him to have vanished from sight, but he stood in the middle of the narrow two-lane street, staring after her.

Kelly let out a long, ragged breath as she turned the corner at the end of the block. Whoever the man was, he intrigued and frightened her as no one ever had.

Lee Roan Horse felt his brows draw together in a frown as he watched the light blue Camaro careen around the corner and disappear from sight.

His first meeting with Miss Kelly McBride hadn't gone quite as planned, he thought wryly. For a moment there, she had looked at him the way most white women did, with a mixture of interest and curiosity, and then, for no reason that he could fathom, she had stared at him as if she were seeing a ghost.

So, he mused, what now?

Hands shoved in the back pockets of his jeans, he crossed the street to where his battered Ford truck was parked and climbed inside, only to sit staring out the windshield, his finger tapping on the steering wheel. She had something he wanted and he had two choices—ask for it, or take it.

He'd tried asking. . . .

A Vampire Romance In The Immortal Tradition Of *Interview with the Vampire.*

A DEEPER HUNGER
SABINE KELLS

For years, Cailie has been haunted by strange, recurring visions of fierce desire and an enigmatic lover who excites her like no other. Obsessed with the overpowering passion of her fantasies, she will do anything, go anywhere to make them real—before it is too late.

Mysterious, romantic, and sophisticated, Tresand is the man of Cailie's dreams. Yet behind the stranger's cultured facade lurk dark secrets that threaten Cailie even as he seduces her very soul.

_3593-6 $4.50 US/$5.50 CAN

Three captivating stories of love in another time, another place.

MADELINE BAKER
"Heart of the Hunter"

A Lakota warrior must defy the boundaries of life itself to claim the spirited beauty he has sought through time.

ANNE AVERY
"Dream Seeker"

On faraway planets, a pilot and a dreamer learn that passion can bridge the heavens, no matter how vast the distance from one heart to another.

KATHLEEN MORGAN
"The Last Gatekeeper"

To save her world, a dazzling temptress must use her powers of enchantment to open a stellar portal—and the heart of a virile but reluctant warrior.

___51974-7 *Enchanted Crossings* (three unforgettable love stories in one volume) $4.99 US/
$5.99 CAN

LEISURE BOOKS
ATTN: Order Department
276 5th Avenue, New York, NY 10001

Please add $1.50 for shipping and handling for the first book and $.35 for each book thereafter. PA., N.Y.S. and N.Y.C. residents, please add appropriate sales tax. No cash, stamps, or C.O.D.s. All orders shipped within 6 weeks via postal service book rate. Canadian orders require $2.00 extra postage and must be paid in U.S. dollars through a U.S. banking facility.

Name _____
Address _____
City _____ State _____ Zip _____
I have enclosed $_____ in payment for the checked book(s).
Payment <u>must</u> accompany all orders.☐ Please send a free catalog.

Futuristic Romance

Love in another time, another place.

New York Times Bestselling Author
Phoebe Conn writing as Cinnamon Burke!

Lady Rogue. Sent to infiltrate Spider Diamond's pirate operation, Drew Jordan finds himself in an impossible situation. Handpicked by Spider as a suitable "pet" for his daughter, Drew has to win Ivory Diamond's love or lose his life. But once he's initiated Ivory into the delights of lovemaking, he knows he can never turn her over to the authorities. For he has found a vulnerable woman's heart within the formidable lady rogue.

_3558-8 $5.99 US/$6.99 CAN

Rapture's Mist. Dedicated to preserving the old ways, Tynan Thorn has led the austere life of a recluse. He has never even laid eyes on a woman until the ravishing Amara sweeps into his bedroom to change his life forever. Daring and uninhabited, Amara sets out to broaden Tynan's viewpoint, but she never expects that the area he will be most interested in exploring is her own sensitive body. As their bodies unite in explosive ecstasy, Tynan and Amara discover a whole new world, where together they can soar among the stars.

_3470-0 $5.99 US/$6.99 CAN

LEISURE BOOKS
ATTN: Order Department
276 5th Avenue, New York, NY 10001

Please add $1.50 for shipping and handling for the first book and $.35 for each book thereafter. PA., N.Y.S. and N.Y.C. residents, please add appropriate sales tax. No cash, stamps, or C.O.D.s. All orders shipped within 6 weeks via postal service book rate. Canadian orders require $2.00 extra postage and must be paid in U.S. dollars through a U.S. banking facility.

Name _____

Address _____

City _____ State _____ Zip _____

I have enclosed $_____in payment for the checked book(s).

Payment <u>must</u> accompany all orders.☐ Please send a free catalog.